IN LOVE WITH THE FIREFIGHTER

AMIE DENMAN

MILLS & BOON

First Published in Great Britain 2018
by Mills & Boon, an imprint of HarperCollins*Publishers*
1 London Bridge Street, London, SE1 9GF

In Love with the Firefighter © 2018 Amie Denman

ISBN: 978-0-263-26515-6

38-0718

MIX
Paper from
responsible sources
FSC
www.fsc.org
FSC™ C007454

Amie Denman is the author of twenty contemporary romances full of humor and heart. A devoted traveler whose parents always kept a suitcase packed, she loves reading and writing books you could take on vacation. Amie believes everything is fun, especially wedding cake, show tunes, roller coasters and falling in love.

Also by Amie Denman

Under the Boardwalk
Carousel Nights
Meet Me on the Midway
Until the Ride Stops
Back to the Lake Breeze Hotel
Her Lucky Catch

Discover more at millsandboon.co.uk

My thanks to all the wonderful people at Mills & Boon, especially my editor, Dana Grimaldi.

CHAPTER ONE

TONY LEANED FORWARD in the passenger seat and braced one hand on the dashboard.

"I think you can make it," he yelled. "But it'll be close."

Kevin kept his hands on the wheel of the rescue truck and frowned, his neck and shoulders tight with concentration. "Wish these tourists would learn to park," he muttered.

A small red car was double-parked on a bustling downtown street. During the height of spring break season in Cape Pursuit. And the driver's-side door was standing open, just asking to be taken off by the rescue truck. Kevin remembered the tense voice dispatching them to a 911 call for a child who wasn't breathing. Every second counted when someone's life was on the line. The siren was loud, even inside the cab, and his adrenaline still rushed as much as it had when he was a new firefighter, over five years ago.

Tony pulled the air horn and the noise reverberated off the commercial buildings lining the street. "You'll barely squeeze by if nobody does anything stupid."

Kevin hoped, as always, that no one would risk their life by stepping into the street. His heart sank when three teenagers on bicycles suddenly swerved off the sidewalk and pedaled against traffic on Kevin's left. No helmets, no brains. *Tourists.*

The teenagers, cords from their earbuds flapping, looked

up in panic at the massive emergency vehicle bearing down on them.

"Anyone in that red car?" Kevin shouted. He knew it was too late to stop, and even slowing down wouldn't help much.

"Not that I can see," his partner said.

Kevin held his breath and veered to miss the cyclists at the last second. The heavy-duty ambulance barely shuddered when it sliced the door off the double-parked red car and deposited it in the street in a sparkling rain of shattered glass.

Tony twisted to look backward out the passenger-side window. "No injuries. Unless you count heart-stopping surprise."

"Call it in," Kevin said. "We can't stop. Other two ambulances are already out."

Tony got on the radio to the local police and reported the non-injury accident. Kevin glanced in the side mirror and saw a blonde woman rush into the street toward the destroyed car. She carried a large box in her arms. He couldn't see her face, but he could guess she'd just learned a valuable lesson about double-parking and leaving her car door open. At least she wasn't hurt. It was bad enough hitting a car, but if he'd hurt someone in the line of duty, he'd turn in his helmet and boots.

"Never gonna live this one down," Tony said.

Kevin breathed heavily through his nose, trying to calm his racing heart and focus on getting to the call. Kid not breathing. The worst. *Focus.*

"Remember how much crap you gave your brother when he backed into a post with the pumper last year?"

"Shut up, Tony."

"This wins. No contest."

"Look for the address," Kevin replied. Not that it would be hard. Cape Pursuit was a town of fifteen thousand year-round residents. Just large enough to have problems, but just small enough for the fire department to know every street in town. During tourist season, the population doubled but was mostly concentrated in the hotels, bars and restaurants that lined the coast along the Atlantic Ocean.

The address the dispatcher gave them was on a street with small cottages usually rented out to tourists. Kevin wasn't worried about finding the place. He'd been to that street before. And with a call this serious, there'd be someone waiting for them out front. Panicked. Waving their arms.

There always was.

"OH, NO!" JANE SAID, surveying her friend's car with wide eyes.

Nicole felt empty. As if the screaming ambulance had either squashed her flat or taken her with it. She stood in the street holding her box, broken glass glistening on the pavement at her feet. The door of her car lay crumpled in front of it. Hysterical laughter bubbled up her esophagus. This could not be happening. She'd been in Cape Pursuit five minutes.

"Say something," Jane said, brows furrowed, staring at Nicole.

"They didn't even stop," Nicole said, her voice sounding far away. "Don't they have to stop?"

"Technically, but maybe they were on their way to a life-threatening emergency. They did have the lights and siren going," Jane said.

A tear slid down Nicole's cheek, but her hands were full so she let the tear drip onto the pavement, which was already shimmering with broken glass. If she'd used her severance package to go to Italy, she was sure this would not be happening. *Mental note: run away to a foreign country next time, not a beach town in Virginia.*

"Not that I'm defending them," Jane added, hands up in the air.

"Firefighters," Nicole huffed, her voice shaky.

"Sorry, honey," Jane said. She took the box Nicole was holding and set it on the sidewalk before returning to give her friend a hug. "It's going to be okay. Just a freak accident. You'll like it here. It's a fresh start."

Nicole gave her friend an openmouthed look. "A fire truck took off my car door on my first day in town."

"It can only get better from here. Right?"

That was what Nicole had been telling herself for the past year. *When one of the worst things that can happen to you happens, your luck has to improve after that.* She took a deep breath and pulled herself into the present. "Maybe I'll get a new car," she said, nodding as if she were encouraging herself. Her chin-length blond hair bobbed with the movement.

"That's the spirit," Jane said. "If I were you, I'd punch whoever was driving that truck right in the gut and then just shake it off. But not until you talk to the city's insurance agent. Make them sweat so they'll replace your whole car." She shook her finger at her friend. "Don't settle for a new door."

Nicole gave a wobbly smile. "I could get a better car. Like a crossover or something with leather seats. This *was* almost paid for." She swiped away tears with the back of her hand. "They owe me."

She stood shoulder to shoulder with Jane, her best friend of six years, staring at the wrecked car. She sighed. *This definitely would not happen in Tuscany or Milan or Naples. They have sunflowers and wine there. Ruined villas with flowery vines. Endless vistas and possibilities.*

A police car approached, its siren echoing off the shops, bars, restaurants and hotels that occupied the strip one block back from the ocean.

"Want me to do the talking?" Jane offered. "I know everyone in the fire and police departments. After all, I'm on the town council that pays their salaries. I'm your muscle."

Nicole looked at her friend. Even at five-five, Nicole towered over Jane. An artist specializing in watercolors, Jane wore a smock and had her long red hair wound up and secured with a pencil.

"I'll see how it goes," Nicole answered. "But I'll call out the big guns if I have to."

An attractive, graying police officer stopped behind Nicole's car, blocking the street completely and leaving his flashing lights on. Now that the initial shock was over, Nicole's stomach lurched and her hands were clammy and cold.

"Any injuries?" the officer asked.

Both women shook their heads. A large crowd had gathered on the sidewalk. Many of them had cell phones in hand, taking pictures of the spectacle. What great spring break stories they were going to have. Someone had probably gotten the actual door destruction on video. Nicole thought it might come in handy for her case, but it was the last thing she wanted to see on social media.

"Want to tell me what happened?" the officer continued.

"A fire truck took off the door of my car," Nicole said. She tried for a competent and neutral tone, one she had practiced in business meetings at her former job in Indianapolis. The tone that said *everything is fine; we just have things to discuss.*

"It was technically an ambulance," Jane interjected. "The big rescue squad. Red."

"Thanks, Jane," the cop said. "How's the painting business?"

"Good. Busy week with spring breakers. My kind of busy. I'd take a whole summer of this."

"I hope you get it." The cop smiled and turned back to Nicole. "So how did the ambulance grab your door?"

"It was open," Nicole said.

"You were just getting out of the car?"

"Not exactly." Nicole was starting to get that *not guilty but not exactly blameless* feeling.

"I see," he said. He raised both eyebrows and wrinkled his forehead. "And was your car parked like this at the time of the accident?"

Nicole felt heat in her cheeks. She was the victim here! The ambulance wrecked her car. But…okay, yes, she was illegally parked. And, sure, she had left the door hanging open. The box with her computer and her desk supplies was heavy. It really was.

Rats.

"Yes, but…" she began.

Jane stepped between her friend and the police officer. "I think I can explain. Nicole just arrived from out of town after a very long drive. She's my new business manager and an old friend. I had her pull up out front to unload a box of stuff. Very heavy stuff. There's a delivery truck behind the grocery store next door. That's where I usually unload. You should really talk to them about hogging the whole loading zone back there. Especially during tourist season." Jane shrugged and smiled at the man. "I'd say it's technically their fault."

The police officer pulled a notepad from his breast pocket and clicked a silver pen against his shiny badge. "Out-of-state license plates, double-parked, left car door open, using the street as an unloading zone," he said aloud as he jotted down notes.

"Hey," Nicole said, hustling over and looking at what he was writing. "The ambulance never even slowed down. There were dozens of witnesses."

The cop raised his eyes and looked at her for a moment before flipping his notepad closed and putting it away.

"I'm usually very responsible," Nicole grumbled. This was true. Her life had been orderly and ordinary at one time. National Honor Society in high school, dean's list in college, excellent credit score, not even a speeding ticket to put a black mark next to her name. But since last summer, she could only make it through a day by hanging on with both hands.

She'd hoped moving to a new town would help her let go. Perhaps she'd chosen the wrong place to start over.

The cop smiled and cocked his head. "I'll send a report to the city's attorney since it involved a city employee, although which one I don't know." He winked at Jane. "You know I'll find out."

"I thought I saw Tony Ruggles in the passenger seat, but I didn't see who was driving," Jane said.

"Chief's son riding shotgun," the officer commented as he wrote the fact in his notepad.

"And will the city replace my car?" Nicole asked. With each question her case grew dimmer.

"That'll be up to the insurance companies. Yours and theirs."

Nicole sighed. Maybe tomorrow would be the day her luck would change.

"Welcome to Cape Pursuit," the police officer added. "I'll call you a tow truck."

HOURS LATER AFTER the art gallery had closed for the day, Nicole got in the passenger seat of Jane's Volkswagen Beetle. The car was sunny yellow and decorated with ads for Jane's art studio, Sea Jane Paint. It also enjoyed the luxury of having all its doors.

"I'll drive next time," Nicole offered, smiling and trying to be cheerful despite the events of the day. "Even if I have to steal a car."

"Tourists leave rentals unlocked sometimes," Jane suggested. "Just a thought."

The spring break weather and happy vibe of the beachside town was something to celebrate. People in colorful shorts and T-shirts strolled the walks, lovers kissed under awnings and the calm sea appeared in glimpses between the buildings they passed.

The evening sky stretching over the Atlantic Ocean nearly transcended the sight of her almost-paid-for car being hauled off by a tow truck, its dismembered door tucked underneath it on the flatbed. Nicole had the feeling she was never going to see it again, but the insurance adjuster on the phone assured her that doors got lopped off all the time. The car might live to ride again—after a few weeks in the body shop.

"We could go to a restaurant," Jane said. "There's at least a dozen of them within walking distance of my studio, some of them really good. But I don't feel like fighting the spring break crowds on the strip." She turned down a residential street, heading away from the ocean. "I'm taking you to a place on the edge of town the locals like."

"Do they have fried food and alcohol?"

"That's all they have," Jane said.

"Perfect."

The low brown building's painted sign said it all: Cape Pursuit Bar & Grill. It was not the kind of place that would attract the tourist crowd. Out of the way and under the radar, it had *local watering hole* written all over it, from the pot-hole-riddled parking lot to the mismatched faux shutters.

Nicole followed Jane inside to a row of dark, high-backed booths and slid in across from her. She picked up a colorful laminated menu and smiled. Fried macaroni bites. Fried mozzarella sticks. French fries. Fried onion straws. Five different kinds of burgers, nearly all with some combination of bacon, cheese, barbecue sauce, fried onions and fried pickles.

Her stomach growled. The car fiasco had robbed her appetite for lunch, but she was starving now. She deserved saturated fat after all she'd been through, and she had a feeling she'd be on her feet working hard in the art gallery. Life in a sunny beach town where she'd be likely to walk everywhere now that she was without a car was a far cry from the sedentary office job she'd left several states behind.

"Thanks for letting me stay with you until I find a place," Nicole said. "I looked at some rental houses and condos on-line, but I was afraid to commit before I actually saw the properties."

"Someone's looking for a place to live?"

A man with a face straight out of a magazine slid into the booth next to Jane. He had blue eyes, rugged cheekbones, a day's growth of beard and dark hair that was just a little too long. He wore a T-shirt with Cape Pursuit Fire Department screen-printed over the left side of his chest.

"Charlie Zimmerman," he said, extending his hand across the table. "I can help you buy or rent a place if you're interested. I'm a part-time Realtor here."

"And a full-time pain in the butt," Jane added.

"Keeps me busy," Charlie agreed, smiling.

"This is Nicole Wheeler," Jane said. "My best friend from college. We both went to Michigan State, but she majored in something far more practical than I did."

Charlie turned his seaglass-blue eyes toward Nicole. "Horseshoeing? Latin?"

Nicole studied their guest and wondered what the heck he was talking about. *Did she look like a horseshoer?*

"Anything's more practical than what my flaky artist friend here does," Charlie explained jovially.

"Hey," Jane said. "I helped personalize gifts for your last three girlfriends, not that it did you much good."

Charlie's smile faded for a moment and he drummed his fingers on the table. "Can't blame a guy for trying," he commented. "And there's no doubt your paintings will easily outlast any of my relationships."

Jane stacked up the menus and folded her napkin into

neat triangles, creasing them mercilessly with one finger. "I hope so," she said.

"So you're not an artist?" Charlie asked, looking at Nicole.

Nicole leaned back in her seat. "I majored in business. I just finished my MBA and I'm trying to figure out what to do with it."

"And you're new in town."

Five or six men, all big, all loud, burst through the door and headed straight for the bar.

"Yes," Nicole said, raising her voice over the noise. "I'm going to be Jane's business manager."

Charlie exchanged a look with Jane, one eyebrow raised just enough to imply a question.

"Lucky me," Jane said. "You know I'm lousy at spreadsheets and paperwork. And Nicole's a great photographer—"

"Hey, Charlie," one of the new arrivals, a big buzz-cut blond at the bar, shouted. "Get over here. You gotta hear this one."

The man next to him on the bar stool turned around and locked eyes with Nicole. From a short distance away, his green eyes reminded her of a stormy sea. His dark hair and shoulders as wide as a truck combined with those stormy eyes mesmerized her. The blond buzz-cut guy slapped stormy-sea man on the shoulder.

"Kevin here has a peach of a story." He paused to laugh. "He took the door off some stupid tourist's car with the squad this afternoon."

Nicole felt her face fall, all the warm blood draining away to be replaced by ice water.

"Those double-parking sons of guns," one of the other guys added.

Charlie laughed and Jane elbowed him in the ribs.

"What?" he said. "I'm joining the cool kids at the bar."

He nodded to Nicole. "Nice meeting you. Jane can give you my number if you're serious about finding a place."

"Thank you," Nicole said coldly. She made brief eye contact with him and then turned back to the group at the bar. So Kevin of the stormy green eyes was the man who welcomed her to Cape Pursuit by slicing off her car's door?

"Maybe this wasn't a good idea," Jane said. "I forgot Thursday night was Testosterone Night."

A waitress appeared at their table, blocking off the bar stool crowd and asking for their drink orders.

"I'm not sure we're staying," Jane said, raising a questioning glance to Nicole.

"Sure we're staying. They have fried everything on the menu, and we're already here," Nicole replied, her tone like that of a lion handler assuring the terrified crowd that everything is just fine. "I'll have wine. Moscato, if you have it."

"Still having your love affair with Italy?" Jane asked. A smile lit her eyes. She turned to the waitress. "Orange soda for me. I'm the driver for the night."

"Rub it in that you still have a car," Nicole said after the waitress left. "After I have that wine, I may just go over there and tell—what was his name? Kevin?—just how much I appreciated the special welcome he gave me this afternoon."

Jane's smile disappeared. "I don't think that's a good idea."

"Why? Will he accuse me of being one of those double-parking sons of guns?"

"Kevin didn't say that. Rick did."

"Rick of the blond buzz cut?"

"Affectionately known by several unflattering names," Jane confirmed.

Loud laughter echoed from the bar. It wasn't much of a mystery what they were all laughing about. Nicole's cheeks heated. She swallowed. Maybe Jane was right. They should leave.

The waitress placed a wine glass on a paper coaster in front of Nicole. Little bubbles rose from the stem to the top. It smelled like heaven. Fermented heaven.

Maybe they could stay.

The twentysomething server parked a steaming basket of french fries in the middle of the table. "They'll keep you company while you decide what to order," she said. "Kitchen's a little backed up tonight and we hate seeing people go hungry."

They were definitely staying.

CHAPTER TWO

NO MATTER HOW much fun the other guys were having, the accident was a dark cloud over Kevin's day. He had no choice. *He knew that*. Kid not breathing, life or death. He couldn't stop, and he couldn't hit those teenagers on bikes. And who the heck had asked that red car to park right there in the street and leave the door open?

But still. He felt bad about it. The two-year-old lying on the sofa in the house where a panicked father had flagged them down was, technically, breathing. But he was unconscious due to a febrile seizure. It was the kind of thing Kevin had seen a number of times, but the child's parents had not. And the terror in their eyes made Kevin wonder if he was ever brave enough to have children of his own.

But everything had worked out. The boy would recover once the hospital got his fever down. The damage to the front bumper of the ambulance was minimal. The department's insurance agent had chalked it up to one more statistic, one more example of the 10 percent of emergency vehicles involved in scrapes and accidents every year. The chief had talked to him, and the write-up in his employee folder declared it not his fault, unavoidable. No disciplinary action assigned. The chief had even congratulated him on following the department's mantra: *life over property*. No exceptions. Ever.

But he was never going to hear the end of it from his fellow public servants who were currently buying him drinks. They weren't impressed by his life-saving defensive driving. They all did that kind of thing every day. The firefighters and cops leaning on the bar were raising their beers over the gritty details.

"Did the door actually get airborne or was it more of a twist-off?" Rick asked. He punctuated his question by twisting the cap off his beer with his bare hand.

Kevin's cousin Tony slid a basket of fries down the counter to Kevin. "No air," he declared. "Saw it all in the side mirror."

Kevin stuffed a handful of fries in his mouth and hoped desperately for a kitchen fire. A false alarm. Anything to change the subject.

"Kev here had his eyes on the road, so I'm the one you should be asking," Tony added. "Barely even felt it when the bumper tore off that door and dropped it right in front of the car. Like roadkill. Glass shattered to hell." He paused and swigged his beer. "Great story for the Wall of Flame. Hope one of the hundreds of tourists who witnessed it got it on video. Maybe they'll put it on social media."

Kevin cringed. The Wall of Flame was likely to be misunderstood by normal people. People who were not in the business of responding to accidents, digging through gutted houses for the cause of the fire, and facing some of the truly lousy things that happen to people. Every day. The Wall of Flame was just a bulletin board with an attached shelf. It hung in the bunk room at the station, where they posted newspaper clippings, photographs, thank-you notes and the occasional artifact. It was a daily reminder of what they did, but its goofiness took the edge off the seriousness of the job. Department humor. It meant survival in a tough field.

Currently the wall had a picture of one of the lieutenants swearing in the newest firefighter, but the lower half of the new recruit's body was a chubby baby wearing a diaper. A picture printed from the internet of Smokey Bear lighting a fat cigar was stapled in the upper corner. A before-and-after photo of the chief as a young recruit with hair, and the current bald version was tacked up next to a colorful photo of a training fire. The house was destroyed by fire on purpose, but the large caption drawn in marker said it all: *Oops*.

"This is not going on the Wall of Flame," Kevin grumbled.

"My cousin drives the tow truck," Ethan said. "He saved the side mirror of the door you took off. We'll put it in the Stupid Tourist section of the board."

Kevin groaned and shook his head.

Rick left his bar stool next to Kevin and headed for the restroom in the back of the restaurant. A gorgeous blonde slid onto the stool, an empty glass of wine in her hand. There was something oddly familiar about her.

"Moscato," she said to the bartender, handing over the empty glass.

She swiveled and faced Kevin, her eyes the color of new plants in spring. He froze. There was definitely something about her.

She had the full attention of the men assembled at the bar, but she was only looking at Kevin.

"I'm Nicole Wheeler," she said.

Could this be happening? Other guys attracted women, even used their badges and uniforms to negotiate themselves into a night in bed. But Kevin's last girlfriend took off eighteen months ago, leaving him an ancient dog and no apologies.

Maybe his luck was changing.

"Kevin Ruggles," he said. "You must be new in town. I'd remember you if we'd met before."

"I'm definitely new. Just arrived this afternoon, in fact."

Something in her tone signaled a warning, but Kevin forged ahead. She was sitting next to him at the bar, waiting for a drink. He should offer to buy. She was beautiful. Her fingers tapped on the bar, with no wedding ring in sight. *What could go wrong?*

"I'd like to personally welcome you to Cape Pursuit," he said.

Her lips formed a cold line. "You already did."

"Uh-oh," Tony said.

Silence replaced the friendly banter at the bar. Kevin's comrades in arms were sharks, waiting for blood they sensed was coming.

The bartender popped a cork and filled Nicole's empty glass, taking his time. He stood still, also waiting.

Kevin felt heat rise up his neck and set his ears on fire. He had a better chance escaping a burning building alive than surviving the next thirty seconds.

He remembered. It was only a glance in the side mirror of the truck. A blonde woman standing in the street staring at the wreckage of her car. The wreckage he had caused.

"You don't happen to own a small red car," he said slowly. "Do you?"

"I do." She sipped her wine, never taking her eyes off his.

"And… I almost hate to ask…but…is it missing a part? Maybe a door?"

"It is."

The silence was how Kevin pictured people waiting tensely in the eye of a hurricane. Hunkered down, knowing the worst was coming, thinking perhaps they should have evacuated when they'd had the chance.

Where is that kitchen fire?

"I'd also like my mirror back," she said, directing her words to Ethan. "So don't bother to add it to your asinine tourist museum."

She picked up her wine glass and returned to her table, only ten feet from the bar and easily within earshot. Close enough to make everyone uncomfortable.

Kevin sat on his bar stool like someone had soaked his

pants in superglue. Even if she'd given him the chance to explain, what would he have said? *Sorry, lady, but your car was in the way. Life over property.*

But she had no use for him or his explanations. She'd made that clear.

JANE SMILED AND waved at the firefighters now silently holding on to their beer bottles as if they were lifelines.

She leaned forward and whispered to Nicole. "I think you ruined Testosterone Night."

"I'll cry myself to sleep tonight," Nicole said quietly. "I know they're your friends, but I just couldn't sit here and listen to their bravado."

"Don't blame you a bit. They'll live." Jane grinned. "It's good for them to get a reminder once in a while that not every female on earth finds them irresistible."

Nicole regarded her friend, one eyebrow raised. "Have you ever dated any of them?"

"Not officially. I briefly dated a cop who left for the bigger department in Virginia Beach. Also dated a firefighter who was only here for the summer. Somehow I got little sister status with that group, so dating is off the table. Maybe I know too much about them."

"Nothing going on between you and Charlie?"

Jane blew out a breath and sat back, crossing her arms. "Nothing I want to burden you with tonight. It's a...well... it's a story."

Their burgers arrived, covered in barbecue sauce, cheese and bacon as promised. "To new beginnings," Nicole said, clinking her nearly empty wine glass against Jane's orange soda.

"Benvenuto," Jane said, laughing. "See, I learned something in that Italian class we took when we were juniors."

While they ate, the firefighters at the bar moved to a corner table closer to a flat-screen television. The baseball game was on, and the noise of the game and the bar patrons covered their conversation. Twice, Nicole's glance strayed to the table in the corner. Both times Kevin was looking at her.

"I'm hoping you can do something about my computer now that you're here. I think I need a new system," Jane said. "Maybe I should put everything in the cloud."

"I'll look at it. You mostly place online orders for supplies, track expenses and print receipts for purchases, right?"

"Yes," Jane said, nodding.

"And you don't have any employees?"

"Nope. Just you."

"Are you sure you actually need me?"

"I definitely do."

When Jane had asked Nicole to move to Cape Pursuit, the timing had seemed too perfect. Just when the top layer of scars from her brother's accident had scabbed over, the foolish office romance Nicole was involved in bubbled over and fizzled out.

It had been far better when she and her boss, Bryan, at the furniture plant were just flirting. Flirting has the potential for danger, but she told herself it was harmless. She ran his human resources department and online sales accounts, was flattered when he asked her to sit next to him at meetings and enjoyed an occasional lunch on his dime. It was a nice distraction.

Until they'd traveled for business and she ended up in his hotel room. The match was struck and burned hotly for about a week. Then it fizzled, and they both discovered there was no fuel left. The cold ashes remaining would make it impossible for her future with Bryan as a boss.

Jane happened to call to say hello at just the right time. Nicole told Jane about the big office mistake and the downward career spiral she was now being flushed along. And Jane begged Nicole to leave Indianapolis behind, swearing she needed someone with a head for business. Getting away from her work, Bryan, her memories, was such a tempting offer, Nicole couldn't refuse.

But she'd worried every day in the weeks since—as she'd finished out her lease, given her notice and packed her things—that Jane was only being nice. Being a friend. That she didn't need a business manager any more than Nicole needed another pair of shoes.

"I know what you're thinking, but you're wrong," Jane said, scrutinizing Nicole. "I really need your help. I have big plans to take my painting business to the internet. When the tourists are gone—nearly half the year—my sales are so dismal I can hardly pay the rent. I want to set up a website and sell online."

"Really?" Nicole brightened.

"Yes. That's where you come in. Since you're also an excellent photographer, I'm hoping you'll photograph and post my pieces on my website that doesn't exist yet."

Nicole felt a weight lift from her chest. "I could do that," she said, energy infusing her voice.

"I've thought of selling my one-of-a-kind stuff online, but I also need your opinion about doing some stock or custom items. I just have to figure out exactly what people want. Market surveys, you think? You know about that."

"I do," Nicole said, thinking of the market research she'd conducted for the furniture company and how excited she'd been to share the results with her former boss. She'd been foolish enough to think that working extra hours for Bryan's approval was some kind of honor.

Working for Jane would be better.

"And I don't know if I'm opening a can of worms offering to do custom pieces," Jane continued. "I've just done a few for close friends, but I'm worried about going online. People can be a real pain. They think they know what they want, but sometimes they only know it when they see it."

"We'll look into it, do a search and see what other art- ists like you are doing."

Jane nodded and scooped the last fries out of the basket.

"I think I'll start tomorrow by securing your web do- main. I have to do a search and see if seajanepaint.com is taken," Nicole said.

"What are the chances?"

"About as good as having the door of your car taken off by a fire truck," Nicole said. She chuckled, the laughter scat- tering the tension from her neck and shoulders. For the first time in a long time, she felt free. Maybe this would work out.

When Jane and Nicole asked their waitress for the check at the end of their meal, she told them it had already been covered. "Tip, too," she added, smiling.

Nicole looked at her friend, eyebrows raised.

"It wasn't me," she said. "Although I was planning to buy since you've had a tough day and I wanted to wine and dine my favorite new employee."

Nicole risked a glance at the corner table where all eyes were on the television. Except for one stormy green pair. It was no mystery who had paid their tab, but Nicole wondered what had motivated the gesture. Guilt? Remorse?

She hadn't seen any of that in the testosterone club at the bar.

"Least they could do," Jane commented. "And don't you dare think of going over there and saying thank you."

"Believe me, that's not what I was thinking," Nicole com- mented. She picked up her purse and followed her friend from the bar, carefully resisting the urge to look at the back corner.

CHAPTER THREE

A PILE OF Nicole's luggage took up a corner of the back room at Sea Jane Paint, hastily unloaded from the trunk of her damaged car before it got hauled away a few days earlier. When Nicole left Indianapolis, she had no definite plans, but she didn't intend to go back anytime soon. Her summer clothes were already unpacked neatly into her closet and dresser drawer at Jane's house. The winter clothes could stay in the heavy suitcase until at least October. If she was still there.

"We should be able to fit it all in my car after we close up today and we'll get you permanently moved into my guest room," Jane said, smiling at Nicole. "I hope you know I'm happy to have you stay as long as you want to."

"Thanks," Nicole said. She handed her friend a diet soda from the mini-fridge. "I appreciate it. Maybe I'll meet your Realtor friend to look at a few places. Now that I'm actually here I think I could commit to something. At least a rental." Nicole cracked open an orange soda. "Not that renting a place is much commitment."

"I rent," Jane said. "It's nice not having to fix the roof or unclog the kitchen drain."

"Did Charlie help you find the place?"

Nicole watched her friend's expression when she mentioned him. She'd noticed a hint of something between them at the bar. Was it her imagination? Jane tapped the top of her aluminum can and then exchanged it for a bottle of water from the fridge, avoiding Nicole's gaze the whole time.

"He did. He was one of the first people I met when I moved to Cape Pursuit five years ago. I had no idea at that time that I'd be renting a house and a running a gallery now."

"To the future," Nicole said, clinking her aluminum can against Jane's bottle. "Whatever it may be."

The front door opened and set off the chime, a foghorn sound that scared Nicole every time. It fit the nautical theme of the gallery and the tourists loved it, but to Nicole it sounded like a freighter about to run over a tiny boat. After the car door incident, she was jumpy about big loud things wreaking havoc on little ones. Too jumpy. There were a lot of things she was trying to get over. That was why she was here in Cape Pursuit.

"I'll get it," Nicole said. "You finish your lunch."

She moved aside the filmy curtain that separated the back room from the gallery and store and stopped in her tracks. It was not a tourist at the door.

Dressed in a navy blue shirt and pants, a fire department insignia over the left side of his chest, Kevin Ruggles stood inside the door of Sea Jane Paint. He shifted from foot to foot, rubbed his forehead with the back of his hand and glanced out the front window. *Uncomfortable*, she noted. *He ought to be.*

Her movement caught his attention and he strode toward her, closing the gap. He was tall, over six feet. Broad chest. A day's growth of beard darkened his square jaw. His dark hair was tousled as if he'd been up all night. He was far more attractive than she wanted him to be, considering that his occupation put him on her *do not touch* list.

He stood in front of her as if he wanted to say something, an expectant look on his face. Maybe the guy was used to a hero's welcome wherever he showed up, but Nicole wasn't handing out any accolades. She waited, giving him no encouragement other than one raised eyebrow.

"I brought you this," he finally said, holding out a plastic grocery bag. He smiled and tucked his chin, the gesture making him appear vulnerable. "It's the side mirror of your car."

He has no right to be so cute. He was about her age, but his demeanor was boyish, eager. Nicole took the bag and looked inside, heat creeping up her neck.

"I know it's broken," he said. "And your insurance company will replace it when they replace your door. But I feel better if it's in your hands and not…"

"On the Wall of Flame?" she asked.

He nodded, a pink flush spreading over his cheeks. "Yes."

"So you brought me this so you'd feel better?"

His flush deepened. He smiled and raised both eyebrows, a goofy, charming look that probably worked on women from his mother to his girlfriend. She glanced at his left hand. No ring, no tan line where a ring had recently been.

"The other guys were giving me all kinds of crap about it. I'm getting rid of the evidence."

It should have annoyed her, his selfish reason for bringing her the mirror. But somehow his raw honesty was cute. Too cute.

She held the bag at arm's length and dropped it in the garbage can by the cash register with a clunk. Kevin swallowed hard, his Adam's apple at her eye level. His smile faded.

He took his dark sea green eyes off hers for a moment and glanced out the front window. He turned slightly so she could see what was behind him. An ugly brown pickup truck with its side window rolled down was parked in front of the gallery. A huge dent marred the bed of the truck. Two wide paws and a nose rested on the open window frame.

"Your dog?" she asked. It was her first attempt at friendly

conversation. She'd have to be a marble statue not to at least ask about the paws and nose. They were adorable.

He nodded, a hint of smile returning. "Arnold. I worked last night and ended up staying over to cover the day shift until they got back from a call. Poor guy was lonely so I brought him with me."

Nicole craned her neck and tried to look around Kevin's very broad shoulders. The dog's head was visible now, and he appeared to be a beagle attempting to climb out the window.

"He loves a car ride," Kevin added.

"Does he ever jump out?"

Kevin laughed, a deep, rumbling laugh. "He tries. Never made it yet and he's at least twelve years old."

Nicole stepped to her right and saw the paws and nose disappear into the truck. "It looks like he gave up."

Kevin nodded. "He's probably tired. He doesn't sleep well when I'm gone all night. Arnold's a worrier. I think he knows I have a dangerous job." Kevin took another glance at his truck. "Dogs are sensitive," he added. "Or he wonders who'll feed him if I die in a fire."

The air left Nicole's lungs, and her shoulders dropped. Of course he had a dangerous job. The same dangerous job that had killed her brother when he was only twenty-one. Robbed him of his future, stole happiness from her parents, her sister and herself. She swallowed. Goose bumps rose along her chilled back.

A breeze behind her told her Jane had swept the curtain aside.

"Shopping for a painting?" Jane asked, her tone chipper and businesslike.

Kevin glanced at Jane and returned his attention to Nicole with a forehead wrinkle. As if he realized he'd said the wrong thing but didn't know what.

"Uh, no. I was bringing something over." He gestured to Nicole, but she had nothing in her hands.

"What did you bring?" Jane asked.

Nicole looked at Kevin, eyebrows raised, wondering what he'd say. She knew Jane had heard the entire exchange through the thin curtain. Jane always had her back and had been on her side since they'd moved into their freshmen dorm in college.

Kevin crossed his arms and faced the two women. Just when Nicole expected him to flee, he surprised her and held out his right hand.

"Let's start over," he said. "I'm Kevin Ruggles. I grew up here in Cape Pursuit. I've been a firefighter for about six years and the worst mistake I've made on the job was two days ago when I crashed into your car."

Shocked, Nicole held out her hand. He took it. His hand was large, warm, rough. But gentle. His touch made her want to withdraw her hand and run for the safety of the back room before he drew her in further than she wanted to go.

"And I really brought you that mirror," he nodded toward the trash can, "so I'd have a good excuse to come by and say I'm sorry. I'm sorry I smashed your car and made your first day in town a lousy one. I'm very glad you weren't in the car and I didn't hurt you."

His solemn expression, eyebrows drawn together, underscored his sincerity.

"I couldn't live with that," he added.

Nicole didn't say anything. Didn't encourage him to go on. But the heat returned to her face and ears.

"We got called to a kid not breathing and I was driving fast. Thought I could make it, but some tourists on bikes swerved into the street," he said, not dropping her hand or taking his eyes off hers. "I couldn't hit them."

Nicole swallowed, pulled her hand back and crossed her arms. She needed a barrier. Something about Kevin made

her want to forget the agony she felt every time she heard
a siren or saw a fire truck. Every time she thought of her
brother, perishing in the flames of a forest fire he'd thought
he could outrun.

"What happened to the kid?" Jane asked, filling the silence.

"He'll be okay," he said, directing his words to Jane. "It
wasn't as bad as his parents thought, but things often look
worse than they really are."

Kevin turned back to Nicole, a sad smile on his face.
"Anyway, I'm sorry about your car. And I hope you like
it here."

She nodded, acknowledging him. "Thank you," she said,
her words hollow.

Kevin pivoted and walked past watercolors propped on
shiny easels. He opened the front door, setting off the foghorn, and got into his truck. Nicole heard his door shut and
watched him put on his seat belt and pet his dog before he
pulled away from the front curb. The dog sat up in the passenger seat and stuck his nose out the window.

"Since you weren't making that easy for him, you should
have asked him to let you drive his truck while your car's
in the shop," Jane commented, grinning. "Would have been
fun to see what he said."

"It's probably a stick shift," Nicole said, disgust in her
voice. "I never learned to drive one of those. He seems like
the kind of man who would drive a standard. It's all about
the ego. And why should I have made that easy for him
anyway?"

Jane shrugged. "Coming in here was a nice gesture. He
wanted to explain himself."

"He probably just felt guilty and wanted to make himself feel better," Nicole huffed. She kicked the trash can
for emphasis.

"You need lunch," Jane said. "Go back and sit down, take your time."

"I'm fine."

Jane leaned one elbow on the glass counter. "If a garbage truck had taken out your car, would you feel better about it?"

"No."

Jane nodded. "So if a sanitation worker came in here in his uniform exuding sweetness and vulnerability, and he told you a sad story about swerving the trash truck to miss a kitten and how sorry he was he'd knocked your car silly, you'd give him the cold shoulder."

"Now you're being ridiculous," Nicole said, a small grin turning up the corners of her mouth.

"But you see my point."

Nicole sighed. "I hate the fire department."

Jane gave her a hug. "I know. And you have a right. But you have to admit fire trucks are sexier than garbage trucks."

"Everything is sexier than a garbage truck." Her shoulders sagged and Nicole felt like crying. "I just thought I would get away and start over. And bam. First thing that happens is I get knocked on my butt by the same guys who took Adam from us."

Jane held her friend by the shoulders. "Not the same guys. Different place. Different situation."

Nicole bit her lip and focused on breathing in through her nose, out through her mouth.

"I know you," Jane said. "When life knocks you down, you get up and dust yourself off."

Nicole swallowed. "I'll have some lunch and then get to work," she said.

"UNCONDITIONAL LOVE, HUH, ARNOLD?" Kevin said, scratching his dog's head between shifting gears on his aging F-150. "That's what everyone says dogs are good for."

Arnold scooted over and surrendered to the temptation of the open truck window, sticking his nose out.

"Fine," Kevin said.

Arnold sneezed and the wind blew snot back into the truck.

"Maybe I should take you to live at the station. You could be the mascot."

Kevin drove to the house he was currently painting on his days off from the station. An irregular schedule of twenty-four on, then thirty-six or twelve on gave him time to work in the sunshine on outside projects. Even if it meant sacrificing sleep.

Charlie Zimmerman stood in the driveway, holding a hammer. He walked up to Kevin's open window as soon as the truck stopped.

"Just got the for-sale sign put up," he said. "The house looks lousy now, but once you get it painted it'll sell fast. Especially with summer coming up."

The house was constructed exactly like the others on the street. Originally beach rentals, they were all one-story, wood-sided, with single-car garages and tiny front yards. Some of the houses had acquired character over the years with brightly painted walls, redesigned front entrances, creative landscaping. This house was like a wallflower cousin asked to the prom out of obligation. It needed color and life.

"Decide on the paint?" Kevin asked.

Charlie nodded. "Come see."

Kevin got out, walked around the truck, and opened the passenger door for Arnold. He lifted the beagle down.

"He doesn't get any better looking with age," Charlie said.

"Neither do you."

"So," Charlie continued, ignoring the insult, "the home-owner thought white was the best choice because it's a standard and it wouldn't scare off any potential buyers. My office thought color would make this place pop. At least that's what the ladies said. So we compromised."

"How?" Kevin asked.

"White with green shutters."

Charlie showed Kevin the buckets of paint stored in the garage, a swipe of color on each lid identifying the contents. The spring green shutter paint was a perfect match for Nicole's eyes. Not that she liked what she saw out of those eyes, at least not when she was looking at him.

He'd blown it. He just didn't know how, aside from the obvious business of wrecking her car.

"While you're here, I wondered if you'd want to think about a little business venture with me. You're a good painter and pretty handy with other stuff. And I've got the inside track on Cape Pursuit real estate."

"No, I don't want to buy and flip houses with you," Kevin said, his tone implying they'd talked about this before.

"You'd make some dough."

"I have enough money. And I'm taking classes this fall to get my fire science degree. So thanks, but no."

"If you change your mind, let me know."

Kevin unloaded a wooden ladder from the bed of his truck and set it next to the paint cans in the garage. He planned to go home and get a few hours' sleep while the sun was hot and then come back in the evening and start in. The house was already pressure washed, the loose paint scraped off. Covering ugly wood with fresh paint was one of Kevin's favorite things. It was just as satisfying as dousing a fire, but the paint lasted longer.

He'd been painting houses in Cape Pursuit since he was a teenager, and he remembered them all, always noticing them when he drove by and evaluating how well their paint was sticking.

"I thought I might see about getting Jane's friend a place to rent," Charlie said, helping unload painting supplies from the truck bed. Drop cloths, brushes, a bucket of paint thinner. "The blonde."

Kevin felt heat under his collar. It was hot in the garage, but that wasn't the only reason. "Did Jane mention how long her friend is staying?"

"Nicole," Charlie said. "Jane implied Nicole was here to stay. Permanently. Making a big move of some kind."

"Good for her. Nice place to live," Kevin commented.

"That all you have to say?"

"At the moment."

"She gave you a hard time at the restaurant. And nobody's seen the mirror that was supposed to go on the wall at the station."

"I think we should leave her alone. She's new in town. She's Jane's best friend. Maybe she's off-limits," Kevin said. "Like Jane is," he added, waiting for a reaction from Charlie. Everyone knew Charlie protected Jane as if she were a little sister.

Arnold bumped into a table in the crowded garage and knocked over a stepladder leaning on it. The ladder clattered to the floor and Arnold stared at it for a moment before lying down and putting his face on his paws.

"He's going blind," Kevin said. "It's worse when he's tired. We're headed home for some sleep, but I'll be back this evening to start in. If I get a coat of primer on before the sun goes down, I can start putting paint on tomorrow."

"Make fun of me if you want, but this place will make me a pile of cash. Think about it, Kevin. You can only fight fires for so long, and the real estate business is a great fallback plan."

Kevin shrugged. "Fighting fires is in my blood. If I ever get too old to do it, I'll hang around the station and bore the young guys with stories about how we used to do things back in my day." He grinned and scratched Arnold's ears while he talked. "Maybe they'll let me toss my walker in the back of the truck and drive them to the fires."

Charlie leaned against the wall. "You putting your name in for a promotion? When the chief retires in a few months, everyone will probably move up a notch. Might open up a lieutenant's job for you, maybe even captain."

"Thought about it," Kevin admitted. His older brother was already a lieutenant with just a few more years than Kevin on the department. "How about you? Are you applying?"

"No thanks," Charlie said. "I'm happy to stay out of paperwork at the station. Leadership is a whole lot of responsibility."

"Fighting fires is a responsibility," Kevin said.

Charlie shook his head. "Not the same thing. When you're an officer, the place owns you, body and soul. And I'm not interested in being owned by anything."

"Or anyone?"

Charlie laughed. "Definitely not. I'm in the rental business for the foreseeable future. Pretty women, ugly houses."

"Give me a few days and this one won't be ugly anymore," Kevin said. He hoisted Arnold into his truck, got in and backed out of the driveway. Charlie waved as he pulled away, and Kevin wondered how his friend could choose selling houses instead of aiming for the top job at the fire department.

CHAPTER FOUR

JANE OPENED HER front door, stepped out of her shoes and dropped her purse on a chair in the living room. Her feet hurt and she was starving, but it had been a good afternoon. Several small paintings and a few gift items had sold, and she'd also enlisted Nicole to rearrange the displays in the front windows of the gallery. Business was picking up on the waves of spring sunshine, and she had a lot to hope for in her future—more than she'd even admitted to her best friend.

"We could order a pizza," Jane said. "I think I could eat the entire thing myself."

"No way. I've been here five days, and I haven't cooked once," Nicole said as she took off her shoes and left them by the front door. "Either I'm living a dream, or I'm being a lousy friend."

Jane wandered into the kitchen with Nicole right behind her. She took a can of cat food from a lower cabinet and smiled at her houseguest. "You're not a lousy friend. You've been busy moving in and helping me build my art empire."

"You look exhausted," Nicole said, giving Jane a long look. "And I like cooking."

"I'm thrilled to have you here, but I'll make you a deal if it'll make you feel better. I'll feed Claudette, and you make dinner for us two."

"Deal," Nicole said.

Nicole took a skillet from a rack near the sink while Jane

found a clean bowl for her cat. It was nice having someone else in her kitchen. As much as she loved owning and running her gallery and living a peaceful life in a seaside town, the loneliness hit her every night when she came home. Having Nicole living with her gave her someone to talk to.

Someone she should confide in. Soon.

As Nicole sliced vegetables, Jane peeled back the metal lid on the can of cat food. Claudette circled her legs, excited about her evening meal. Without warning, the sight and smell of the wet food hit Jane like a wave of filthy water. She put her hand to her mouth, nearly retching, and dropped the can on the counter. It rolled, crashing loudly into the stainless steel sink.

"What's the matter?" Nicole asked, rushing over. "Did you cut yourself on the lid?"

Jane shook her head and gripped the edge of the counter, fighting nausea. She heard a chair scrape the kitchen floor and felt Nicole pressing her into it.

"Jane, say something," Nicole said. "Do you need a cold cloth or a drink?"

"I'm all right," she protested. "The cat food smell just got me there for a minute."

Claudette danced around the chair legs, sniffing the air, and then jumped into Jane's lap. Nicole grabbed the cat and set her gently on the floor. She wound through Jane's legs and tickled her bare feet.

"She's hungry," Jane whispered.

"She can wait a minute. What's going on with you? You've smelled cat food a million times, and if I know Claudette, she's been eating the same kind of food since we were in college. She knows her own mind."

Jane sat back and took a deep breath. "I'm okay now. It was a passing thing."

Nicole put the food in the cat's bowl and set it on the

floor on the far side of the kitchen. She grabbed a chair and pulled it close to Jane's.

"Talk to me," Nicole commanded.

Before she could say a word, Jane's tears betrayed her. "I was planning to tell you, but I wanted you to get settled in first."

Nicole put an arm around Jane's shoulders. "Tell me what? Oh, God, are you sick? What's wrong?"

Noticing the worry in her friend's eyes, Jane tried to smile. "I'm not sick. At least not permanently." She sucked in a deep breath. "I'm pregnant."

It was the first time she had said the words aloud. Jane hadn't spoken of it to anyone, even after her doctor confirmed it several weeks ago. It was her secret, the new life growing in her body. She hadn't even told her parents, though she knew she couldn't conceal it from them much longer. They lived an hour away, and she was surprised her mother hadn't already figured out there was something going on, just from her voice over the phone.

"I wondered," Nicole said.

"You did?"

"There were just a few things that didn't seem…right."

"You can say that again," Jane said, sniffing and swiping at her tears. She'd already accepted the change her life was taking. A baby. For the past few weeks, the thought had come over her like sunshine through a window. Exciting, warming, but illuminating, too. How was she going to manage a baby along with her gallery? Was she ready to be a single mother? Or a mother at all?

Jane had found her own peace and joy about the child, but her emotions overwhelmed her as she tried talking about it for the first time. It was liberating but frightening, and she choked back sobs. Nicole jumped up and came back with a box of tissues.

"It'll be okay," Nicole said.

Jane wiped her eyes while Nicole rubbed her back and didn't ask questions. "I'm not crying because I'm sad," Jane mumbled from behind her tissues. "Having a baby isn't a tragedy."

"Of course not," Nicole assured her. "And you're not alone. I'm here. And Claudette will be a wonderful baby-sitter while we're at the gallery."

Jane laughed and wadded up her tissues. She looked at her friend's sincere, supportive smile. "What am I going to do?"

"Be a wonderful mother."

"I hope so," she whispered. "At first I was stunned. Couldn't believe it. But then I realized there was only one thing I could do. Be excited that I'm getting a wonderful and unexpected gift."

"Can I be Aunt Nicole?"

"Of course. I'm an only child, so you're the only aunt my baby is going to get."

Nicole nodded and waited silently, hands on her knees.

"You know you want to ask," Jane said. She would have been dying to ask if the tables were turned.

"Ask what?" Nicole said. "I'm here for you, and that's all I need to know."

"The father."

Nicole got up and poured two glasses of water. "You only have to tell me what you want to tell me."

Jane took a long, soothing drink. There was no reason to keep the truth from Nicole. Perhaps her best friend could help her figure out what to do.

"Charlie Zimmerman," she said. "Realtor, firefighter, baby daddy."

Nicole sucked in her lower lip but didn't say anything.

"I've known him for five years. We're friends," Jane said swiftly. "He's funny and attractive…but I didn't think he was interested in me other than my status as the kid sister of the fire department. And then…"

"Then?"

"Stupid Valentine's Day," Jane muttered. "What a dumb holiday. It should be outlawed. It just makes single people feel unworthy and couples feel like they have to come up with some magical present or date. And then sometimes you go on dates you never would have accepted if it weren't Valentine's Day."

"True," Nicole conceded. "I spent it watching my favorite movie and drinking wine by myself this year."

"Under the Tuscan Sun?"

Nicole nodded. "I swear I'm going to run away to Italy one of these days."

"I wish I had been there watching it with you," Jane said. "I wouldn't have ended up single and pregnant."

"So you went on a date with Charlie on Valentine's Day?"

"No. We both had dates with other people."

Nicole leaned back. "This is getting interesting."

Jane laughed. "It's not funny."

"I'll be the judge of that. Right after I get our dinner cooking." She stood and turned on the burner. "You need to eat, and I'm happy to listen and cook at the same time."

Jane watched Nicole scoop ingredients into the pan, and the aroma reminded her she was actually hungry. The sick feeling from the cat food was long gone. Poor Claudette. She might need to switch to dry food for a few months. And when the baby came along…how would an aging house cat, set in her ways, adjust to the change?

How would *she* adjust to the change?

"He doesn't know," Jane said as Nicole stirred.

"I assumed. When he sat with us at the bar, I thought there might be something between you." She turned and held a large spoon in the air. "But I had no idea."

"I have to tell him."

"You do," Nicole agreed. "But not tonight."

Jane laughed. "No, not tonight. But it's not the kind of thing you can hide forever. Not that I'd want to."

"And what do you think he'll say?"

"I have almost no doubt about it. He'll ask me to marry him."

"That jerk!" Nicole said, grinning. "And everyone thinks those firefighters are such heroes. Everyone except me, of course."

"That's exactly the problem. He'll offer to do what he thinks is the right thing without a second thought."

"But you'd have second thoughts."

"Of course I would. I've known him a long time, and he's no fan of commitment. Dated one girl after another, never staying with anyone for long. He would only marry me out of obligation, and I don't want to be someone's obligation. I'm worth more than that."

FOLLOWING POLICE ORDERS, Charlie and Ethan waited behind the shelter of the fire truck while several officers entered the dilapidated home in a neglected section of Cape Pursuit. Far from the eyes of tourists, it was a five-minute ride from the fire station. Calls to the Dune Heights area of town often ended in a refusal of treatment, and domestic violence calls left Charlie and his fellow firefighters with the sick feeling that someone needed their help but wasn't going to get it.

"I hate these calls," Ethan muttered.

Charlie nodded. Everyone hated seeing drunk guys threaten their wives and families. His father would have cut off his own arm before threatening his wife and son. He would also have given that arm to have more years with Charlie's mother, who died far too young of breast cancer.

"Maybe it's a false alarm," Charlie said. He listened closely for any sounds coming from the house. "It happens."

Ethan blew out a breath and leaned against the truck. The

midday sun flashed off the chrome pump. Charlie peered through the open middle of the truck, where the pump operator usually stood. Both he and Ethan wore full turnout gear and smelled like smoke. The Dumpster fire behind a fast-food restaurant in town hadn't taken long to put out, and they were returning to the station when the call came in. The rest of their crew had returned to the station to grab the ambulance, but Ethan and Charlie went straight to the scene. The massive pumper truck was stocked with first aid and rescue equipment.

"I'd take a false alarm," Ethan said. "Police only came to my house once when I was a kid, despite my parents constantly drinking and fighting. It wasn't a false alarm that day."

Charlie knew Ethan had a tough background. Instead of letting it destroy his life, he funneled every ounce of pain into doing the right thing. He fought fires, saved lives and never touched alcohol. He went along to the bar with his friends, and he drove them all home every single time. The eight-passenger SUV he owned probably cost him a fortune in car payments and gas.

"My dad spent the night in jail and it educated him for quite a while about his drinking limit." Ethan took off his helmet and ran his fingers through his damp hair. "I can't believe some days they're both still alive." Ethan shrugged and sat on the chrome step on the side of the truck. "Well, I don't see them much even though they live right up the street."

Charlie sat next to him and rested his elbows on his knees. It was hot on the shiny chrome bumper, blistering in his turnout gear. A cool shower at the station sounded like heaven, but he and Ethan would stay and sweat it out, hoping for the chance to help.

A police officer stepped around the front of the truck, and Charlie and Ethan jumped to their feet. "You better come in here," he said. "We took out the husband in cuffs, but the wife could use some attention."

Charlie hoisted the medical bag on his shoulder, and he and Ethan trudged up to the house behind the cop. The front steps had a missing board and one of the numbers over the front door was missing. A faded outline of the number *two* indicated where it had been. Still wearing his helmet, Charlie ducked out of habit as he went through the front door.

A woman sat on the only cushion left on a decrepit couch. She held a kitchen towel to her head. Charlie knelt in front of her and quickly snapped on the gloves his partner handed him. "I'm Charlie," he said gently. "I'm a firefighter and I'm here to help you. Can I look at your injury?"

He heard Ethan talking with one of the police officers, asking if there were any other injured people in the house. The room looked like a battlefield. A table was overturned, a window was broken and there was a sizable hole in the wall above the couch.

The woman looked warily at Charlie. He took off his helmet and set it next to him on the floor so she could see him better. He opened his hands and held them in front of her so she could see there was nothing in them. "I'm not going to hurt you," he said.

She lowered the towel and Charlie didn't flinch when he saw the bloody mess on the side of her face. Although he'd seen worse at fire scenes and car accidents, the wounds inflicted by a person's supposed loved ones always seemed to be the ugliest.

The police officers had left the room so Ethan and Charlie could help the victim. Ethan snapped open an ice pack and handed it to Charlie. He stood back, letting Charlie take the lead because he was the first person to talk to the patient. Charlie heard the ambulance's siren approaching. "A few of my partners are coming, and they'll take you to the hospital."

"What makes you think I'm goin'?" the woman asked. Her lip quivered when she spoke.

"You need to," he said gently. "Your cut needs a few stitches."

"I don't know."

"I'll go with you," Charlie said, hoping he'd gained some of her trust. Ethan could take the truck back. He could wear his heavy turnout gear just a little longer. He placed sterile gauze on the open wound on her temple and held the ice pack over the bandage. She didn't object. Her dirty hair, streaked with gray, had already stuck to the drying blood on the side of her face. Charlie was afraid she'd crumple if they tried to pick her up.

"What's your name?" he asked.

"Karleen," she said.

"Hey," a loud voice yelled in the adjoining room. Charlie glanced up in time to see a massive bearded man staggering into the living room. He was shirtless and disheveled. "You can't take my brother to jail just for beating up this—"

Charlie stood and shielded the woman on the couch, and Ethan moved swiftly and pinned the large man against the door frame. He fought back, and a lamp crashed to the floor, but Ethan was almost as large and had the advantage of a thick suit of turnout gear. Charlie wanted to jump into the fight, but his first duty was to protect his patient, so he stood his ground. Ethan was winning anyway.

At the sound of the scuffle, two cops rushed back into the living room and were followed by Tony Ruggles and his father, the fire chief. When the assailant saw he was outnumbered by six men ready to fight, he backed off.

"I ain't going to jail, too," the bearded man said. "I was just sayin' it ain't right to take her word over his. She's just as drunk."

Charlie turned to Karleen, keeping his body between her and the other man.

"Can we go?" the woman whispered to Charlie. "I need to get away from him."

He offered her a hand. "Ready when you are."

As Charlie helped his patient out of the house and into the back of the ambulance, he mentally reviewed any rental properties he owned that were empty. He'd do anything it took to help Karleen find a new home. Even though he'd never be half the man his father was, he could try.

CHAPTER FIVE

NICOLE AWOKE TO the sound of sirens. Wailing sirens. She lay awake listening for a moment and then drifted into a dream that was her worst nightmare—a startlingly realistic memory of her brother.

TALL, HANDSOME ADAM. He was blond and green-eyed like her and had the gift of long limbs and broad shoulders. The last time she saw him, he was boarding a plane in Indianapolis to go out West for his summer job with the forestry service. He already wore the T-shirt with the fire insignia on the front and one large word on the back: FIRE.

In the dream, he smiled and waved to her and her parents as they stood in the area just before the airport security line. They watched him navigate bag check, walk through the metal detector and head off to fight flames and save lives. He turned and smiled at her one last time.

NICOLE AWOKE AGAIN, sweat drenching her nightshirt. She had never seen him alive again.

The sound of noise in the kitchen, clanging pots, metal on metal, had awakened her this time. She pulled on a thin robe and headed toward the clamor.

Claudette lay curled on a kitchen chair, watching Jane pour coffee into a large thermos. The tabby cat kept one sleepy eye open, and Jane herself was wide awake and zipping around her small kitchen.

"Sorry to wake you up," Jane said. She screwed the lid on the thermos and filled another, smaller carafe.

"You're making coffee at one in the morning?" Nicole asked. Her dream still made her feel disoriented, almost as if someone was going to knock on the door and deliver the news that was every family's nightmare.

"Fire down the street, and it looks like they'll be there awhile." Jane opened the cabinet over the sink and pulled out two sleeves of disposable white cups. "I'm taking the guys coffee."

Jane was already dressed in jeans and a long-sleeved T-shirt. Although it was early May, the nights on the Virginia coast were still chilly.

"Can I help?" Nicole asked.

"Spare blankets. I keep them in the closet outside the bathroom, bottom shelf. Would you grab three or four? And you could throw on some clothes if you want to help carry this stuff."

Jane flipped the switch to brew another pot. She glanced up and met Nicole's eyes. "I'll understand if you don't want to."

Nicole hesitated. She wanted to help. But her dream was still so raw, her damp nightshirt clinging to her and chilling her. She swallowed and steadied her breathing. "I'll get dressed and grab the blankets," she said.

Claudette followed her down the hall, winding between her legs and apparently hoping for something interesting to happen. Nicole dressed quickly in jeans and a sweatshirt, slipped into sneakers, and went to the linen closet. She wanted to hurry, but her legs were lead. The door creaked in the nighttime silence and she pulled the chain to turn on the bulb in the closet. Claudette crept stealthily inside, her tail twitching. A stack of industrial-looking rough blankets were on the lower shelf. Nicole pulled out four of them, toed the cat out of the closet, turned off the light and closed the door.

She gathered the blankets in her arms and steeled herself. She was going to a fire in the middle of the night. There would be firefighters, flashing lights, danger. Was anyone hurt? She nearly lost her nerve, but she took solace in the fact that Jane would be there with her. It would be okay. Starting over in a new place meant she had to face the things that were holding her back. But she wasn't sure she could.

As they went through the front door, Jane lugging the big thermos and cups and Nicole holding blankets, they saw the flashing lights and spotlights of the fire scene only eight houses down the street.

The house on fire was a large one, a storybook house with fancy trim and detailed paint. White with rose, sage and soft gold accents. She'd snapped a photo of it two days ago when she took an evening walk with her camera slung over her shoulder.

Fire trucks with hoses snaking from hydrants robbed the house of its fairy-tale quality. Neighbors gathered, their faces red and white in the flashing lights. Jane walked quickly, but Nicole lagged a few steps behind. Lights were on in houses they passed even though it was the middle of the night. It appeared the whole neighborhood had beaten them to the scene.

But Nicole and Jane had an advantage. They had coffee and blankets.

A small group of people wearing bathrobes and sweatshirts, clothing disheveled and untucked, gathered just outside the fire scene. Nicole stopped, but Jane stepped over a hose and walked right up to a firefighter in full gear. A reflective stripe defined the bottom of his heavy yellow coat. The word *Zimmerman* flashed in reflective letters across his back. Jane put her thermos on the truck's silver running board and waited next to Charlie while he listened to a radio pressed against his ear and adjusted gauges on the massive pump on the side of the truck.

Nicole felt like she was in a war zone. She didn't follow Jane, hanging back and mutely holding on to the blankets. How could Jane be so brave? Not only had she marched up to the scene, but she was talking with the father of her baby. Putting other people's problems before her own—that was the source of Jane's bravery.

"Can I borrow those?" A police officer, an older man whom Nicole recognized as the officer who wrote the report on her car, stood at her elbow. "The family would sure appreciate it."

He took two blankets off the top and cocked his head, indicating she should follow him. She wanted to help, wanted to offer comfort to people whose house had windows broken out, charred furniture on the lawn, smoke seething from the upper floors. She took a breath and followed the police officer, resolving to be strong. Her brother would be in there fighting the fire.

If he were here.

If he were alive.

"Here you go," the police officer said. He handed a blanket to a woman wearing a nightgown and a man's coat that was much too large for her. She wrapped the blanket around a little girl and tucked in the folds in front. The girl sat down, the long tails of the blanket spreading around her as if she were on a picnic.

A firefighter came over. Kevin Ruggles. "Any accelerants in the garage or basement? Gas cans, propane tanks, anything like that?"

The little girl's father shook his head. "No gas cans. We have a lawn service. Nothing else like that."

Kevin nodded, his helmet bobbing. He pushed his helmet up and nodded to Nicole.

"Thanks," he said. He turned and trudged back to the front porch where a man in a red helmet was giving orders.

The little girl got up and followed him, her blanket dragging on the ground. Her parents didn't notice, but Nicole did. She waited, watching. The girl wasn't in danger. Kevin was talking with the man who appeared to be in charge of the fire scene, and the worst seemed to be over. The girl pulled on the edge of Kevin's coat and looked up at him. He leaned down and put his ear as close to her as he could manage with his helmet on, listening and nodding. Then he turned the girl around by her shoulders and pointed at her parents.

"Where did you go?" the mother asked, panic and despair in her voice as her daughter approached. "I told you to stay close by, honey. It's dangerous."

"I was asking him to look for Eddie," she said, and started to cry. "I can't find him. What if he died in the fire?"

The parents exchanged pained looks.

Oh, God, Nicole thought. *Who is Eddie? Her brother?* She felt tears stinging her eyes as she relived the pain of losing Adam.

"He was sleeping on my bed when the smoke alarm woke me up," the girl continued.

"Maybe he followed us out," her father said, putting an arm around his daughter. "He can see really well in the dark."

Nicole let out the breath she was holding. *Okay, we're obviously talking about a pet. Breathe.*

"I asked the fireman to look for him and he promised he would," the child continued.

"I'm sure he will, baby," her father said.

"I'll help you look," Nicole offered. "Is Eddie a dog or a cat?"

"Cat," the girl said.

"Maybe he followed you, just like your dad said. We could stay out of the way and look around together."

Nicole had no idea why she was insisting on searching for a cat that probably perished in the fire. But in a way, she understood the girl's grief. Knew what it was like to hope someone or something you loved had somehow survived against the odds.

"I'm Nicole," she told the girl's parents. "I'm staying with my friend Jane who owns the art gallery in town."

"We know Jane," the mom said. To her daughter, she said, "If you stay far away from the firemen and the trucks, you can go with this nice lady and look around." Her face softened. "Maybe he climbed a tree to hide and he's just waiting for you to come get him."

Nicole took the girl's hand. "What color is your cat?"

"Black. He's all black."

Great. Looking for a panicked black cat that may or may not even be alive. In the darkness. At least it was better than watching the firefighters systematically carry out smoldering furniture and other belongings. Anything was better than that.

"I'm Julia," the girl said, her voice small. Her dark hair fell around her face and she looked tiny under the rough blanket. "Do you think we'll find Eddie?"

"Yes," Nicole said, trying to sound convincing. "He could be sound asleep in the mailbox."

"Or my sandbox."

"I'll bet you're right. We'll check those places and then start looking under plants and in trees. Is Eddie a good climber?"

Julia wrinkled her forehead. "He never goes out of the house. He usually sleeps all day unless I'm playing with him."

"So," Nicole said. "He's a beginner climber. That's good. He won't be too far up. But we're going to need a flashlight."

Nicole took the child's hand and approached Kevin, who

was now digging through a cabinet on the side of one of the fire trucks.

"Excuse me," she said. "Do you have a flashlight in there we can borrow?"

At the sight of Nicole and the little girl, his brows came together in a skeptical look. "What are you planning to do with it? You can't go in the house."

"I'm not a fool," Nicole said. "We're looking for Eddie."

Kevin glanced at the little girl. "The cat?" he asked.

"Uh-huh," Julia said. "Nicole is helping me find him. We're looking in the mailbox and up in the trees."

Kevin smiled. "That's really nice of Nicole, and I'm sure you'll find him. He's probably just scared. Fires are scary."

He took a flashlight from the large front pocket of his heavy coat and handed it to Nicole.

"I'll bring it back," she said.

"I know where to find you," he replied, smiling at her and holding eye contact as if he wanted to emphasize that they were on the same side.

"Thank you," Nicole said. She took the child's hand and they crept around the edge of the property, checking every hiding place they could find on the lawn. Trying to ignore the damp, smoky smell of the fire, she swept the flashlight into trees, under shrubs and beneath the swing set. Nicole smiled encouragingly at the little girl even though it seemed hopeless.

One set of searchlights went off. A fire truck left, and neighbors went home. It had to be two in the morning at least, but there was no sign of Eddie. Nicole felt tears of frustration, exhaustion and something she didn't want to think about well in her eyes. Julia's mother found them in the backyard and claimed her daughter's hand. "Sorry we didn't find Eddie tonight," Nicole told the girl, "but I'm sure he'll come back tomorrow."

"We're staying with my sister across town," the mother

said. "If you happen to see a lonely black cat around, here's her number."

Nicole took the scrap of paper and promised to keep an eye out. She watched the family climb wearily into an SUV with only the clothes and blankets on their backs. The fire chief and another firefighter put up yellow caution tape across the doors.

Nicole still had the flashlight and most of the trucks had left, so she approached the man in the red helmet. "Please give this to Kevin Ruggles," she said, her voice faint with disappointment and unshed tears.

"He's right here," the chief said, handing the light over Nicole's head to a man behind her. She turned and faced him.

Although he was covered in black grime, the light from the remaining fire truck illuminated his smile. "Did you find the cat?" he asked.

She shook her head, not wanting to talk about the cat or anything else related to the fire.

"Hope he didn't die," Kevin said, "but I'm afraid it's pretty likely. Animals tend to hide and the flames go right over them."

Nicole thought her heart would explode. Her brother, when he realized he couldn't outrun the forest fire, had hunkered down with his partners under fire-resistant blankets. Two of his partners survived, although seriously burned. Adam did not. He was lying under the blanket when they found him.

She couldn't help it. Tears ran down her cheeks and a sob choked her.

"Hey," Kevin said, touching her arm. "Sorry. I didn't think you knew the…uh…cat."

Jane appeared out of the darkness. "Ready to go home?" she asked.

Nicole nodded, unable to speak. Kevin took off his helmet and ran a hand through his hair. "I think we're all ready for this night to be over," he said.

Jane glanced at Nicole and she knew her teary face must look a mess.

"Okay, Nikki?"

In answer, Nicole turned and headed toward the street. She heard Jane murmur something to Kevin and then her friend was at her side, arm around her, as they trudged home.

KEVIN AND THE chief were the last two on scene, finishing cleanup for the time being. There would be plenty to do tomorrow when the fire and insurance inspectors showed up.

"Call it a night," the chief said.

Kevin tossed the flashlight Nicole had returned to him into the side compartment of the truck. It bounced against the back of the bin and rolled out, falling on the ground and rolling under the truck.

"Dangit," Kevin said, dropping to his knees to look for it. The flashlight was hidden in the grass, but he saw something else under the truck. A black blob. The black blob moved and light reflected off a pair of eyes.

"Hey, buddy. You must be Eddie."

He ducked low and reached for the cat, but the frightened animal recoiled and slunk farther back.

"Don't make this hard on me, cat."

He extended his arm slowly toward the animal and then made a quick lunge, grabbing the cat before he could run away, but whacking his head on the running board of the truck at the same time. He held the cat in one hand and got up. Tucking the cat inside his coat, he glanced down the street toward Jane's house. It had only been a half hour since the women left. Could they still be awake?

"Got everything?" the chief said.

"Yup. And I think I found the homeowners' cat under the truck."

"We didn't run over it, did we?" the chief asked. "I hate when we do that."

"No, he's alive. Can we stop by Jane's house on the way back to the station? If she's still up, I think she can help us with it."

The chief stared at the lump inside Kevin's turnout coat. "Didn't know you were such a cat person," he said.

Kevin shrugged. "You drive."

They parked in the street in front of Jane's house. Lights were still on inside. "Be right back," he said.

Approaching the front door, Kevin tried to gauge which rooms had lights on. He guessed they were the kitchen and living room. A good sign.

He tapped on the door just loud enough so anyone who was already awake would hear him. A moment later, someone moved a curtain, and the porch light came on overhead. Jane opened the door wide.

"What happened to you?" she asked.

Not what Kevin expected. "Happened?"

"Your head. It's bleeding. Come in."

Kevin stepped into the house, keeping one hand on the warm lump inside his coat. He toed the door shut and swiped the other one over his forehead. Blood smeared his grimy hand. "Oh," he said. "I guess I did that when I was trying to fish the cat out from under the fire truck."

"You found Eddie?" Jane exclaimed.

Nicole appeared behind Jane wearing only a short pink nightshirt. Her hair was wet and her bare feet and legs under the short edge of the shirt riveted Kevin's attention. "You found Eddie?" she echoed.

Kevin pulled open the flap of his coat and revealed black fur. "He's been fighting me under here." Eddie stuck his head out and hissed.

"Did he claw your head?" Nicole asked, gesturing over Kevin's eye.

"Nope. That happened while I was trying to catch him. He was hiding under the pumper. He's fast for a house cat."

"Poor Eddie," Nicole said. She approached and reached toward him, her fingers brushing his neck. Her wet blond hair tickled his chin.

He would bring home a wild cat every night of the week for attention like that. But it was over too soon. Nicole unsnapped his coat and pulled out the cat, cuddling him against her chest. His coat flapped open and he wished he could think of a reason for her to reach in again. Her green eyes were darker in the dim light of the entryway. She smelled like shampoo, as if she'd just stepped from a shower to erase the soot and smoke of the night.

The cat enjoyed Nicole's attention for a moment and then struggled to get down.

"Close the door behind you," Jane said. "Want to come in for something to eat?"

"Love to, but the chief's waiting in the truck." He watched Nicole's every move as she bent over to put the cat on the rug. He cleared his throat. "We have to clean hoses and write reports until dawn. Then at least one of us will be back in the morning combing through the mess with the fire inspector and probably the insurance claims person."

Jane's tabby cat came around the corner, back up, tail high. She saw Eddie, and a low growl emanated from her throat. Eddie bounced to his feet and fled, a black blur down the hallway, the tabby right on his tail.

Kevin rubbed his head. "Think you could keep that little devil for the night and get him back to the owners tomorrow?"

"Will you stop rubbing your cut with your filthy hands?" Jane said. "And yes, Nicole has the number where they're staying. We'll call in the morning and meet up with them."

"That little girl will be so happy," Nicole said, smiling at Kevin as if he'd just made a rainbow appear over Cape Pursuit. It was the happiest he'd seen her in the short time he'd known her. "Thank you for catching him. And for bringing him over. I can sleep now."

"You're welcome. I really got lucky. I dropped that flashlight you borrowed and it rolled under the truck right to the cat's hiding place. Like it was meant to be."

A searchlight shone through the glass on the door and toggled back and forth.

"I think my uncle's ready to get back to the station," Kevin said. "Can't blame him."

"Good night," Nicole said.

"Night," he replied, staring at her bare feet and nightshirt. "Thanks for bringing blankets and coffee," he said, directing his words to both Nicole and Jane. "We always appreciate it."

He opened the door just wide enough to slip outside, in case the cats came racing back through. As he walked down the front sidewalk toward the fire truck on the street, he had the feeling a set of green eyes was on his back. And the feeling cleared the smoke from his head and lifted his heart.

CHAPTER SIX

KEVIN PULLED THE ladder truck out of the station and parked it on the front concrete apron. He got out, slid the wheel chocks under the rear dual wheels and headed for the cab of the pumper. One by one, he pulled the pumper, light rescue pickup and heavy rescue squad out and parked in front of the station's four bays. He drove the Jeep with the dive trailer and then three ambulances out the huge overhead doors in the back, totally clearing out the Cape Pursuit fire station.

"You're serious about cleaning," Tyler Ruggles remarked. "Something on your mind?"

"Tracked in sand from that call on the beach and lots of debris from the house fire two nights ago," Kevin said. "This place is a mess." He used a wide broom and made passes across the concrete.

His brother opened the rear doors of the ambulance. He sat on the bench seat in the back of the vehicle, clipboard on his lap, and reached into cabinets with sliding doors. Kevin knew he was inventorying every bandage, mask, tube and sterile pad. It was part of the daily drill.

"You're off in an hour," Tyler remarked. "Hope you plan to finish your housecleaning and put all the trucks back."

"Nope," Kevin said. "I plan to leave you with a mess. Payback for sharing a room with you for fifteen years. Does your wife put up with your pigsty habits?"

Tyler rubbed his forehead while simultaneously flipping

off his younger brother. "Does your fat old dog like your neat-freakery?"

"Arnold's not fat," Kevin said. "He's just short."

Kevin unrolled a hose from a hanger on a post by the large overhead doors. He started by an entry door leading into the bunk room and offices and continued hosing a careful pattern over the wide floor. Drains ran front to back between the parking bays, and Kevin directed the stream toward them. He rolled up the hose and then got a wide squeegee from a hook, using a long, sweeping stroke to shove the remaining water off the station floor.

His brother leaned against the water rescue trailer, arms crossed, watching. "You need a wife," Tyler commented. "And some kids. You'd learn to appreciate a mess that way."

"When I'm chief someday, I'm going to make you do this," Kevin told him. He got in the cab of the heavy rescue truck and backed it slowly into the station. He followed it with the pumper. As he went outside and pulled the wheel chocks from under the rear tires of the ladder truck, he caught a glimpse of a blonde woman on a bicycle.

She slowed then stopped by the door of the truck, planting both her feet. She smiled. Kevin's heart raced as if he were responding to a five-alarm fire.

"Hi," she said. "Are you leaving on an emergency call?"

Kevin tossed the rubber chocks in the cabinet over the rear wheels. "No, I was just cleaning the station floor."

Nicole glanced at the wide brick fire station with its bay doors in the front and back standing open.

"Quite a job," she commented.

"Trying to stay awake for the last part of my shift," Kevin said. "It was a long night."

"Again?"

"It goes in streaks," Kevin said. He leaned against the front fender of the massive ladder truck. "Did you have any trouble getting the cat back to the girl's family?"

Nicole smiled. "Nope. We called the next morning and they came by to pick him up. You should have seen that little girl's face. I told her the nice fireman rescued the cat."

"A bit of an exaggeration."

"I thought it might make her feel better. You never know what part of an event a child will focus on. I'm hoping she remembers her house cat getting a ride in a fire truck. I glamorized that part a little bit for her sake."

"Where are you going?" he asked, pointing at her bike. "I could give you a ride in the fire truck. If nobody's looking."

Nicole laughed. "Better not. It's my first day off from the gallery. This is my only mode of transportation right now unless I ride with Jane."

Kevin bit his lip. "I hate to ask how much longer until they put the door back on your car."

"And replace the windshield. And repaint that whole side," Nicole said.

"Did I mention how sorry I am?"

She smiled. "I figured it out. Did you get your rescue truck fixed?"

Kevin pointed through the station to the ambulances parked side by side. Their body styles and sizes were different. One had wide tires and a heavy truck frame; the other two were smaller and lighter. The smaller ones might have made it past Nicole's car, but the big one hadn't stood a chance.

"It hardly got scratched," he said, gesturing at the larger one. "Never had to take it out of service."

"Lucky for it."

Kevin nodded. Scratched his jaw. Shifted his feet. "So what are you doing on your day off?"

"Beach. Just like all the tourists." She shrugged. "I'm from Indianapolis, so the ocean is a treat."

"I grew up here, and I never get tired of it," he said. He would also never get tired of Nicole's eyes and the way her face softened when she smiled. If only he could start over with her.

A loud ringing in the station echoed through the open bay doors. A dispatcher intoned an ambulance call for a possible heart attack at one of the hotels along the strip. Tyler and another officer barreled out an interior door and headed for the smaller ambulance.

"We got this one, baby brother," Tyler yelled. "Don't want you to have to take off your cleaning apron." He got in the cab of the ambulance and pulled out the back of the driveway, lights flashing and siren blaring.

"Baby brother?" Nicole asked.

"Tyler is three years older than I am and he never lets me forget it. He's my best friend, but he's a pain in the rear."

Something changed in Nicole's face. Her eyes dropped and her smile faded. Maybe she didn't like hearing people complain about their relatives. If that was the case, she wouldn't want to make a habit of hanging around the fire department where they acted like one big family and many of them were, in fact, related.

"Believe it or not, my uncle is the chief and my cousin Tony is in the department. If we ever had a family feud, this place would be a mess."

"It sounds like this—" she waved her hand at the trucks and station "—is a family tradition for you."

Her voice was flat, as if she were showing her kitchen to someone and explaining where she kept the baking soda. Kevin did not consider her attitude encouraging, and he wondered what it would take to impress her. Finding the cat had helped, but Nicole seemed to have a wall when it came to him—or was it his profession? His colleagues operated on the assumption that women were enthralled by their uniforms, but Kevin's one long-term relationship so far had ended partially because of his dedication to his job. But she'd left him Arnold. The dog was more understanding of his late nights and smoke-stained clothes than Janelle had ever been.

"At least my brother doesn't outrank me," Kevin said, attempting to lighten the mood. "And I'm trying to make sure he never does. I'm going to take classes in fire science this fall and get my degree so I can jump in front of him in line for promotion."

"Good plan," she said, again with the here's-my-canola-oil-shelf tone.

The bunk room door opened and Captain Dan Bauer came out. Kevin waved at him as he climbed into one of the trucks on the rear apron. He backed it into the station and closed the overhead door before moving on to the next one.

"You should probably get back to work," Nicole said.

Kevin nodded. "Nice of the captain to help out, but I should get things put away before I leave for the day."

Nicole put one foot on her bike's pedal.

"If you want the opinion of a local," Kevin said, "I'd go past the Oceanfront Hotel and use the beach entrance by the big mermaid statue. Not as many tourists down that far."

Nicole smiled. "That's the same thing Jane said."

Kevin wanted to reach out and touch the exposed skin on her arm. Brush his fingers over her full lips. Feel her hair against his cheek.

"See you around," she said. She rolled away, unknowingly preventing Kevin from making a fool of himself.

NICOLE LOCKED HER borrowed bike on a rack by the giant mermaid statue. Jane had told her part of the legend of Cape Pursuit. While being chased by a rival, a pirate had stashed his gold somewhere along the shore. One version of the tale claimed he took to the sea for his own safety. Another said it was supposedly because he was in love with a mermaid. Of course it was a local legend, but there were those who believed the treasure might be somewhere just waiting to be discovered. More than the idea of riches, Nicole liked the story of how the pirate gave up his treasure to return to the woman he loved.

Pausing under the mermaid statue, she skimmed the engraved sign with a tourist-friendly version of the romantic story. The mermaid herself, made of copper grown green with age, leaned on a rock and looked wistfully out to sea. Her tail curled elegantly around the base of the statue, but it was her eyes that dug into Nicole's imagination. She'd have to get a few pictures of the statue when the midday light softened.

She slung her striped beach bag over one shoulder, took off her sandals and held them in her free hand. She had only taken a dozen or so pictures in the few weeks she'd been in Cape Pursuit, and looking at the view reminded her it was time to remove her lens cap and start seeing the world in a fresh way.

The Atlantic Ocean was one of the most beautiful things she'd seen. Nicole crossed the sand, feeling it squish between her toes. When was the last time she'd had a foot rub or bothered to pamper herself at all? She chose a spot on the sand, spread out a green blanket and sat, knees drawn up in front of her. She pulled her camera from the bag, got out the water bottle and book, and settled in to enjoy hours of solitude.

Balancing the camera on her knees, she focused on a gray-and-white seagull walking stiff-legged across the sand. A bright red surfboard nosed up on the beach. A weather-beaten wooden pier stretching into the water. Two boys throwing a ball. A mother and small daughter holding hands and wading into the ocean.

She zoomed in on the water next, its azure waves lapping at the sand. She took a string of pictures, promising herself she'd open them on her computer later and play with the lighting and color. Editing was one of her favorite parts of photography. She loved taking something that existed for a moment in time and improving it. That was where her artist's streak came in, and she wished life could be improved so easily. She'd love to change the colors and textures of her past—making some of them disappear and some of them shine more brightly forever—if only she could.

Maybe she should take Jane up on the offer to display her photographs in the gallery. Perhaps it was the next step, part of her journey to filter the past and focus on where she wanted to be.

The sun touched her bare shoulders. The breeze cooled her face and kept her hair off her neck. She sighed, looking as far over the ocean as she could see.

On the other side of the Atlantic, Italy waited for her. Her dream vacation. Under the sun in Tuscany, beneath fields of sunflowers, beside ancient villas, along the sparkling Mediterranean. It was there waiting for her to rebuild her courage and repurchase the plane ticket she'd forfeited last summer when her brother was killed.

"What are you thinking about?"

She glanced up, startled at the voice right over her head. It was Kevin. He stood barefoot on the sand, blue uniform pants cuffed a few inches, heavy black boots in one hand. He blocked the sun and his face was deeply shadowed.

"Italy," she said.

"Mind if I share your spot?"

Nicole shook her head, and Kevin sat next to her on the blanket, spreading his long legs in front of him. "Never been to Italy."

"Me neither."

"But I'm guessing you want to," he said. He leaned close and looked at her camera. He smelled like a man who worked for a living, a little salty mixed with something like engine oil or exhaust. The breeze whispered between them, but he was still very close. A shadow darkened his jaw. Nicole pictured him sleeping at the fire station, not bothering to shave.

"That's a nice camera," he said. His voice was low, but he was so close that she heard it just fine.

The breeze blew a lock of her hair across his cheek.

"Would you like to look at my pictures?" she asked.

She'd had no intention of showing anyone these pictures a minute ago. At least not until she'd filtered and edited them. The string of images were like a stream of consciousness glimpse inside her brain. Her impressions. Her art. Personal.

But something about Kevin made her trust him enough to offer him a flip-through on the LCD screen.

"Love to. You have to show me how to work it, though. I don't even own a camera. Usually just use the one on my phone if I need a picture of something."

She handed over the Nikon, which she'd spent a fortune on when she was looking forward to and planning the trip of a lifetime with Jane. They had sketched out the whole ten-day journey. Art galleries where Jane could see the master painters, scenic day trips for photography and fun. A wine tour.

Adam was killed right before their departure, and their plans were crushed. Nicole had encouraged Jane to go without her, arguing that an artist owed herself the chance to see the European masters. Jane had deferred, claiming she'd purchased the travel insurance and would get her money back. She put all the funds into improving her gallery instead and suggested they go another time.

Nicole wasn't sure when she'd be ready to pursue her dream of going to Italy. Each day in Cape Pursuit was a chance for a new beginning, but she had a long way to go.

"It's not hard," she told Kevin, settling the camera in his outstretched hands. His hands were giant compared to hers and he held the camera as if it would explode if he pushed the wrong button. "Just use this dial to scroll through the pictures. Go as fast or slow as you want."

He shaded the LCD screen with one hand and took his time looking at each picture before moving on to the next.

"Really good," he said.

"Thanks. Do you have a hobby? Something you do when you're not saving the world?"

Kevin smiled, showing even, white teeth with a hint of a dimple in his cheek. "I don't usually save the world," he said. "Seventy-five percent of my job is less dramatic than it seems. Most problems will resolve themselves if you give them time."

Nicole nodded.

"But I do have a hobby," he said. "I paint."

"You do?" she exclaimed. She could not picture Kevin painting a beach scene or a sailboat in the bay at sunset. Kevin in a painting smock making delicate brush strokes on canvas? "That's a surprising habit for someone who is so…"

"So what?"

Rats. She was thinking *masculine*. Manly. Muscular. "Busy," she said.

"We work twenty-four on, twenty-four off most of the time, sometimes twelve or thirty-six off, depending on the rotation. That's plenty of time off for me to paint houses on the side."

Oh. That explains it. Nicole laughed. "You paint houses?"

He wrinkled his forehead. "What did you think I painted? Pictures?"

"Yes."

He laughed. "I'm definitely no artist. Nope. I paint the exteriors of houses. I've been doing it since I was a teenager."

"Do you have your own business?"

Kevin leaned back on his elbows, his long, lean body spread out on the blanket. Nicole admired how at ease he appeared. Was that what it was like for someone who knew exactly where he belonged?

"Sort of. But I'm the only employee. Unless you count Arnold. He likes to go along, but he usually sleeps on the job. I mostly paint houses when someone hires me, like my friend Charlie who's in the real estate business. It's easier to sell a place with fresh paint, so I stay busy."

"Charlie seems like an ambitious guy," Nicole commented. Maybe Jane was wrong about him avoiding commitment. A man who had a full-time job and another on the side…maybe he was just very busy. Kevin and his firefighter friends probably knew Charlie really well. "I believe he's a friend of Jane's," Nicole said casually, hoping it might spark some revelation she could use to help Jane.

Kevin laughed. "He's a friend of every woman in Cape Pursuit. If you believe the rumors."

Nicole looked back at the water and tried to focus on helping Jane and pursuing her own dreams. Her future. That was what she'd come to the beach today to begin sorting out. What did she want? Did she plan to stay in Cape Pursuit and use her expensive business degree to sell paintings in a gallery? The sand, sun and sound of the sea made ever going back to an office very unappealing. And Jane needed her.

She sighed, lost in her own thoughts. The beach blanket shifted and Kevin stood. "I'm sorry I intruded on your day off." He looked down at her, his eyebrows drawn together. "I know you have a lot going on in your life, and I have to get going anyway. Arnold and I have a cottage to paint."

Nicole looked up at him and nodded. "If you ever give up firefighting, it sounds like you have a fallback career," she said.

He shook his head, his expression serious. "I'll never give up firefighting."

CHAPTER SEVEN

MAYBE IT WAS a sneaky move, going to the gallery when he knew Nicole was at the beach, but he wanted a chance to talk to Jane. She was a friend. Of his and Nicole's. And she was probably the one person who could tell him what was causing the clouds to pass over Nicole's eyes whenever he talked to her. He'd rather see her spring-green eyes clear. And happy. He didn't know what it was about her in particular, but she made him want to protect her. Make her happy.

He always wanted to protect people, save them, keep them safe from physical danger. But Nicole brought out something more in him.

Kevin had only been in the gallery a few times, and the foghorn door chime got him every time. At least no one was there to see him jump. Except Jane, who was one of the least judgmental people he knew. That was why he was here.

"Sorry about that. The foghorn scares me once in a while, too, when I think I've snuck past it without triggering it," Jane said. She wore a painting smock and a name tag with the Sea Jane Paint logo—a girl with a swinging red ponytail in front of an easel.

"Why do you keep it around?" Kevin asked. "You could get a chime or a regular doorbell."

Jane shrugged. "Tourists like it. I'm hoping they'll remember my shop year after year if they come back on vacation. Sea Jane Paint, home of exceptional watercolors and a door chime that sounds like you're about to be sliced in half by an aircraft carrier."

"Good marketing," Kevin said.

"I like a little danger in my life."

"Me, too."

"So what brings you into my watercolor lair?"

"Officially, I'm shopping for a gift for my mother's six-tieth birthday. My brother and I want to get her something nice and personal. Any ideas?"

"You should get her a painting."

Kevin laughed. "Thanks, genius."

Jane smiled, ignoring his barb. Being friends with most of the firefighters and police, she was used to joking around with them. She'd called them worse things.

"I may have a painting hanging around she would like. They're mostly of the local area, of course. What does your mother enjoy most about Cape Pursuit? Any particular place she likes?"

Kevin thought about it. He hadn't lived in his parents' home since he'd graduated from high school. He'd gone to the state fire academy, then rented his own place. But he saw his parents all the time. Dropped by to say hello, helped with cleaning gutters and replacing window screens. All the things that were getting tough for them as they aged, espe-cially considering his father's health.

"She likes her house. Hanging out on the front porch. Taking the grandkids to the beach," he brainstormed. "The lighthouse. Having lunch out on the pier. Not the mermaid statue, she hates that for some reason, we always thought it was the bare…uh…top on the statue."

"I'm not crazy about it either. The scale is way off, makes it look tacky and touristy. I'm sure the city leaders had good intentions when they hired that sculptor fifty years ago, but I keep arguing for a change at the council meetings."

"Any luck?"

"Not yet. So back to your mom's present. Tyler is your only brother, right?"

Kevin nodded.

"Did your mom take you to the beach and lighthouse when you were kids?"

"All the time."

"Follow me," Jane said. She led him to a group of paintings hanging over a table with a model ship, conch shell and miniature fisherman's net. She pointed to a watercolor depicting a woman in a straw hat and two little boys, holding one of their hands in each of hers. The lighthouse stood to the left and the wide blue ocean spread across the center and right. The three figures in the painting were facing the sea.

"That could be us," Kevin said. "When we were smaller, of course."

"That's the idea," Jane said, smiling. "In addition to loving the beach and the lighthouse, she probably loves you and your brother. When you're behaving."

They briefly discussed the price, and Kevin continued looking at the picture. "This is really nice. I can see it hanging over her fireplace. Will you take this down and set it aside for us? I'll have my brother stop in and take a look at it, but I think it's perfect. Her party is next week at the house. She'll probably cry and make my dad get a hammer and hang it up right away."

"Mission accomplished," Jane said as she carefully took down the framed painting and put it on a shelf behind the cash register. Kevin followed her.

He wanted to find a good way of asking her more about her friend Nicole, but he struggled with how to bring it up. He scratched the stubble on his jaw and waited.

"So you said this gift was your official reason for being here," Jane said, "leading me to believe there is also an unofficial one. And since you've happened to come by when Nicole isn't here, I don't really need my decoder ring. Do I?"

Kevin felt the heat in his face. Jane was teasing him, but she was also taking it easy on him by getting to the point.

"I like her," he said.

"I like her, too. She's been my best friend since she helped me survive freshman math. She's smart about numbers."

"Sometimes I think I've said the wrong thing in front of her, but I don't know why," Kevin confessed. His heart raced. Talking about this was more disconcerting than strapping on a breathing tank and heading into a fire.

"You took the door off her car in the first five minutes she was in town," Jane said. "Maybe she hates you."

"Do you think she hates me?"

"No."

"So she likes me?"

"Nicole's nice. She likes everybody."

That was not very encouraging. "I see," Kevin said. He pulled his truck keys from his pocket. "Thanks."

He took five long steps toward the door before Jane stopped him.

"I shouldn't be telling you this," she said.

Kevin stopped, cold dread sinking around his heart.

"It's Nicole's story to tell. But I feel sorry for you. I also think telling you what happened to her brother will prevent you from hurting her feelings. And since she's my best friend, I'm going to do what I think is in her best interest."

Kevin turned and walked back to the cash register, his heart still racing but cautiously now. "What happened to her brother?"

"Nicole has a sister two years younger than she is and she had a brother, Adam, who was about four years younger. At the end of his junior year in college, Adam saw a job posting. The forestry service out West was hiring college students to work alongside the experienced forest fire guys for the summer."

Kevin took a deep breath. "I don't like where this is going."

"Adam was with a group that got trapped fighting a fire near Yellowstone. Some of them made it out in a Jeep, some of them got separated. Apparently, his group was on the wrong side of the fire line, fighting for their lives. The fire was racing toward them and they had no place to hide. Their leader had them get under the fireproof lifesaving blankets." Jane paused, emotion choking her voice. "A few of them were injured pretty bad but lived. Adam and two others died."

"Man," Kevin said quietly.

"They said it was the heat," Jane added. "Either way, I've never seen anyone so devastated. Adam was her baby brother and they'd been close all their lives. They looked a lot alike."

He took a moment to absorb the story. Tried to picture a blond young man with green eyes like Nicole's. Imagined him dying under one of those blankets, felt the scorching heat, knew the fear.

"I understand," he said, mentally reviewing everything he'd said to Nicole. The clouds passing over her expression were all too understandable now.

There were tears in Jane's eyes. Kevin had known her for several years, seen her at fire scenes and around the station helping with coffee, dinners and fund-raisers.

He'd never seen her cry.

"I went to Indianapolis for the funeral. This was just last summer, so the wound is still raw. Nicole and I actually had a trip planned for the week after Adam died, but we canceled our plans."

Something flashed through Kevin's mind. A memory clicked. "Were you going to Italy?" he asked.

Jane glanced up quickly, her mouth open. "How did you know that?"

"Just a hunch. Something Nicole said this afternoon on the beach."

Jane's expression changed. "You went to the beach with Nicole?"

"Not exactly. I sort of…followed her there."

"Stalker."

"Stalker with good intentions."

Jane narrowed her eyes at him. "Have I mentioned I used to like you?"

"Yes, but I have no idea why."

Jane shrugged. "I have a soft spot for firefighters. My dad was the fire chief where I grew up, so I hung around the station a lot when I was a kid. That's where I got interested in art. Drawing pictures of fires and fire trucks. Always starring my dad as the hero."

Kevin smiled. He'd grown up hanging around the station, watching his uncle work. And he'd always wanted to be a hero and save people, coming to the rescue on a flashing red truck.

But his sinking gut told him Nicole had no interest in a hero like him.

JANE WAS RIGHT. Hanging up artwork was like putting a little piece of your soul on a wall for people to examine. But Nicole straightened the edges of the frames, resolving to brave it out. Her subjects—the Cape Pursuit lighthouse, beach, hotel skyline, pier and sunrise—would have been beautiful even in the hands of an amateur photographer.

She just hoped her work was as professional and aesthetically pleasing as Jane had assured her it was. Giving her a wall near the front of the shop, Jane had insisted Nicole was ready to exhibit. She even had a plaque made up with *Nicole Wheeler, local photographer* printed on it.

Local photographer. Apparently the fact that Nicole lived in her friend's guest room made her a local. Nicole propped a picture of the Cape Pursuit pier on a small easel on a table below the group of framed photographs. Did she want to be a local? See the sunrise from the beach every morning? When she came to town almost a month ago, she'd had no timeline. No goal except to get away. And now?

Jane had taken the day off to visit her parents, who lived about an hour down the coast. Alone in the shop, Nicole had ridden her bike to work early to take advantage of the morning quiet and hang up her photographs. She wanted to get the display right before anyone else saw it.

The foghorn attached to the front door blasted its warning, not even raising a hair on Nicole's neck. She'd gotten used to it. But the two men standing in the front door both jumped like they'd been shot.

"Dang it," one said, "that thing would wake the dead."

Kevin elbowed the man who Nicole recognized as his brother. The morning sun behind the men highlighted their almost identical crew cuts and square shoulders.

"Hi, Kevin," Nicole said.

"Good morning," Kevin said. He smiled at her, keeping his eyes on hers. He looked handsome. Clean shaven, a slightly younger and more rugged version of his brother.

"We came to look at the painting Jane set aside," Kevin said. "I brought my brother along so he could say he had something to do with picking it out. Mom will know it was all my idea anyway."

"Because you're the thoughtful son?" she guessed.

"He's the son with free time," the brother said. "I have two daughters who usually have me tied up with tea parties, dance classes and piano lessons. Kevin only has a fat old dog to take care of."

"Arnold's short, not fat," Kevin objected. From the tone, Nicole could tell this was an old argument.

"Whatever," his brother grumbled. "I'm Tyler. I saw you

at the station the other day, but my little brother didn't introduce you." He held out his hand.

"I believe you were running off to an emergency while he tidied up," Nicole said, her tone light and teasing.

Nicole shook Tyler's hand and glanced out the front window. The red fire department pickup truck was at the curb in front of the shop next door, and both brothers wore navy blue uniforms. "Are you on duty?" she asked.

"Yes," Kevin said. "We're officially on our way to pick up donuts for the rest of the crew." He held up a radio. "On call."

"Then I better show you the painting and get you on your way," Nicole said. "Jane mentioned you'd come by the other day."

Nicole had thought it odd that Kevin left the beach and went straight to the gallery, but Jane hadn't made much of it. Just commented that he had to take advantage of his days off. She started to lead them over to the counter where the painting waited, but Kevin stopped her, his hand on her arm.

"Are these your pictures?"

Heat tinged Nicole's face. His fingers on her arm were light, only exerting enough pressure so she'd know they were there. Just her luck, the first visitors to the gallery to see her artwork were two firefighters. One of whom made her feel hot all over.

She took a breath while both brothers stared at her pictures. "They are," she said. "Jane thought I should display them."

"Are they for sale?" Kevin asked.

"Technically, yes," Nicole said. More heat warmed her cheeks and her heart was on a roller-coaster ride. "But I hadn't consulted Jane about a price yet. It's her gallery."

"But it's your work," Tyler said. "You could do well with these. They're good."

"Thank you."

Kevin continued to stare at the photograph of the pier. "Did you take this one the other day when we met on the beach?"

Nicole noticed Tyler's quick glance at his brother.

"The lighting and the sky look the same as they did that day," Kevin continued.

"You have a good eye," Nicole said, smiling. "Yes, I took it right before you sat down."

"Thought so."

Tyler punched Kevin on the shoulder. "We better look at Mom's present and get back to the station," he said. "The crew's waiting for donuts."

"Right over here," Nicole said. She was glad to have the attention focused on Jane's art and away from her photographs.

She slid the painting from its shelf and laid it on the counter for the two brothers to see. She stood behind the counter, giving herself a little breathing room. She recognized the painting, but had hardly paid attention to it hanging in a group of beach portraits. Now that she looked more closely at it, she saw why Jane had suggested it. A mother and two sons at the beach. Perfect for a mother's birthday present.

"Are there just two sons in your family?" she asked.

Kevin nodded, making eye contact with her while his brother looked at the price tag on the edge of the frame.

"No sisters?"

"Nope."

"Then this is perfect. Two boys at the beach with their mom," Nicole said. Both boys in the picture appeared to be about the same age but were dressed in different colors. Only their backs were visible as they faced the ocean and the lighthouse. One wore a ball cap and had bare feet. The other one carried a bucket with sand toys sticking out the top. "Which one are you?" she asked.

She looked up and met Kevin's eyes. The counter wasn't

helping. He was plenty close anyway. His hand rested on the surface and she could move her fingers only inches and touch his.

"I'm the cuter one," he said.

"Hard to tell from behind," his brother said. "Unless that's your best asset." He stressed the first part of the word and grinned at Kevin.

"Try to have some class. You're in an art gallery," Kevin said.

"But I'm hungry."

Kevin sighed. "Fine. Yes or no on the painting for Mom?"

"Yes," Tyler said. "I can't believe you had to drag me in here to ask. It's perfect. She'll love it. My wife will be so impressed I thought of it."

Kevin ignored his brother. "Can you gift wrap it? I'll pick it up later when I'm not on duty. I don't want to put it in the back of the truck or let it sit around the fire station."

"Of course," Nicole said.

Kevin stood, hands on counter, looking at Nicole as if he wanted to say something.

"Tyler, if I buy the donuts, will you wait in the truck?"

"Insurance, please."

Kevin took out his wallet and handed his brother a ten-dollar bill.

Tyler grinned at Nicole and left, the foghorn punctuating his exit.

Kevin pulled a credit card from his wallet and handed it to Nicole. She ran it through the machine and waited for the receipt to print. Without a word, she slid the paper across the table. She watched his fingers as he signed, and thought about the way she'd felt when he touched her.

There was no one else in the gallery. Morning light poured through the front windows. Nicole and Kevin faced each other over the narrow counter. Almost close enough to touch. Her heart pounded in her ears. This was a mistake, letting herself be attracted to him. He was all wrong for her. But it would be a lot easier to ignore him if he didn't have broad shoulders, a dimple when he smiled and stormy green eyes that were also incredibly sweet.

"Jane told me about your brother," he said. "And I want to tell you how sorry I am."

All the air whooshed out of Nicole's chest. That was the last thing she thought he was going to say. She stepped backward, reaching out a hand to a low table for balance. Kevin stepped around the counter and pulled her into his arms, holding her tight. Tears pricked her eyes. It felt so good to be held by someone with strong arms. A sweet smile, sensitive eyes. Someone who smelled of soap and aftershave.

Someone who did the same thing her brother died doing. *Why did Jane tell Kevin about Adam?* She must have had a reason, but right now it felt like betrayal.

Nicole opened her eyes. The fire department symbol on his chest was right under her cheek. A vivid memory of hugging her brother at the airport, the same symbol on his chest, shook her.

She put both hands on Kevin's chest and pushed him away.

"I'm sorry," he said.

Nicole shook her head, trying to clear it. Trying to make him go away. He was not the kind of man who would leave unless he thought she was okay. Unless she made him.

She had to make him.

"Thank you," she said, trying to keep her voice steady. "I have work to do. You should go."

The radio on his belt crackled. *Good. He'll have to leave in a hurry.*

"Just static," he said, dismissing the sound. "I didn't mean to upset you. I just wanted to tell you I understand. Finally. Why firefighters aren't your favorite people."

Nicole didn't say anything. Adam had been one of her

favorite people. Would he think she should give Kevin a chance? What would he tell her now, if he were here?

But he wasn't.

"You should go," she repeated.

Kevin looked at her for five long seconds. His glance made her think he'd seen a lot of things in his time as a rescuer. Maybe he thought she needed saving.

Maybe she did.

But not by him.

He turned and walked out the front door, not even breaking stride when the foghorn blasted.

CHAPTER EIGHT

JANE AND NICOLE admired the new awning over Sea Jane Paint. With pink-and-white stripes, it gave the shop a vintage beach look. Nicole had talked her into the new addition, and had also suggested the white wicker chairs on the sidewalk out front. Guests might sit in the awning's shade and perhaps linger long enough to purchase a painting. Jane was glad her friend had persuaded her to make the physical improvements as well as the back end improvements in her computer system no one would actually see.

"I can't believe I waited two years to improve the storefront," Jane said.

"You were being cautious and responsible, making sure your business would be viable before you put more money into it," Nicole said.

"That's me." Jane pointed a subtle finger toward her belly. "Cautious and responsible."

Nicole laughed. "I meant fiscal responsibility. It has nothing to do with Valentine's Day or misguided hormones."

Was spending the night with Charlie misguided? She loved him as a friend…and more than that…well, she had to admit to herself that they would never have become entangled physically if there wasn't something already there. At least for her.

Jane crossed her arms and surveyed her gallery, the culmination of a dream she'd chased since high school. Being able to support herself as an artist had seemed out of reach so many times, and now it was right in front of her, but she didn't have just herself to support. Would she be able to run the store and take care of a baby?

"When are you going to tell him?" Nicole asked.

Good friend that she was, Nicole had asked no further questions for over a week, only offered support and an ear when Jane wanted to talk about it. Until now.

"I'm waiting for the right time."

"Any idea when that will be?"

Jane shook her head. "He wants me to meet him across the street at the end of the day today. He's bought one of the downtown storefronts and has some idea about putting in a coffee shop."

"Really?"

"That's what he says. He wants a mural painted on an interior wall, a beach scene of Cape Pursuit."

"That sounds nice. It will also give you an excuse to spend time with him."

Jane grabbed Nicole's arm, sudden panic gripping her. Maybe it was the thought of finding the words to tell him. "Come with me. Please. I'm so nervous around him now... I know it's ridiculous." She released Nicole's arm and rubbed her own temples. "I'm carrying his child—I should be able to talk to him about a painting. I've got to get it together."

A group of tourists walked down the sidewalk and paused under the new awning. Two of the men in the group sat in the wicker chairs while the women went inside.

"It's working already," Nicole whispered. "I'll go help those customers, and when we lock up for the day, we'll go meet Charlie. I'm your business manager, so I'll negotiate a good deal for you for the custom artwork he's ordering."

"I don't know what I'd do without you."

"You'd be fine. One day at a time."

As Nicole went inside, Jane remembered giving her

friend the same advice during the past year. Take things one day at a time…she'd helped Nicole survive losing her brother. And now Nicole was helping her as she came to terms with her own little family. A friendship like that couldn't be beat.

Jane worked steadily throughout the day, and, a few minutes after six that evening, Jane and Nicole crossed the street and peered through the wide front window of a vacant storefront.

"This is a mistake," Jane said. "I'm too tired and hungry, and I won't be able to think."

"It will probably take seven minutes. Just focus on breathing, and remain calm for four hundred and twenty seconds."

Jane sighed. "You're so much better at math than I am."

Charlie opened the front door and held it wide. "Come in and see this place. It looks bad now, but I've got you and Kevin on my side."

"Kevin's helping?" Nicole asked.

"He's my painter. He's going to do the inside and just enough of the outside to make it appealing. He'll be here in a few minutes. I asked him to pick up a pizza on the way."

Jane's mouth watered at the thought of pizza. Maybe Charlie wasn't the carefree playboy she'd believed him to be. He'd thought to buy dinner, knowing she'd be hungry after a long day of work.

"Kevin's been on duty all day and they didn't have time for lunch, so I had to bribe him somehow or he'd be a whiny baby," Charlie explained. "No time for that."

Back to the playboy man of business *persona.*

Charlie turned and gestured to a long side wall. "Ugly as sin right now, but the right paint job will make all the difference, and I'll have tourists dropping money here all season long."

Jane didn't answer. She was busy evaluating the sunlight that would come in the front window at different times of day, the width and length of the room, and the antique lighting fixtures. It was a beautiful space, one of the historic shopfronts that had hardly seen any remodeling in the century it had existed. Her own store across the street was from an era of much newer construction after a fire had swept through downtown forty years earlier. It had modern advantages but lacked the charm of Charlie's property.

"Do you like it?" Charlie asked. "Or do you think I'm making a huge mistake? Maybe I rushed into this, but I grabbed it right before it was going on the market."

If only they'd thought ahead eleven weeks ago when they'd rushed their relationship from friendship to the bedroom without stopping to consider the consequences.

"Not a mistake. It could be beautiful," Jane said. "I'm imagining a seascape all along that wall." She waved her hand. "Water here, shoreline and sand along there, maybe a lighthouse or colorful beachfront homes."

"Sounds fantastic," Charlie agreed. "Why haven't you done a mural in your gallery?"

"Because it would detract from the art I'm trying to sell," Jane said. "I don't want people looking at the walls—I want them looking at the paintings. The walls aren't for sale."

"What exactly is your business plan?" Nicole asked. She nudged a loose floor tile near the front entrance. "If you don't mind my asking."

Jane appreciated her friend jumping in. It freed her up to use her imagination on the future mural. It was a long wall, and the ceilings were high. She would need a ladder and a lot of energy to complete it after busy days in her gallery. Was it wise to commit to a big project in her situation?

"Coffee and donuts in the morning, maybe sandwiches and cookies later," Charlie said. "Didn't you ever notice this street has no place to get something quick to eat?"

"I haven't been here long enough to notice the local holes

in the marketplace. Have you ever owned a restaurant?" Nicole asked. "Any relevant experience?"

"Never really owned anything. I've been buying and selling houses for a while, and I thought it was time to get my hands on something more permanent."

Jane and Nicole exchanged a quick glance. *Charlie wants to do something with permanence?* Before they could ask any more questions, the front door opened and Kevin came in with empty hands.

"Where's the pizza?" Charlie asked. "I was going to provide dinner."

"I was just giving you a hard time when I said you had to buy me pizza," Kevin said. "This won't take long, and I should get home and feed Arnold. He's into this canned meat and gravy stuff lately. Smells awful, but he loves it."

Jane thought about feeding Claudette, and the canned food's aroma came over her with a wave of nausea. She put a hand on the wall and tried to breathe. How many more seconds until they got to four hundred and twenty? She was just hungry…and she had to stop thinking about gross things for a few months. Especially canned meat and gravy dog food. Yuck.

"Jane?" She heard someone saying her name but it sounded as if it was coming through a tunnel. She opened her eyes and saw Charlie's face only inches from hers. "Are you okay?"

"Too hungry," she said, her voice shaking.

Charlie put a hand on her back. "We can do this later. I'm not anywhere close to opening this place, though I thought I might try for midsummer."

"We're here now," Jane said, forcing herself to breathe and straightening up. "Let me get a rough idea what you're looking for, and I can come up with a few sketches to fit the space."

"You've seen it," Charlie said, concern drawing a line

between his eyebrows. "Let's talk over dinner. You want to come, too?" he said, gesturing to Nicole and Kevin.

Kevin shook his head. "I'm headed home. I already looked at the front façade, and the interior is just like another one I painted not long ago. I'll work up a price for you based on that."

"Are you hungry, Nicole?" Charlie asked.

"I'll pass," Nicole said, holding up one hand. "I was thinking of taking some pictures while the evening light is so beautiful."

Nicole is bailing and leaving me alone for dinner with Charlie? Panic rushed through Jane's chest and her heart thumped.

"I can give you a ride," Kevin offered, smiling at Nicole.

Jane was ready to protest, knowing how sensitive Nicole was about Kevin. She wasn't really going to accept a ride home with Kevin, was she?

"That would be great," Nicole said brightly. She turned to Jane and Charlie. "You two have plenty to talk about over dinner."

With one meaningful glance, Nicole turned and left with Kevin.

"Where to?" Charlie asked in the silence that followed the door closing. "Burgers? Italian?"

She had to tell him. There would never be a better time. Nicole had set her up perfectly.

"Pancakes?" he prodded. "Mexican?"

Jane shook her head. She couldn't tell him in a restaurant. Not with other people around.

"My gallery. We'll order something, and you can look around and tell me what you like. All my samples and portfolio work are right across the street."

THE FOGHORN BLASTED as Charlie followed Jane through the front door, but he hardly noticed. What was going on with

Jane? She was pale and nervous. He'd never seen her like that before, and he thought he knew her better than he knew anyone else. Their relationship had provoked questions from his friends for years, and he'd always claimed there was nothing more than friendship between them.

It was a lot harder to make that claim now, after the night she'd spent at his place, in his arms a few months ago. He'd tried to forget, tried to honor the pact they'd made that it wouldn't change their friendship. It was just one foolish night.

Forgetting had been tough every time he saw her and remembered the way she'd made him feel—as if he belonged somewhere…to someone…for the first time in years. All the other women he'd dated as he'd tried to fill the hole in his heart had never made him feel complete.

Jane locked the front door behind them. "Chinese?" she asked without looking at him.

"Sure. You want the usual?"

He knew what she liked. Orange chicken and rice, a side of snow peas and two fortune cookies.

She nodded and he searched for the number on his cell phone and called in the order.

"Fifteen minutes," he said. "They'll deliver. Must be a slow night."

"That should be enough time."

"Enough for what?" Since when was she in a hurry to get away from him?

"Why don't you look around and take note of what sort of images you would like in your mural? I'll go in the back room and work on a framing project so you can wander in peace."

Charlie walked around her shop, taking a close look at the works on display. He'd been in here dozens of times, had stood over her shoulder and talked with her when she'd painted outside, had visited her booth at the Art in the Park show the previous summer. He'd even purchased small paintings as gifts for more than one girlfriend.

He wanted to look at Jane's watercolors with fresh eyes. Since Valentine's Day, he'd seen her as a woman, not just a friend. A brave, passionate woman who cared about the town and poured herself into whatever she was doing. Her passion and bravery showed in her work. Even the sunsets over the water in her paintings glowed with life. The ships at rest in the harbor seemed to have an energy, as if they were waiting to take to the open water.

After he'd spent enough time looking to satisfy Jane that he'd given the project adequate thought, he pushed aside the curtain and entered the back room where Jane leaned over a worktable with a mat knife and a ruler.

When she saw him, she took two bottles of water from the small fridge and put them on the table. "Have a seat," she said as she took one of the chairs. Her posture was rigid, hands folded on the table in front of her.

"What's going on, Jane?"

She unfolded her hands and laced her fingers. She didn't look at him. "There's a lot going on."

"Early summer in a beach town."

Jane met his eyes. Her lip trembled. "It's not about the season or the town."

Charlie reached across and put his hands over hers. "Are you all right? Is this about what happened between us a few months ago?"

"Yes. No." She pulled her hands from under his and jumped to her feet but then swayed and paled.

He was out of his seat in an instant and took her in his arms. She trembled against him, her head pressed against the center of his chest.

"Whatever it is, please tell me." Dark thoughts raced through his mind. He remembered that horrible night when his parents had sat on his bed and told him his mother had cancer. She fought it for almost two years before she lost. His father had been strong enough for all of them throughout it.

He would be strong for Jane no matter what she had to tell him.

"I'm pregnant," she whispered. "We're pregnant."

Charlie sucked in a long breath and held Jane tight against him. She was sobbing now. Was she sad? Angry? He couldn't tell. Didn't know how to react. Like an animal frozen by something unexpected, he remained perfectly still.

Jane was warm, alive, emotion rolling off her in waves. But he was afraid to move or speak. All he could do was hold her tight and wait—wait for the correct words to come. He'd held his emotions and tears in tight during the long months of watching his mother slowly leave them. He never saw his father cry; instead, he'd faced it with squared shoulders and quiet calm.

Charlie could follow his father's example. Strength. Fortitude. Doing the right thing without painful and useless emotion.

"I'll take care of you," he said. It was the only thing he could do. "And the...the baby."

Jane stiffened and pushed back. "Is that all you have to say?"

"I don't know what else to say. I'll take responsibility. I can provide for us."

"Responsibility? Provide for us?" she said, turning her tearstained face up to his.

"You know I'd never let you down, Jane."

She stepped back but kept a hand on his chest, still using him for strength but not leaning against him. He wanted to pull her close again. This was Jane, his friend. He knew and trusted her more than anyone he'd met in Cape Pursuit.

There was only one thing to do. Charlie took her hand.

"We'll get married," he said.

Jane stared at him and opened her mouth.

Someone knocked loudly on the glass door of the art gallery, but Charlie ignored it. The delivery guy could wait. He needed to make sure Jane knew he was serious when he said he would take care of her.

"Our dinner is here," she said.

How could she say that as if nothing had just happened?

"I just asked you to marry me."

Jane nodded. "I know. Thank you. It's a very nice offer."

The knocking grew louder.

"What do you say?" Charlie asked.

Jane took her hand back. "We should answer the door."

"The heck with the door. Will you marry me?"

"Why did you ask?"

Charlie thought he must be in the middle of a terrible practical joke. The driver was pounding on the door, and the woman carrying his child wanted to know why he wanted to marry her.

"It's obvious why."

Jane sat in the nearby chair. "Will you please go pay for our food?"

She was hungry. Pregnant and hungry, and he was harassing her for an answer. Charlie dug his wallet from his back pocket and strode to the front door. He handed the kid a much larger bill than necessary and took the bag back to the table where Jane sat looking stunned.

"I'm sorry," Charlie said. "Eat something and we'll talk." He unpacked the food and set it neatly in front of her, then placed a napkin and plastic fork on her right. He sat across from her and took a bite of his eggroll. They were sharing a rational meal. Two adults facing a problem with friendship and bravery.

"Eat, Jane. You need it."

She took a forkful of rice and chewed it slowly.

"What do you think?" he asked.

"It's fine."

"Not the food. What do you think about getting married?"

Jane put down her fork. "Thank you for asking, but no. I won't marry you."

CHAPTER NINE

"I FIND IT hard to believe that the woman who could calmly turn down a marriage proposal and then eat her orange chicken and fortune cookies could be in such a panic over a picture frame," Nicole observed. When Jane had gotten home a few nights earlier and told her friend the bomb-shell and proposal story, they had stayed up late talking it through. Although Jane had asked how Nicole's ride home with Kevin went, Nicole had downplayed it as a quick drop-off.

But it had been more than that. Being alone with him in his pickup had felt as if they were becoming friends. It had reminded her Kevin was not just a firefighter—he was a man. She'd wondered what he had in his refrigerator and what he watched on television after a long day. They'd hardly spoken on the short drive. He'd waited in her drive-way until she was safely inside the house before backing onto the street and driving away.

"It's my fault we're down to the wire on this," Jane said. "I decided to put a nicer frame on that painting and now it's the day of the party."

Jane finished gift wrapping Kevin's painting, tied a rib-bon around it and used a pair of scissors to curl the tails. A week had gone by since Kevin and his brother came to the shop, and Nicole found it hard to believe Jane had put off the project until the last minute, even if they'd been busy.

"I told him we'd deliver it this afternoon. To his house," Jane said.

Nicole wrinkled her brow. "Why can't he pick it up?"

"We close in fifteen minutes. I thought it would be no problem to drop it off on the way home. He worked late because of an emergency, so he rushed home to clean up. His mother's party is at six."

The foghorn sounded and a group of tourists came in. It had been a busy Friday, with more crowds arriving for the upcoming weekend. There were already a half dozen people in the shop. Several of them had asked questions about the paintings and appeared interested.

Business was gaining speed. Two of Nicole's photographs had sold the day before and she and Jane had celebrated with comfort food and *Under the Tuscan Sun*.

Jane left the gift-wrapped painting on the counter behind the register and greeted the new arrivals, offering to help them select a piece of art. The clock ticked toward closing time, but Nicole knew from experience Jane would stay open as long as there was a paying customer in the gallery. Every sale counted.

Nicole approached Jane and an older couple who were dressed in expensive clothing. They were asking questions about a very large and pricy painting. As Nicole tried to catch Jane's eye to point out the time, the older gentleman asked about changing the matting.

"Excuse me just one moment," Jane said to them. She took Nicole's arm and led her toward the register. "I think I'm going to sell the big one," she whispered. "Can you deliver Kevin's painting?"

Nicole sucked in a breath. Of course she would. Jane was her best friend, and she wouldn't stand in the way of making a sale that would pay her rent for the month. She realized she had no idea where Kevin lived.

"I know he's not your favorite," Jane said. "But it was my fault for blabbing your business to him, not his."

"I'm not mad about that," Nicole said. "I understand why you told him. You were trying to protect me. Don't worry. I can handle this if you just give me directions to his house."

Jane put a hand on Nicole's arm. "Are you sure?"

No.

"Completely."

Nicole laid the wrapped painting on the back seat of her car and made sure it couldn't slide around by fencing it in place with an old blanket. She hadn't written down Jane's directions. A navy blue house with a red front door was not going to be hard to find. Especially on a street of beachy-colored rentals just a few blocks from the fire station.

She saw his brown pickup truck when she was several houses away. The dent on the driver's side activated her curiosity. But not as much as the house. Dark navy blue, white trim around the windows, glaring white garage door—she guessed the garage was too small for his truck or was full of junk—and a bright red front door.

The colors would look great in a wardrobe for a cruise or a resort vacation, but they were all wrong for a house. Nicole parked next to Kevin's truck, took the neat, narrow walk to the front door and rang the bell. She didn't hear the bell ring inside the house, but she did hear howling. Beagle howling.

Maybe the guy didn't need a doorbell with his dog around.

The red door swung open and Kevin stood there in black dress pants and bare feet. His white shirt was unbuttoned all the way, flapping open and showing off his impressive chest and abs. His hair was wet.

"Nicole," he said, surprised.

She held up the painting. It was easier than trying to think of anything to say. He took the painting, his fingers brushing hers on the edge of the frame.

"Thank you. You saved my life by bringing this over."

"I thought lifesaving was your job."

He grinned. "Not always."

Arnold scooted under Kevin's feet and whined. Nicole leaned over and scratched his head, glad to have a distraction.

"Can you come in?" he asked.

Definitely not.

"Just for a minute," she answered, emotion trumping brains. "I see you're in a hurry."

"I'll be on time now that you delivered the gift." He glanced toward the driveway. "You got your car back!"

He laid the painting on a table just inside the door and stepped past Nicole. "Is it okay? Did they do a nice job?" He'd already walked around to the driver's side. He examined the door, running his fingers along it.

"All better," she said. "I picked it up a few days ago." She smiled. "It took six weeks, just like they said. Apparently they had to order a whole new door and it came on a slow truck from Michigan."

Kevin dipped his head until his chin almost touched his chest. "Sorry," he said.

That chin-dipping look of his was irresistible. She was going to have to try hard to resist it.

"When I picked it up, I expected to have to pay my five hundred dollar deductible, but the manager said it had been taken care of. He refused to give me any information about who paid it. Do you know anything about that?"

Kevin reddened and ran his fingers through his wet hair.

"I thought so," Nicole said. "Thank you."

"You shouldn't have to pay for someone else's mistakes."

"But it was *my* mistake. That's what I get for being one of those double-parking sons of guns."

Kevin laughed. "Come in. I'll pour you a soda if you'll help me pick out a tie."

Nicole waited for Arnold to hoist himself over the threshold and then went inside as Kevin held the door.

"Nice place," she said.

"Except for the color."

She shrugged. "It's unusual."

"It was a failure in judgment. Navy blue is my favorite color, so I thought it would look great on a house. I couldn't understand why no one else had a dark blue house." He grinned. "Now I know."

"You could always repaint it."

He shrugged. "I could. And I probably will when I get time. It seems to bother other people more than it bothers me. Like my landlord. He thought it was great that I was painting the house for free until he saw it. I may never get my deposit back."

He led the way to the kitchen. His house looked like a magazine ad for cleaning products. Shining floors. Clean windows. No dog hair on the navy blue living room couch. Same story in the kitchen. White cabinets with no finger smudges, stainless refrigerator with no smudges, dog food bowl by a back door, no mess around the bowl. Table for two, no junk stacked on the table. Not even unopened mail. Keys hung neatly on a wood plaque shaped and painted like a fire truck.

"Your house is very clean," she said.

"Easy to keep it that way. It's tiny, it's just me and Arnold and I'm not home much."

"Have you had Arnold since he was a puppy?" Nicole asked.

Kevin opened a cabinet over the toaster and took a clean glass from a neat row. He opened the fridge and looked inside, his back to her.

"He was left with me by someone who was…going away."

"Recently?"

"She left almost two years ago," he said. "Arnold was

the best thing I got from that relationship." He turned and faced Nicole. "I have root beer and iced tea," he continued, eyebrows raised in a question.

"Iced tea."

He poured her glass full and handed it to her.

"Have you sold any of your pictures at the gallery?"

He has no right to be so attractive and thoughtful. It wasn't fair. She sipped her tea. "Two sold yesterday."

He smiled. "That's great. On top of being a business guru, you're an artist, too."

A business guru? Was that what he thought of her? If he only knew that Jane didn't need a business manager any more than she needed a full-time roofer or plumber on staff. It had taken Nicole about a day and a half to realize Jane was doing just fine with her accounts.

"I have an MBA, but I've discovered I don't really need it to run a tourist gallery."

"Doesn't hurt."

"No, but I'm spending more time on Jane's web page than her tax records. We're going online with sales and promotion."

"We?"

"Mostly Jane."

"And what do you want to do?"

"I'm trying to figure that out," Nicole admitted.

Kevin pulled out a chair for her. "I hope now that you've got your car back you don't plan to leave Cape Pursuit."

She shook her head. "No plans to go anywhere. Except home. I should head out. You're on your way to a party."

"Can you wait just a second?" he asked. He dashed out of the kitchen. Nicole set her glass on the table and was considering sitting down when he loped back in.

He had three neckties dangling from his outstretched hand. All solid colors: red, blue and dark green.

"Which one?"

Nicole fingered the ties. Somewhat industrial material. His shirt was still open in front and he was standing very close to her, waiting.

"Red or blue would work. But I like the green one best." She raised her face to look at him. His lips were eye level. Begging for her touch, her kiss. "It matches your eyes," she whispered. She was a breathless fool but she couldn't help it. Without the uniform he'd worn every other time she'd seen him, he was just a man. An attractive man.

And she was in his kitchen helping him pick out a tie.

She wished she had her camera to capture the way he looked. Instead of taking a picture, she put her hand on his bare chest.

That was all it took. His lips touched hers, gently at first, as if they were questioning their right to be there. She slipped her hand behind his head, touching his wet hair and pulling him closer. He dropped the ties on the floor and crushed her against his chest, kissing her as if he'd been waiting to do so for a year.

Her senses were on fire. Heat crept over her, ripples of sensation spreading from her lips to her feet. She'd had other kisses, other boyfriends. But it was very easy to forget them when all she could think about was wanting more of this.

This was a huge mistake.

Nicole pulled back and opened her eyes. She hadn't realized they were closed. Kevin's stormy green eyes were dark with desire.

"Are you coming up for air or should I start apologizing?" he asked. He dipped his chin and smiled, eyes still darkened.

"I started it," she said. "I think."

"How would you like it to end?"

It's already over. She could not let herself go any further without losing herself.

She blew out a breath. "You need to get dressed and go to your party," she said. As she spoke, she started buttoning his shirt. Her fingers shook, but she needed to cover up that bare skin, conceal those muscles before she lost any more control.

He stood still, watching her fasten his buttons. She finished the long row down the front and reached for his cuffs, turning his hand over to focus on his wrists. She did the same with both sleeves. Neither of them said a word.

Methodically dressing a man she had a hard time resisting was like carefully wrapping a present she wanted to keep for herself. She had to give this one away. Letting herself fall for a firefighter would open an old wound she'd been working hard to close ever since she got to Cape Pursuit.

She bent and picked up the green tie. Slid it around his collar and started to tie it.

"Confession," he said. His skin was hot under her fingers, even with the white broadcloth between them. She could only imagine what he was going to confess to. She had plenty of things she would regret in a saner moment.

"I can tie all kinds of rope knots, but I'm lousy at tying a necktie," he said. He raised his chin to give her room to work. "I was hoping a beautiful woman would come along and save me. Especially one I've been crazy about since the first day I saw her."

Nicole stopped. *Since the first day?* "You mean when you wrecked my car?"

He laughed, his Adam's apple bobbing under her fingers as she tightened the tie. "That night in the bar when you sat next to me and let me have it."

She smiled.

"I liked you right away," he said. "Even if you did scare the pants off me."

"That was my goal."

"Getting me to like you?"

She straightened his tie and stepped back.

"How do I look?" he asked.

Like a fabulous gift I'm shipping off to someone else.
"Good enough for your mother's birthday party."

He caught her hand. "Come with me."

No way. "Can't," she said, shaking her head.

"Sure you can. We'll have dinner, open gifts, take some pictures. My dad will eat too much cake and Mom will nag him about his blood sugar."

"Is your dad a diabetic?"

He nodded. "Type 1, had it since he was a kid. Lives on an insulin pump. It's why he never became a firefighter like his brother and…uh…well, it's a family tradition."

And it was time to be going. That was a family tradition she could never be part of.

CHAPTER TEN

DESCRIBING THE WEATHER in Cape Pursuit to her parents would just be mean, Nicole thought. The second week in June was sultry, the kind of weather Indianapolis only got for about two weeks a year—usually the first two weeks of the school year when it was as welcome as a sliver under a fingernail. Summer usually went too fast in her hometown, and she always tried to grab it before it got away. But last summer, grief sucked the joy out of every sunny day.

Not this year. Nicole eyed the tent she'd organized in the front yard of a formerly abandoned house on a side street in Cape Pursuit. Summer weather stretched from April until Thanksgiving in a coastal Virginia town. She didn't have to hurry up and grab it before the snow fell. And she was starting to remember to slow down and enjoy it. Tonight was a perfect example.

"It looks great," Jane said. Like the other members of the Cape Pursuit city council, Jane was dressed up and wearing a name tag. "Have I told you how glad I am you're here? This is the part of being on the city council I have a love-hate relationship with. I love the project we did and I love a party, but figuring out how many chairs to set up and how much food to order and sending out invitations and calling the media…it freaks me out."

"That's my specialty," Nicole said. She handed Jane a glass of water from the neat rows on the white-clothed table.

"I used to organize travel and meetings all the time, and I was always in charge of putting together the holiday party and the summer barbecue for all the factory employees."

"You're a pro," Jane said. "If I had to do this myself, we'd be eating pizza on the front porch and drinking out of cans."

Nicole shrugged. "I like pizza and cans, too. This is just fancier."

"And elegant. This is what I love about living in Cape Pursuit. It's why I serve on the council. This town actually cares about the people who live here."

"Even people like me who are still bunking with friends while they figure out their lives."

Jane smiled at her. "Like I have it all together? You'll figure it out."

The church parking lot across the street, vacant on a Friday night, began to fill with cars. The Cape Pursuit city council made a goal a year ago that was finalized and being feted tonight. Three houses on this residential street had been foreclosed upon or otherwise abandoned in the mortgage crisis a few years back. Instead of letting them be auctioned, sold for a fraction of their value or carved up into apartments, the city council had bought them from the bank.

Using community volunteers, the three houses had been refurbished and would soon be available for sale. Real estate had recovered in the area, and the city leaders hoped to recoup their investment and hand over the keys to people who would be future citizens.

"The photographer from the *Cape News* is coming over," Jane whispered. "You have to be in the picture with me."

Nicole and Jane smiled for the picture. *Glad I finally got a tan*, Nicole thought as she listened to Jane answer questions about the project.

"We'd better be on the front page," Jane said when the photographer had moved on to another member of the city council. "The front page article last week was about the man who drives the tractor raking the beach every night."

"I think that sounds very important," Nicole said, a grin lighting up her face.

"Of course," Jane replied. She hooked an arm through Nicole's and turned toward the tent exit. "But we're much prettier."

In addition to the grand opening and community tour of the homes, there was a silent auction to benefit this project and future ones like it. Jane and Nicole strolled over to the row of donated items for the silent auction. Jane had painted a street scene from Cape Pursuit to donate. It could have been any street in a coastal town, but this painting had the three renovated houses right in the middle.

"This one is beautiful," Nicole said, pointing to the lavender house in the painting. "The color is risky, but it looks so perfect between the white and yellow houses."

"That's the nice thing about redoing three houses in a row," Jane said. "You can coordinate them. Not many people get that chance."

"I guess that's why you don't see too many lavender houses," Nicole said. "It might cause friction with the neighbors."

"There's another reason," a deep voice said behind them. Nicole turned and found Kevin looking over both their shoulders at the painting. He wore his fire department uniform and towered over her and Jane. "Some poor man has to go home with purple paint on his hands."

Jane turned and clinked her glass against his can of soda. "Lavender looks good with your skin tone," she said. "It takes a real man to pull it off. And besides, there was no one at your house except Arnold." She paused and grinned. "I doubt he complained about it."

"I took some teasing at the station when I showed up with purple paint in my hair."

Jane put her hand on Kevin's arm. "You poor thing. I'll tell the other boys to stop picking on you."

"Did you paint all these houses?" Nicole asked.

He nodded. "Took me most of the spring, working it in between my job and my other houses."

"Thank you for volunteering all that time," Jane said. "I really mean it. You're mentioned in the official program for tonight, but I don't think any of the guys on the city council realize how many hours it took to paint those houses. Especially the lavender Victorian with all the fancy trim."

Nicole took another look at the houses and pictured Kevin way up on ladders filling in all the intricate details. It was an astonishing amount of work. And clearly not fair. *Why does a man who is sexy, sweet, dedicated to his community, available and apparently interested in me have to be a firefighter? The universe is trying to torture me by dangling something right in front of me I'm afraid to take.*

Kevin shrugged. "We were lucky with dry weather this spring. And Arnold always enjoys getting out of the house." He pointed to a large southern oak in the front yard of the yellow house. "He spent hours under that tree. Probably killed the grass."

"I can't imagine all that work in your spare time," Nicole said.

"I can't stand seeing houses with peeling paint." He shuddered. "Drives me crazy."

"He's a spontaneous painter," Jane said. "Known to scrape and paint people's front doors without being asked." She raised both eyebrows. "I could tell you stories."

"That story about me being arrested for trespassing is not true," Kevin said. "Urban legend."

"That's what they all say," Jane said.

The three of them stood in silence for a moment, sipping their drinks and casting sideways glances at the people arriving, the row of silent auction items and each other. Nicole wondered if she should have told Jane about the kiss she'd exchanged with Kevin. When Jane had asked her how the picture drop-off went, Nicole didn't divulge any information, but she guessed her face probably betrayed her. There was no reason *not* to tell her best friend, except that saying it out loud made it more real. And she was afraid of letting her feelings for Kevin be real.

Silence hung like an anchor between the three of them now, and Kevin kept glancing at her as if he wanted to say something. Would he bring it up in front of Jane? And had Charlie confided in Kevin about Jane's pregnancy? Firefighters were like brothers in arms…did they tell each other everything?

"I'm going to talk to the mayor and make sure he has an appropriate speech," Jane announced. "His wife usually tells him what to say, but she's out of town." She swiveled and headed for a group of people assembled near a stage inside the large white tent.

And now they were alone. Not counting the dozens of people congregating on the front lawn and circulating in and out of the tent. Nicole pointed to Kevin's uniform. "Either all your clothes were in the dryer or you're on duty."

"On the clock," Kevin said. "Ethan and I are driving Big Red tonight." He gestured across the street where the red ambulance was parked right at the exit of the church lot.

"Do you usually attend events with an ambulance?"

"Depends," he said. "If we have the manpower, we send a squad to athletic events and things like the Homecoming Festival. That's the first weekend in August. People come out of the woodwork and find all kinds of foolish ways to need our help. You'll see for yourself."

Nicole laughed. "I'm looking forward to it already."

"This year's Homecoming Festival is also the one hundredth anniversary of the fire department, so there's going to be a big fuss. We should probably hire whoever put this party together to set up our party."

Nicole considered telling him she was the one who organized this event to help out her friend, but she didn't want to volunteer herself into throwing a party at the fire station. *For so many reasons.*

The evening sun tinted the tent and houses with coral and rose. Guests streamed across the street from the parking lot. Jane had advised Nicole to dress up because the silent auction and champagne crowd in Cape Pursuit tended to arrive in expensive cars and cashmere. She was right. There was also plenty of sparkly jewelry to complement the designer handbags. Men wore collared shirts and jackets, even in the heat of the June evening.

She felt Kevin refocus on her. She touched her simple necklace, the one with the gold heart her mother had given her for her birthday. She'd skipped carrying a purse so she'd have her hands free to take pictures.

"You look beautiful," he said. "As always."

"Really? Like the time I showed up to a house fire at two in the morning?"

"Absolutely."

Nicole flushed at the compliment. The sleeveless black dress had a low neckline and she had almost chickened out of wearing it. Jane persuaded her to put on heels and show a little skin, and now she was glad she did.

Even though she *shouldn't* be thinking about stepping closer to Kevin and inviting him to glance down the front of her dress. She also *shouldn't* be thinking about that kiss in his kitchen two weeks ago. She'd tried hard not to think about it every day. Every time she heard a siren going past, every time a tall, dark-haired man walked past the gallery.

"I've been thinking about you," Kevin said, his voice so low only Nicole could hear it.

"I don't know how you find time to think with your job and your house painting on the side," she said.

"That's what my last girlfriend said," Kevin said. He lowered his chin and chuckled. "But I've reformed in the past two years. Arnold's helped me. I take time to think now."

I used to think all the time. Planning out my day, my future, everything. And then I learned the hard way that life laughs at well-laid plans.

"I'm trying the opposite approach this summer," Nicole said. "Relaxing and enjoying it."

"Easy to do on an evening like this." He pointed to the camera slung over her shoulder. "Are you the official photographer?"

"Unofficial. I did take pictures of each of the houses earlier this week. We framed them and they're hanging in the entryway of each one."

"If I get a chance to take the tour of the interiors, I'll look for them."

"And I thought I'd take some shots tonight. Maybe I'll put them together in a collage for whoever buys the houses."

"I think they'd like it. Nice to have a little history to go with a new house."

They sipped their drinks. Champagne bubbles tickled Nicole's throat and reminded her that tonight was a celebration. Kevin stepped a little closer.

"Did you help organize this party?" he asked. "I heard Jane was in charge, but I can't picture her putting it together. She's more the creative type."

"She provided the vision, but I did the paperwork and crunched the numbers."

"You two are a great team."

Nicole smiled. It was so easy, chatting with Kevin. More than one woman looked him over as she walked past. Was she crazy for resisting him and not giving him a chance? Especially now that she knew what a great kisser he was?

Great kisser or not, he was still a firefighter. And her heart contracted in pain every time she thought about her brother. She doubted that would ever change.

"Make sure you try the food," Nicole said. "The champagne is pretty good, too, but I think your chief would frown on that since you're on duty."

"The mayor, too," Kevin said. He nodded toward the tent where Jane and the mayor were both looking closely at a piece of paper. "He's technically my employer. And the city council."

"So that's why you're nice to Jane."

"It's easy to be nice to Jane. And you." Kevin reached out and touched Nicole's bare upper arm. "Nicole, I was serious when I said I was thinking of you. I wonder if you might consider having a drink with me or grabbing dinner one of these nights."

The rush of warmth through her body at his touch made her consider it, but her brain—despite the champagne—still prevailed. She took a long breath before answering, hating to quash the look in Kevin's eyes. It was interest mingled with hope and genuine…something. Everything.

It would be so nice to say yes.

"Sorry," she said. "I don't think that would be a good idea."

He dropped his arm and nodded, looking at the ground. His shoulders lowered and Nicole was on the verge of changing her answer just to see his smile and his eyes light up again. Maybe she was wrong to write the guy off just because of his profession. Because of what happened. Because of her own fear. Maybe she should consider giving him a chance.

The radio on his belt beeped and a dispatcher's voice said something Nicole didn't catch. Kevin snatched it and held it to his ear. He stood straighter and scanned the crowd, waving at Ethan when he found him. Nicole glanced over at the tent. Ethan had a pastry in one hand and his radio in the other. He had the same alert posture as Kevin. Both of them looked as if they could face down a wild animal or stop a train. *Testosterone in action.*

Ethan approached, parting the crowd with his rapid movement. He didn't even notice Nicole as he and Kevin strode across the street. The two men wore the same uniform, but there was something about Kevin that made Nicole's heart pick up speed and want to match his quick steps. Made her want to follow along just for a moment, just to make sure he was safe.

Kevin opened the driver's-side door of the ambulance, glanced over at Nicole and raised one hand in a wave. He drove out of the church lot and roared down the street, the noise of the siren echoing off the quiet housefronts. Everyone in the crowd turned to watch the emergency vehicle depart, and then they went back to their conversations, drinks and food.

Nicole continued to watch the ambulance until it drove out of sight, and then Jane nudged her as she came up alongside her. "Well?"

"Well what?"

"What's going on between you and Kevin? I felt like I was chaperoning the prom when I was standing between you two. I took my chances with the mayor and his horrible speech instead."

Nicole laughed, glad to let her tension go. "Nothing is going on. As you are well aware, guys like Kevin are not on my list of eligible bachelors."

"If you're looking for an eligible bachelor, let's start your search at the dessert table. I'm starved," Jane said. "We need something to sustain us during the speeches."

Nicole followed Jane toward the tent, but her mind was on the way Kevin had looked as he took off in the ambulance. *That's what it would be like*, she thought. If she dated someone like Kevin. When duty called, he'd race off in a blur of lights and sirens. Where were they going? A medical call? Or were they driving to the station to jump in a fire truck and head into God knows what?

It was the *not knowing* she couldn't face. It was a good thing she'd said no to a date with Firefighter Kevin Ruggles.

CHAPTER ELEVEN

TWENTY FULL-TIME GUYS on the department, and he got stuck with the new guy on a Saturday night. Saturday nights always sucked during the summer. Drunk tourists fell out of their flip-flops or started fights in bars that didn't end in their favor. Parents let their kids play too long in the hot sand and put in a call from a hotel over a sunburned and dehydrated toddler. Narrow streets in a town made for fifteen thousand people became the venue for reckless driving with out-of-towners looking for a good time and a parking place.

For some reason, the chief thought Kevin was the man to train Travis Bennett. The new guy was barely twenty-one and full of enthusiasm, but he'd only been in the department a few weeks. A Saturday night in June could be an ugly proving ground. Despite the kid's new boots, Kevin liked the guy. He wanted to save people, wanted to be a hero. They all did.

There was a big-name local band on the beach until midnight. There would be fireworks after that. It was a long summer evening, the light taking forever to fade, and there were too many teenagers clogging the beach and the sidewalks. He and Travis had already been on an EMS call to the area and it wasn't even seven o'clock. That case was just a cut foot from a broken bottle in the sand. The boy needed stitches and a ride to the local hospital. Kevin let Travis take the lead on patient care and do the paperwork.

Sometimes it was nice to step back and just drive the ambulance, and it was good to let the new guy get experience on the less serious runs.

The call the dispatcher described now was different. "I'll drive," Kevin told Travis as they headed for the squad. They were going back to the beach, but this was a lights-and-siren call.

"You on the boat, Tony?" Kevin yelled to his cousin.

"Yep." His face was grim. Tony and his shift partner got in the truck and peeled out of the station, heading for the downtown marina to the fireboat.

"Traffic is going to be a nightmare," Kevin said. His new partner already had the lights going and flipped on the siren before they cleared the station. "You saw the way people were parked on our last call. That was an hour ago. They're drunker now."

"What's our plan of attack?"

"I'm starting with hoping the caller gave the dispatcher the wrong story. Drunk girl walked away from a fight with her boyfriend, last seen heading toward the water. If we're lucky, the girl went home with someone else."

Three police cars were already on scene when Kevin maneuvered the heavy rescue squad through an access gate. He dodged cars and tourists and drove directly onto the beach where a couple of uniforms, guys he knew, directed him. A clump of teens were talking with police officers, pointing and gesticulating. It was not a good sign.

The cop waved Kevin and his partner over. "They think she's in the water," the cop said, his face like a funeral. "Sixteen. Last seen entering the water just about right here. Another witness thought she saw someone out in the water but lost sight of her." The cop pointed straight out from the spot on the beach.

Kevin pulled off his boots and handed his radio to Travis. "Stay here. Mark the spot where I entered the water.

Don't move, no matter what. Radio the fireboat and tell them to haul ass."

Four years of swim team in high school. Five years belonging to the Cape Pursuit Water Rescue Division. And his chances were still slim to none. There were already two cops and a few bystanders in the shallow water, searching.

Kevin ran as far as he could before he started swimming, strong strokes taking him toward the spot where a bystander had seen someone. The sun slanted low, stabbing out from behind the hotels. Even full daylight wouldn't help him see below the water. He stopped swimming for a second, treading water and checking his orientation from his partner's position on the beach. Travis was new, but he followed directions. He stood like a statue, watching Kevin and talking on the radio.

Where the hell is the fireboat? The city marina was just down the strip.

Small waves slid past him, and Kevin eyed their direction, trying to reason and feel at the same time. Where would a girl be if she slipped under the water right here? He let himself sink. Bobbing up and down, he mapped out a pattern on the sandy bottom, hoping desperately not to find someone down there.

He took on water, felt his stomach filling up with air even as his lungs fought for oxygen. Travis was still his marker on the beach; a large crowd had gathered at the water's edge. More bystanders entered the water.

Please, no more victims.

Kevin moved out a little farther, continued bobbing and diving, searching the water's surface and the bottom. He didn't know how much longer he could keep up this search. He glanced toward the shore. A cop he knew swam toward him, wearing a bright yellow life vest. Kevin had no flotation device. It would slow him down and prevent him from searching below the water.

It might also save his life if he was too tired to make it to shore, and he recognized the dangerous fatigue settling into his muscles.

Where is that fireboat and the rest of the dive team? An eternity had gone by since he parked the rescue squad on the beach.

He took a deep breath and dove below the surface, a glance toward the crowded shore and the approaching cop the last thing he saw before he went below. He was not going to stop until he found her. If she was even under the water.

Kevin felt the bottom, seaweed and shells falling through his fingers. He searched for ten seconds, fifteen seconds. And he touched something. Something cold and solid. He used both hands, palpating the object. It was a leg.

With nothing left in his lungs, Kevin grabbed the torso and pulled, dragging the body to the surface. It was heavy. He knew it would be. He'd trained for this dozens of times.

There was no way he could do this alone. He'd end up a victim, too.

The cop with the yellow life jacket was only a few yards away, struggling for breath, but ready. The cops trained with the fire department a few times a year, so Kevin knew the guy and didn't have to say anything. Couldn't have found the breath to shout.

The cop grabbed the girl under one arm, her long, dark hair swirling in the water. She was lifeless, pale. *How long was she under?*

Kevin filled his lungs enough to give her a rescue breath, grabbed an arm and started swimming. The cop kept up with him, the two of them towing the girl to shore and stopping every few feet for Kevin to breathe for her. It wasn't helping.

It wasn't helping. He'd found her, but a deep chill of realization settled in his limbs with every stroke.

It was too late.

As the water grew shallower, Kevin staggered to his feet and gathered up the girl. He carried her out of the ocean to the waiting ambulance, and her dead weight taunted him with every step. Travis met him and put a strong arm under his, supporting Kevin the rest of the way to the backup squad that had just arrived.

Sharp pain streaked through Kevin's leg, but he didn't stop until he'd handed over the girl to his newly arrived partners. Charlie and Ethan shoved a backboard under her and began CPR instantly while Kevin crashed onto the sand. He rolled onto his back, gasping for breath. He didn't want to watch the desperate attempt to revive her.

"Stay with him," he heard his uncle's voice bark. The chief was on scene even if he was technically off duty. Patrick Ruggles slept with his radio next to his pillow and showed up to every scene that had the potential to be ugly.

And this was ugly. A call for a missing person, upgraded to possible drowning.

Kevin opened his eyes and saw Travis standing over him, looking lost. He rolled to his knees, trying to get up in case they needed a driver for the backup squad. Chief Ruggles shot a long look at Kevin and nodded before getting into the driver's seat. The nod told Kevin his uncle had it under control.

Of course he did. He'd never seen his uncle fail to control a scene or handle a tense situation. What would Chief Ruggles say about the way Kevin handled this call? There was nothing else he could have done. No fireboat on scene, victim in the water. What was he supposed to do?

Ethan and Charlie had the patient loaded, back doors closed. The squad barreled off the beach, Kevin's uncle at the wheel, leaving sand and silence in its wake. The huge crowd on the beach gaped at the departing ambulance. On all fours, trying not to puke from all the water and air in his stomach, adrenaline rushed through Kevin and nearly blinded him. He pounded his fist into the sand.

Why couldn't he have found her sooner? And where was that fireboat?

"Tell me what you need, Ruggles," Travis said, leaning close. "Oxygen?"

Kevin shook his head, trying to clear it and slow his breathing.

"Help me up."

Travis pulled Kevin up. The pain in his left leg nearly knocked him back down. He leaned on his partner.

"Okay?" Travis asked.

"Not sure." His soaked clothes clung to him. Seaweed tangled around his toes. And he wanted to punch something. But even adrenaline couldn't mask the pain radiating from his ankle.

The back doors of the remaining ambulance hung open. Kevin leaned on his partner and limped over. He sat on the bumper and pulled his heavy, wet pants away from his ankle.

He didn't remember how he did it, but his ankle was already swollen. *Come on.* Five years on the job and the only injury he'd had was a paper cut. A Band-Aid wasn't going to fix this.

But he was a heck of a lot better off than that dark-haired girl he'd tried to breathe life into. *And failed.*

WHAT HAD STARTED as a fun night out at a beach party had turned heart-wrenching as soon as Nicole and Jane heard the sirens. They abandoned their place by the stage, where the band was playing, and hurried to the water's edge.

When Nicole had seen Kevin race into the water, she'd wanted to run in, too. There had to be a way she could help. Jane had stopped her. "Not a chance," Jane said when she suggested it. "The firefighters hate that. You'd just be one more potential victim."

Nicole and Jane had stood watching along with the rest of the silent, shocked crowd. A few teenagers talked with two police officers on the edge of the beach. They were crying. *Friends of the missing person. Poor kids. No one should have to see a friend die. At any age.*

Shock and relief had rushed through her when she saw Kevin stagger from the water, carrying a girl whose dark hair swung with every one of his uneven steps. She watched him hand over the girl and collapse on the sand. Jane's hand was tight on her arm. Kevin's partner, the man who had stood guard on the beach, leaned over him as the rest of their colleagues took the girl away in the ambulance.

When he'd pounded his fist into the sand, she'd wanted to go to him.

When he'd gotten up and staggered, walking painfully to the ambulance, she'd wanted to go to him. Wanted to offer comfort.

"Are you okay?" Jane had asked. Even in the deepening sunset shadows, Nicole could see her concern. She knew what Jane was thinking—that Nicole was reliving the death of her brother. And she was. She would always live with that. It was part of her as if it were written in marker on every nerve in her body.

But there was something else wrestling with her grief. She wanted to go to Kevin and take away *his* grief, even a little part of it. Anything to ease the expression on his face.

She knew that terrible agony. Wished she could tell him it would be okay. It would just take a while.

She *knew.*

"I'm okay," she said. "I really am. Just devastated for that girl and her family. Do you think she'll live?"

Jane bit her lip, dug her foot around in the sand.

"You never know," Jane said.

Nicole glanced back at the water's edge, trying to imagine what would make a person walk into the waves and not come back. But she saw no answers there. Just a pair of heavy black boots.

She tapped Jane's arm to get her attention and pointed to the boots.

"Probably Kevin's," Jane said.

Without a word, Nicole walked toward them. The sand was firmly packed close to the water and waves lapped within inches of the boots, but they remained dry. She picked them up and brushed the sand off them, then walked to the ambulance. Jane followed.

Kevin's head was down. He only looked up when she stopped next to him, her pink flip-flops probably cluing him in. His expression was of exhaustion and pain. She dropped to her knees so she could look him in the eye as he sat on the back bumper.

She put his boots on the ground next to his bare feet and put both her hands on his knees. "What you did out there was incredible."

Kevin dropped his eyes and shook his head. "It wasn't enough."

Nicole squeezed his knees. "You don't know that. The girl may live. You gave her a chance, at least."

Kevin swallowed hard. Met her eyes. "Maybe."

"Are you okay?"

His partner stepped out of the ambulance with an instant ice pack and an elastic bandage. Kevin swung his leg up on the bumper, causing Nicole to sit back on her heels. He reached out and touched her shoulder, trying to steady her. "Sorry."

He left his hand on her shoulder. It was ice-cold against her bare skin. Looking at his swollen and already bruising ankle made her even colder.

"Is it broken?" she asked.

"I don't think so. Probably get an X-ray just in case."

"Are you hurt anywhere else?"

Kevin looked at her, surprise wrinkling his brow as if he hadn't considered the question.

"Don't worry," the other firefighter said. "They'll look him over at the hospital."

The younger man fumbled with the medical supplies, trying to hold the ice pack on with one hand while unrolling the bandage with the other.

"Give me that," Kevin grumbled. He took the ice pack and bandage, leaned toward his ankle and took care of it himself. Nicole wanted to help, but he obviously didn't need it. The set of his jaw was probably pain, but something else, too, and it made Nicole back off.

Kevin swung his leg down. "We should get going. Get this squad back in service."

"Can I help you up?" Nicole offered. She expected him to growl at her and refuse. Instead, he held out his hand.

"I'm wet and sandy," he said. "I'll try not to get it on you."

Jane took one of his arms and Nicole pulled his other arm over her shoulders. They walked him to the passenger seat of the ambulance and helped him in. Nicole pushed the red door shut, feeling that there must be something more to say. Kevin's partner closed the back doors and got in the driver's seat.

"Don't you dare turn on the siren," Kevin grumbled. He looked at Nicole, reached through the open window of the truck and touched her hand.

"Thanks," he said.

"Take care of yourself."

He met her eyes. "It's my job to take care of other people." He sighed while his partner pulled on his seat belt. He shook his head, eyebrows drawn tight together, and stared at the floor of the ambulance.

"I think you're a hero," Nicole whispered. She didn't know if Kevin heard her because his partner turned on the engine as she said it. It didn't matter if he'd heard. What mattered was how she felt.

CHAPTER TWELVE

"IT'S ONLY FOR a week," the chief had said. "You can't shove your bum foot in a fire boot or climb a ladder."

Only for a week. A nice long week for him to think about the ways he wished the water rescue had turned out differently. Wished that poor girl, just a child, had lived.

But she didn't. Every second he'd searched had equaled too much time in the water. She'd been robbed of her life, no matter how desperately he'd tried to save her.

He couldn't fight fires, respond to emergencies or climb a ladder, but he could still paint. The one-story home he was currently working on had plenty of trim and shutters, no climbing required. Kevin set up sawhorses in the driveway of the half-painted yellow house and waited for Charlie to drop off the sky blue paint for the shutters and the rest of the yellow house paint.

He sat on the open tailgate of his truck. Arnold slept under the truck in its shade, even though it was too early in the morning to be hot. The dog was old enough to think ahead. Kevin dangled his feet, frustrated by waiting. Frustrated by missing work. Frustrated by life.

A yellow VW Beetle pulled in the driveway and Jane got out. "I just stopped by the station to talk with the chief about the big event later this summer," she said. "Then Charlie drafted me into delivering paint. He had it in his truck but got called in to cover a shift."

"Probably my shift," Kevin said. "I'm off for a week."

"And this is your idea of recovering?"

Kevin shrugged. It was impossible not to like Jane, but he had a hard time liking anything right now.

Jane crossed her arms and stared him down for a minute. The dog wandered out from under the truck, stretching his hind legs and taking his time greeting her. "Sorry to wake you, Arnold." She knelt and scratched his floppy ears.

"So you have paint for me?" Kevin finally asked. "I'll help you unload it."

Jane gave the dog a final pat and popped open the trunk of her Beetle. "One gallon of sky blue, three gallons of sunshine yellow."

Kevin grimaced. "Charlie's choice. He thinks it will sell better if it looks like the weather forecast."

"Maybe he's right," Jane said. "It's certainly more cheerful than you are."

With two of the cans in each hand, Kevin walked slowly to the tarp under the sawhorses. He tried not to limp, didn't need or want any attention.

"I saw that," Jane said. "It's only been three days. You should stay off your ankle."

"Thanks for coming by, Jane. I think your gallery opens in five minutes."

"Nice try. I've got a half hour." She leaned on the side of her car. "Just in case you feel like talking about what happened."

"Looks like you'll have twenty-nine minutes to get coffee and donuts before you open your doors," he said gruffly.

Jane stalked over and snatched the paint can opener right out of his hand. "My dad was a fire chief my whole life. I'm an expert at listening to crybabies like you."

Kevin glanced up sharply. Jane was smiling.

"You'll drive yourself crazy if you bottle up all those feelings," she continued.

Kevin sat on the tailgate of his truck, leaving enough room for Jane. She hoisted herself up next to him. Usually the guys at the fire station found their own therapy when something terrible happened. Dark humor, talking about it in their own way, throwing themselves into the next call. The problem was that he wasn't at the station. Not since the drowning, and not for another five days at least. Maybe it wasn't a bad idea to talk to someone.

"That wasn't the first time you saw someone die," she said, her tone gentle.

He shook his head. "Not by a long shot."

"But there was something different about it."

He nodded.

"Because she was just a kid?" Jane prodded.

Kevin inclined his head.

"And you fought so hard to find her. To save her. Practically by yourself. I heard what happened with the fireboat. Lousy time for it not to start."

Wow. Jane was good at this.

"And it doesn't seem fair that you can try so hard, do everything right, and you still can't save everyone," Jane said.

He swallowed. Stared at the mailbox, the cracks in the driveway, the neighbor's tree with one dead, swinging branch somebody ought to trim.

"You can't save everyone," Jane said. "But I'm sure glad there are guys like you who try."

Kevin had not said one word. Didn't have to.

She patted him on the back. "Time for paint therapy. That house isn't going to paint itself," she said. "Unless you can train your fat old dog to do it."

Jane hopped down and headed for her car. "Jane, wait," Kevin said.

She turned. "I know. Arnold's short, not fat."

He smiled. "Thanks."

"Any time."

She got in her car and backed out of the driveway. Kevin popped the lid off the sky blue paint and stirred it, watching the colors blend for a long time before he got back to work.

NICOLE'S SISTER, LAURA, was tall like their brother, Adam, had been. She also had green eyes, but her long hair was a darker blond. When Nicole picked her up at the airport in Norfolk, she noticed some changes. Laura had dyed her hair a chestnut brown. It was attractive. But it didn't do anything to conceal the dark circles under her eyes.

"Vacation," Laura squealed when Nicole hugged her in the luggage area. "Screw Indianapolis. I need to get away from that place."

"That's what I'm doing," Nicole said. "Cape Pursuit is wonderful."

"No kidding. You look fantastic," her sister said. "Not that you were a hag before or anything, but you've got some color and you look—" her sister held her at arm's length for a minute, scrutinizing her face "—happy."

Nicole felt a twinge of guilt. Was she happy? Did she have a right to be happy? Her family had lived with such grief for the year since they lost Adam that she hadn't known anything else. Until she came to Cape Pursuit just over two months ago. Every day the sadness ebbed away as if the waves lapping at the sand were taking it out to sea.

And she was starting to realize her feelings for Kevin were wrapped up in that. As if her lungs could finally expand and she could breathe. As if her eyes opened to the sunlight a little wider than they had before. This new feeling was like walking into her parents' house after school and smelling her favorite dinner cooking. How much of her newfound happiness was Kevin and how much was getting away, starting over in Cape Pursuit? She wasn't ready to confide in Laura. Not yet. She'd have to assess where her sister was before she started talking about rainbows and unicorns.

"It's the beach," Nicole said, thinking she should offer some reason to her sister. "And my job. I love working with Jane and I'm even displaying some of my photography."

"Are you sure it's okay with Jane if I stay with you for the week?"

"Of course. She insisted. While you're here, you can help me look at houses. I've decided to rent my own place for now—before I wear out my welcome with Jane—but I'm seriously considering buying."

"You're not coming home?" Laura asked. Her shoulders drooped and she stopped towing her suitcase.

"Honey, I'm sorry. I know I said moving here was temporary, but…well, I'm not sure about that anymore."

Laura half smiled and rubbed her sister's arm. "Do they have a high school here in Cape Pursuit? Maybe I could get a job. The teenagers here can't be any snottier than they are back home."

"You've only been teaching one year. Give it a chance," Nicole said.

"Teenagers are mean." Laura sighed and continued rolling her red suitcase toward the parking garage. "I need a new life."

They loaded Laura's luggage in the trunk and spent the hour's drive catching up. As they approached Cape Pursuit, Nicole's cell phone chimed with a message. "Will you read that for me?" she asked. "It's illegal, and I'm too old anyway to master texting and driving."

"You're twenty-six." Laura reached into the back seat and pulled her sister's cell phone from the front pocket of her purse. "It's from a man named Charlie Z," she said. She narrowed her eyes at her older sister. "Sounds like a drug dealer's name. Do I need to tell Mom and Dad anything?"

Nicole laughed. "He's my Realtor. His last name is Zimmerman, but I didn't bother to type the whole thing in. The Z section of my address book isn't that complicated."

Laura tapped the text and read it aloud. "'I'm at a great house for you right now. Are you available for a quick look?'"

Nicole took the exit into Cape Pursuit and thought about it for a second. Was she serious about a place of her own? She loved the town, loved working in the gallery, but was it a permanent or even semipermanent choice? What about the MBA from the state college in Indiana she'd just paid the last loan on? Was she using that investment working in an art gallery and selling a few photographs on the side? Did it matter?

"Do you want me to answer him?" her sister prompted.

"Am I crazy for looking at a house? I've never owned anything big except this car."

"This car is small," Laura said. She pulled a chocolate bar from her purse, broke it in two, and gave Nicole half. "You look better than you have in a long time. Since…you know when. If you're happy here, then…"

Nicole bit off a chunk of the chocolate crisp bar from the locally famous candy factory in her hometown. It was one of the things she missed about Indianapolis, but there weren't many others. Except her family, of course.

"Life is short," Laura said, interrupting her thoughts.

"Ask him the address, if you don't mind a little detour."

"I'm on vacation. I have plenty of time." Laura tapped out a message on her sister's phone. "Is Charlie Z hot?" Laura asked after she sent the message.

"Yes," Nicole said. "Very."

"Taken?"

"Sort of. I believe he's involved with someone." Nicole wouldn't divulge Jane's secret; there would be plenty of time during her sister's visit if Jane wanted to talk about it.

Nicole's phone beeped and her sister read the address in the message.

"Too bad the hot Realtor's taken. He actually answers messages, unlike the last loser I dated."

Nicole laughed. "It's business for him, so of course he communicates fast. Plus he's on a tight timetable. Realty is only his part-time job. He's a full-time firefighter," Nicole said. She wondered if and how he would balance being a parent along with his work. But Jane could do it, and so could he.

"Not interested in a firefighter no matter how hot he is." Laura sighed and shoved her sister's phone back in her purse. "Guess we'll keep our eyes on the house instead."

KEVIN WAS ON day three of his painting job. Yellow covered the house except for the high parts under the eaves and the two dormers perched on the roof. He'd need a ladder for those parts. Another day and he planned to try his ankle's strength by standing on a ladder. The swelling was down, the black and blue fading. But he wasn't sure he could trust it.

Maybe the chief had been right about making him take a week off. With the way the shifts ran, he would actually end up with nine days off. By that time, this place should look like a cottage befitting a beach town. He stood on the front porch and balanced a sky blue shutter in one hand, his cordless drill in the other. It was the last shutter to go on the front of the house, and the blue contrasting with the yellow made a nice combination.

He hated admitting Charlie Zimmerman was right about the colors, but it was a cheerful house. Inviting. Made his own dark blue house look like a dungeon, even though the style and floor plan were almost the same. Most of the houses on the side streets in Cape Pursuit were similar because of their origins as beach rentals. With his remaining three days off, he could repaint his own house and make his landlord happy.

Paint therapy. That was what Jane had called it.

He wondered if Jane had told Nicole about their talk. Even though she might not realize it, he'd heard Nicole's whisper as his partner turned the ignition on the squad. *I think you're a hero.* Fighting fires and rescuing people takes bravery, but it was nothing compared to what it must have taken Nicole to say those words. As he'd mulled over the drowning and limped through the past six days, remembering Nicole's quiet admission had been powerful.

That still didn't mean he'd been brave enough to call her or stop by the gallery. It was an embarrassing cowardice, and he should kick his own ass, but he was afraid of breaking the fragile relationship he had with Nicole. If his former relationships—all one and a half of them—were any indication, he wasn't good at reading minds. He and Arnold had both had the same stunned expression when his girlfriend had moved out almost as quickly as she moved in, leaving him, the dog and a note. That was two years ago, and he hadn't made it past buying a drink for a woman since.

Charlie was inside, opening windows and getting ready to show the place to someone. A young couple had been there two days ago to check it out, but the paint was covering the house in patches and the shutters were propped all around the driveway and yard, their sky blue paint drying. It probably hadn't made a great impression. A family with three children came yesterday. The paint looked better, but the dearth of square footage sent them packing in their minivan.

Perhaps it would be perfect for whoever Charlie was pitching it to today.

Kevin carried four shutters and stacked them against the side of the house to complete the two windows there. Charlie had given Kevin a tour before he started painting, so he knew the side windows provided light for a kitchen and small dining area.

He heard two car doors shut in the driveway, Charlie greet someone and the front screen door snap shut. It was his job to make the place look good but stay out of the way. Charlie was the schmoozer, using his charm to talk people into the right bed, bath and closet combo.

A higher selling price often meant a bonus for Kevin, a deal he and Charlie had shared for several years, but he still wasn't interested in becoming partners with him. Although Charlie balanced his time and energy between his two jobs, Kevin preferred to think of firefighting as his main occupation. His calling.

Kevin surveyed the side windows and decided they were too high to reach from the ground. Without the benefit of the front porch to stand on, he needed an extra three feet of height. He stacked up a few concrete blocks, balanced a scrap board on top and stepped carefully onto the platform, trying to shift his weight off his tender ankle. Holding a shutter against the house next to the kitchen window, he leaned close to the glass and screwed the shutter fast.

He noticed movement inside the kitchen and hoped his drill's noise wouldn't wreck Charlie's sales pitch. He held a shutter up on the other side of the window. The old wood shutters were heavy, but they had character. A bead of sweat ran down his forehead, but he didn't let go of the shutter. He got the two top screws in and paused to wipe his face with the sleeve of his T-shirt.

A face in the window stopped him. A pretty woman with dark brown hair stood over the kitchen sink and watched him work. He smiled at her, hoping he wasn't such a disgusting sight that she'd move on to the next house for sale. The woman turned and said something to someone else in the room, probably Charlie.

Kevin held a screw in place and drilled it in. He fished

the last screw out of his chest pocket and glanced in the window again. It was hard to avoid looking since he was standing on a makeshift platform right outside the window.

There was another face. A familiar one. What the heck was Nicole doing here? As he watched, she flipped two latches and shoved the lower half of the window up.

"What are you doing?" she asked. "I thought you were staying off your ankle."

Kevin grinned. "I'm standing on the other foot."

Nicole smiled. She was just as beautiful through a dark window screen as she was in the sunshine. There was something so right about seeing her in this house. Perhaps it was the sunny yellow color.

Did she still think he was a hero now that a week had gone by since the water rescue?

"I like the color you're painting this," she said.

"Charlie's idea. I can't take credit."

"It looks like it belongs on the Mediterranean," she said. "Like an Italian villa."

"Glad you like it. Are you seriously thinking of buying it?"

That's a very good sign.

"I'm coming out to talk to you before we leave," she said. She shut the window without giving him a chance to respond.

Kevin moved his platform below the next window and continued hanging shutters, all the while keeping an eye open for Nicole. Was she serious about settling down in Cape Pursuit?

More importantly, why did she want to talk with him before she left?

He finished affixing the shutters to the other side of the house. A half hour had gone by. If he didn't want to climb a ladder and paint the eaves today, he was out of things to do. He stacked his tools in the garage, refilled Arnold's water bucket under the truck and listened to the voices inside the house. Who was the woman with Nicole?

The door from the house into the garage opened and the two women followed Charlie out. Nicole wore shorts and a close-fitting green top that matched her eyes. Kevin took quick stock of his own appearance, knowing he looked like a man who hadn't shaved or glanced in a mirror in days.

"Try to picture the garage without all the ladders and paint cans and the troll I hired to paint it," Charlie said. "Plenty of room for your car, a lawnmower, a bike."

Nicole wasn't looking at the garage. She was looking straight at Kevin. The woman with her had the same eyes but was several inches taller with much darker hair. Nicole came straight to him as he hovered near the bed of his truck.

"Kevin," she said. Was her breathing a little too fast? He was trained to notice things like that when he assessed people with medical emergencies. Was he the cause of the flush creeping over Nicole's neck? "I want you to meet my sister, Laura," Nicole continued. "She's here for a week's vacation."

Kevin turned to Laura, shook hands and exchanged greetings. *That explains the resemblance.* He saw the curious glance Nicole's sister gave her, as if to ask how she knew this house painter guy.

"Kevin is—"

Nicole hesitated and Kevin wondered how she was going to fill in the blank. What was he to her? He knew what he'd like to be, but he also knew how unlikely that was.

Charlie, the schmoozer, filled in the gap. "Kevin's the guy who took the door off your sister's car the first day she got to Cape Pursuit. If I were you," Charlie said, "I'd watch out for this guy. And I'd certainly keep my car doors closed."

Charlie grinned, but Laura drew her eyebrows together and frowned. She turned to Nicole. "I thought you said your car got hit by a fire truck?"

"It did," Nicole said. Her flush deepened and she shuffled the papers in her hands, probably realty documents from Charlie.

Kevin wasn't sure how to read Nicole's reaction. He knew this was a delicate topic for her, and it likely was for her sister, too. He saw Laura's eyes focus on the embroidery on his Cape Pursuit Fire Department T-shirt.

Laura's eyes traveled back to his face. "So did you steal a fire truck and wreck it or do you have two jobs?" Laura asked. The wrinkles in her forehead relaxed, but only a little. It was hot in the garage. But this would not be the time to have a bead of sweat roll off his nose, not when he was trying to come up with the right answer.

"Stole it," he said.

Laura gave him a hint of smile. "Good."

CHAPTER THIRTEEN

GETTING OUT OF his house and having company other than his dog was worth the effort of showering, shaving and putting on clean clothes. Seeing Nicole across the bar was a bonus. When Tony, Ethan, Charlie and Tyler stopped by his house and wouldn't take no for an answer, Kevin cleaned himself up, agreeing to a night at the Cape Pursuit Bar & Grill. It was Thursday, their usual time to blow off steam. The previous Thursday Kevin hadn't felt like talking. Now that more than a week had gone by since the drowning, he was ready to put it in perspective over a glass of whatever was on draft.

Tyler sat next to Kevin. "How are you doing?"

"Fine," Kevin said.

"Ankle better?"

"Yep."

"Good," Ethan said. "We're tired of covering for your butt at work. About time you pulled on your pants and showed up." Ethan slid a glass of beer across the table to Kevin as he spoke, his smile showing he didn't mean any harm.

"You're buying, right?" Tony asked.

"Sure," Kevin said. "Any excitement at the station this week?"

Tyler shrugged. "Lots of minor runs. Little stuff. Smoke alarm at the Marriott, Dumpster fire at the Holiday Inn."

"Bunch of squad calls," Tony added. "Usual stuff. And some tourists tangled in their rental cars. None of those guys ever look where they're going."

"So I haven't missed much."

"I wouldn't say that," Ethan said. "Chief's getting worked up about the big party in August." The other three men glanced at Tony. The chief was his father.

"Go ahead and say it. I know what he's like."

As Kevin had mentioned to Nicole, the Cape Pursuit Fire Department one hundredth birthday was coming up—one hundred years since they officially put out their first fire with a steamer truck and four volunteers. Coinciding with the Cape Pursuit Homecoming Festival, they were planning a big celebration and open house in August, and Chief Ruggles had become a bridezilla planning the reception.

"Chief misses you," Tyler said. "I think I saw him wearing your cleaning apron the other day."

"Screw you," Kevin grumbled.

"This week we cleaned out the squad room and the equipment locker. He's talking about having the carpet in the meeting room professionally cleaned. Now he wants us to repaint the whole interior, bays and all," Ethan said.

"When are you coming back?" Tony asked.

"Couple of days."

"Good. We'll save the painting for you. I'll tell Dad you volunteered and it's some kind of light duty transition period for you."

"Why is he so worked up over the party?" Kevin asked. "Unless it rains, no one will even notice the inside of the station."

Tony shrugged. "He's getting ready to retire, probably wants to leave on a high note."

Kevin wondered how many of his friends were considering applying for the promotions that would open up with his uncle's retirement. Tyler wasn't interested. As he'd put it, the higher up the ladder a guy gets, the more meetings and headaches he has. Kevin was willing to put in extra hours to advance in a career he loved.

He took a long drink and glanced over at Nicole's booth. She was with Jane and Laura. Meeting Laura yesterday reminded him why he was treading on dangerous territory trying to have a relationship with Nicole. The sisters shared their brother's loss and probably the same feelings about firefighters.

"You going over there?" Tyler elbowed him in the ribs and nodded toward the table he'd been staring at.

"Don't know."

"If you are, you should send drinks first," Tyler advised. "Makes you look better when you show up."

"Is that how you got Hillary to marry you?"

"Yes. And I'm better looking than you."

Kevin signaled the waitress and asked her to take a bottle of Moscato to Nicole's table. He waited, watching for Nicole's reaction when the Italian wine she'd ordered the first night they'd met arrived at her table. Even if it didn't soften her feelings toward him, he could at least try to say thank you for her words the night of the drowning.

His partners exchanged glances and grinned at him. He would have expected Charlie to rib him about it, but Charlie stared pensively at the women's table.

"Is Jane doing that mural for your new shop downtown?" Kevin asked.

"I don't know," Charlie said.

"I thought you two worked all that out."

"Not by a long shot," he said grimly.

"Wait a minute," Tyler cut in. "Is there something going on between you and Jane? Have you managed to piss off the one woman in town who still respects you?"

"Like I'd tell you," Charlie said. He got up and headed toward the restroom.

"WHO WOULD SEND us a bottle of Moscato?" Jane asked, raising her eyebrows and smiling at Nicole.

Nicole carefully avoided looking in Kevin's direction when the waitress brought the bottle and told them it was from another table. Nicole and Jane knew who sent it. Kevin was like the ocean breeze always present in Cape Pursuit. Since her first day in town, he'd been right over her shoulder and right around the corner. It had gone on for over two months at this point. She was going to have to do something about it.

Like kiss him again.

"Seriously, who?" Laura asked, her open expression conveying her confusion.

Jane turned and waved at the table of firefighters in the corner by the television. "Charlie disappeared," she said to Nicole. "And he's obviously not sending me a bottle of alcohol."

"I don't think it's Charlie," Nicole said.

"Of course I have other friends at that table," Jane said, "but I'd say this is for you."

"Fine," Laura said, "don't tell me. I'm drinking it anyway." She filled up her glass and downed half of it.

"It's Kevin," Nicole said. She hoped she would remove some of the mystery and slow her racing heart by sounding matter-of-fact about it.

Laura cocked her head and looked at her sister. "Kevin who?"

"Remember the guy who was painting the house we toured?"

"Uh-huh. He's here?"

Nicole glanced over at the table of testosterone. Kevin was looking at her at the same moment. *Of course.*

Laura swiveled and stared. "He looks way better now. But he's a firefighter. Those guys live on adrenaline." She was already finished with her glass of wine. "Until they die on it."

Nicole felt like a birthday balloon that had floated away from the backyard party and popped on a tree branch. Her sister was right. Kevin would give his life for his job. She'd seen him going under the water over and over to look for that girl. That was his life, his passion. Did she really want to take one step closer to a man who wouldn't walk away from daily risk?

She sipped her wine and toyed with her food.

"I like the website," Jane said. "I had no idea you knew how to write HTML code."

Nicole laughed. "Only a little. I bought one of those pre-made template-driven sites where you plug in your stuff. Anyone could do it."

"I doubt it," Laura said. "We're supposed to be using all kinds of technology at my high school, but most of the teachers haven't even mastered our online attendance program."

"How's teaching?" Jane asked. "History, right?"

Laura sighed and shoved her salad plate away. "I love history, but I hate teenagers. I need a new job."

Nicole and Jane exchanged glances. In the two days her sister had been in town, Nicole had felt her sister's sadness like a heavy winter coat hanging over her shoulders. She'd been there, too. Adam's death last summer shocked them both into rethinking how they wanted to live.

For Nicole, the picture had come into focus. Cape Pursuit with its sunrises and fresh air touched a nerve and switched on a light for her. And Laura? Nicole wished she knew how to help her sister, who was refilling her wine glass. Again.

"Maybe you could write about history? Or get your PhD and teach college?" Jane suggested.

Laura shrugged. "I don't know, maybe. I like history because it's safe. You know what did happen instead of worrying about what will."

Nicole exchanged another worried look with Jane. Nicole signaled the waitress and asked for a pitcher of water. *Maybe we should dilute the wine.*

"The online store should be ready to open in a few days now that I've uploaded pictures of the pieces of art for sale. I have to make sure the commerce end of the site is totally secure before I open it up for business," Nicole said.

"Next I'll be launching a chain of art galleries," Jane said.

"Need a manager for any of them?" Laura asked, a smile erasing her earlier gloom.

Nicole saw movement in her peripheral vision. With a subtle twist of her head, she determined the source. Yes, Santa Claus was coming to town. And she had five seconds to prepare.

Jane shot her a warning glance, a small lift of one eyebrow.

Kevin stood at the edge of their booth's table. He bestowed a quick smile on Jane and Laura and turned his focus on Nicole like a searchlight. He looked like a different man than the paint-splattered, half-bearded version she saw yesterday. It didn't matter. Kevin, with his broad shoulders and stormy green eyes, would be attractive if he were frozen in ice for a century and thawed over her grandmother's old Maytag stove.

It wasn't fair.

"Thank you for the wine," Nicole said, congratulating herself on her even, rational tone of voice. Her internal thought of *would you consider kissing me in front of this whole bar?* temporarily lost the battle. Not the war, though. She still wanted him in an irrational way.

"Not sure if it's an actual Italian vintage, but it's probably the closest thing they have," he said.

"It's nice."

He turned to Laura. "How do you like Cape Pursuit? Good vacation so far?"

This was a good sign. He was making small talk with her sister. While he chatted, Nicole glanced over to the fire-fighter table. Empty glasses stood on the table and a game played on the television, but all eyes at the table were looking in her direction. Maybe they were mentally sending encouragement to Kevin for whatever mission he was on. Or maybe they were just waiting to see him make a fool of himself so they could entertain themselves giving him grief about it later.

"So far, so good," Laura told Kevin. "I may never want to go home. No beach in Indianapolis."

"So you're staying awhile?"

"Just a week, according to my plane ticket. But my sister here was only staying for the summer and now she's looking at houses." Laura smiled, a little crookedly and a lot drunkenly. "Ask me in a week."

He nodded and returned his attention to Nicole. She wasn't disappointed to be in the search beam of the stormy eyes, but she wondered if he had something special to say. After all, he'd abandoned man-land and trekked across the bar, even though he hadn't made an effort to see her in the past week.

Maybe he'd needed time to let the wound of the tragic drowning heal over a little. She understood that well.

"Can I call you later?" he asked. "There's something I want to ask you."

"Sure," she said, smiling. Unlike her sister, she'd only had one glass of Moscato and she was in full awareness mode. "But you could ask me now...unless you're planning a surprise gift for Jane to thank her for being such a good listener."

He grinned, his shoulders relaxing a solid inch. "She told you about that, huh?"

Nicole shrugged. "We're friends. We talk."

"Talking is good," he said.

"Do you talk at the fire station?"

"All the time." He raised one eyebrow at Jane. "But your friend here is a whole lot more polite. And intuitive."

"Do you talk about your personal lives?" Jane asked.

"Only if we have to," Kevin said. "And only if it's really interesting."

Nicole knew she and Jane were wondering the same thing. Had Charlie confided in any of his friends at the station? Had he told anyone he would become a father in a matter of months? She wanted to ask Kevin, but she couldn't just blurt out the question no matter how much wine she had drunk.

Even though her attention was on Kevin, Nicole noticed her sister's speculative glance. She hadn't told Laura anything about Kevin—not about the brief flirtations or the scene in his kitchen. Or the lying-awake longing she'd felt for weeks. She'd been standing outside the bakery looking at cupcakes, when all along she'd had enough money in her purse to buy out the whole tray of sweets. *What was she waiting for?*

Maybe it was time.

"What did you want to ask me?"

Kevin glanced at Jane and Laura, who were listening intently.

"I'm afraid of getting rejected again," Kevin said. "Maybe I should go sit down."

"Give it a try," Jane said. "I'm not drinking tonight so I could use some entertainment."

Nicole returned her attention to Kevin and tried to appear encouraging, even though she probably shouldn't. If she wanted to preserve her sanity, she should be preparing a speech that would gently decline whatever he was asking.

"When you have time, that is, maybe after your sister's visit…would you have dinner with me?"

Nicole considered it. *Why was she considering it?* What

had changed since the last time he'd asked her out? Maybe it was seeing him in action, seeing him put his heart and soul into trying to save that girl. A man with a heart like that...

No. No matter how big his heart was, it belonged to fire-fighting.

She shook her head and tried for a pleasant smile. "Sorry. It's very nice of you to ask, but I don't think it's a good idea."

Kevin nodded and swallowed. His fingers played with the edge of the table. Nicole was almost on the verge of changing her mind. Jane and Laura seemed to be holding their breaths.

"I understand," Kevin said. He turned and walked back to his table of friends, his shoulders squared but his steps slow.

CHAPTER FOURTEEN

A WEEK LATER, Nicole reminded herself that what she was about to do with Kevin was not a date. It was business.

The owner of the largest marina and boat dealership in Cape Pursuit had seen her pictures in the gallery and asked her to photograph his business and boats for an upcoming feature in a local tourist magazine. If she wanted to save money to get a place of her own, freelance photography was a great opportunity.

"Are you sure you don't mind being left alone?" Nicole asked her sister. "I could see if the marina could postpone the photo shoot until next week."

"The weather today is perfect, and this is your big chance to get your pictures in a magazine. I'll be fine," Laura said. "You're leaving me your car and I know how to get any place I want to go in Cape Pursuit."

"Do you plan to go anywhere?"

"Probably the beach and carryout food. Maybe pick up a souvenir for Mom before I head out on Tuesday. Are you planning to keep your cool with the hot firefighter who's picking you up?"

"Absolutely. I only accepted his offer of a ride because I didn't want to leave you with no wheels. His dad is a boat dealer with the marina, and that's the only reason Kevin is my ride."

The bell rang. Nicole opened the door and almost gasped.

Kevin wore a blue polo shirt and tan shorts. Boat shoes. No socks. He didn't look the least bit like a firefighter. He looked like a man on vacation. A muscular, well-built, dark-haired, handsome man.

"Hi," he said, his eyes doing a quick survey of Nicole. "I forgot to ask you if you have boat shoes."

"I didn't know we were getting on the boats," Nicole said.

Kevin laughed. "What fun would it be if we didn't?"

"I think it's supposed to be work, not fun, but I'll grab some different shoes."

Nicole ducked around the corner and dug in the bottom of the hall closet. She and Jane wore the same size, and she hoped her friend owned boat shoes.

"You're still here," Kevin said to her sister, Laura, his tone friendly but questioning.

"I decided to stay a few more days," Laura said. "There's over a month until school starts, and I'm not sure I'm going back to high school teaching anyway."

Nicole wondered what Kevin would think of her sister's career crisis. He'd probably never wavered in what he wanted to be when he grew up and never considered changing his occupation. She doubted he dreaded going to work every day, unlike the guys she'd seen trudging into the furniture factory back home. They hauled their hard-sided lunchboxes through the gates as if they were going to their own funeral.

"How can you not go back?" Kevin asked. "It's your job."

"Easy. I just won't," Laura answered, her tone flippant and bitter. "There's always somebody who wants a job. Some other poor schmuck can try to make teenagers give a darn about history instead of their smartphones."

Over the past week, her sister had talked a lot about how she dreaded angsty adolescents, homework, hall passes and bus duty. *Had Nicole hated her former job and trudged in every day?* Never. Quite foolishly, she'd popped into her office each morning, hoping to catch her boss's eye. It made the days go faster until reality surfaced and she discovered her boss had only been using her devotion. That was a mistake she wouldn't make again.

"It's an important job," Kevin said, continuing his conversation with Laura while Nicole dug through sandals and mismatched sneakers in the bottom of the closet. She really should organize it for Jane before baby and toddler shoes joined the pile. "Don't you like being a teacher?" Kevin asked.

Nicole found two matching boat shoes with white soles and slipped them on. She heard her sister sigh as she came up behind her.

"Still working on what I like," Laura said.

Nicole squeezed her sister's shoulder. "Behave yourself today."

"You, too."

The sisters exchanged a quick smile and Nicole followed Kevin through the door. He opened the passenger door of his truck for her.

As Nicole hoisted herself into the passenger seat, she noticed a leash and a plastic water bowl on the floor. Apparently Arnold was not going along on this ride.

"Does your dog like boats?" she asked, clicking her seat belt in place.

"Definitely not," Kevin said. He shut her door, went around to the driver's side, climbed in and started the truck. "We took him out just one time. He's got a stomach made for land, not sea. He's just as bad as my brother, the puker." Kevin laid a long arm across the seat back as he backed out of the driveway. "Tyler never goes out on the fireboat. It would be bad."

He shifted gears and then swung his gaze toward Nicole, concern wrinkling his brow. "You don't get seasick, do you?"

"I've never been seasick," she said, smiling reassuringly at him. "I went on a cruise with my family when I was sixteen. My dad won the trip from some promotional thing at work."

"Where did you go?"

"Nassau in the Bahamas. It was a short cruise, but there was one really rough day. My mom and my sister got sick, so my dad and my brother and I had the dinner table all to ourselves."

"Calm today."

"That's probably good. I haven't been out on a small boat on the ocean, so it'll be an adventure."

"Thanks for helping out my dad's marina. They worked with a photographer from Virginia Beach last year, but I guess he didn't have much imagination and the pictures were just...flat."

Nicole admired Kevin's smooth shifting on the way down the shoreline from Cape Pursuit. He was easy on the clutch, and the truck moved through gears almost as if it were an automatic. *The man has good hands.* No matter how many days had passed since their unexpected kiss in his kitchen, she hadn't forgotten how good he was at that skill, too.

Had he forgotten? Or was he giving her space, doing what she said she wanted and not pushing her to go out with him?

I'm out with him now.

"How is your ankle?" she asked, keeping her tone on the business side of friendly.

"Fine," he said, glancing briefly at her. "It was just a sprain."

"And you're back to work full-time now?"

"Yes," he said, his tone implying he'd escaped some terrible threat.

Back to work risking his life. Despite Nicole's reservations about his career, it was clear that it was Kevin's idea of living.

They passed small seafood restaurants and oceanfront homes on the seaside drive.

"I'm curious about something," Nicole said. "How did you get the dent on your truck?"

"My mom backed into it in her driveway."

Nicole laughed. "How did that happen?"

"Last fall, my dad's insulin pump failed and he went into insulin shock. It's a scary thing. Mom called the ambulance, but I beat them there when I heard the call over the radio."

"It must have been frightening hearing your parents' address," Nicole commented. She pictured Kevin racing to their house.

"It was. I parked alongside the driveway so I'd be out of the way of the squad. After the ambulance took Dad to the hospital—I went along—Mom backed out of the garage to follow them and didn't notice my truck."

"Why didn't you get it fixed?"

For a man whose house looked like an advertisement for cleaning products, it didn't make sense.

Kevin shrugged. "I only have collision and liability insurance because it's a pretty old truck. And it's my painting truck. I hate to have it in the body shop for weeks."

Nicole laughed. "I can understand that." She'd had the convenience of getting rides with Jane while her car was in for repair, but with Kevin's two jobs, being without a vehicle would make life impossible.

He turned off the highway into a large marina. Gleaming white boats bobbed at docks along both sides of the driveway. A large building with wide porches rose from an expansive parking lot. The whole place was upscale.

"Nice," she said. "You were never tempted to get a job here like you father and spend your days on the water?"

Kevin pulled into a parking spot and set the brake. He turned to her and smiled. "It's not for me. My dad's diabetes made firefighting an unhealthy career option for him, so he went with his other love. Boats."

Too bad Kevin didn't love boats as much as he loved fighting fires.

"Go ahead and take as many shots as you want from the docks, and then we're going out on a boat to get a perspective of the marina from the water."

"I have a list from the magazine of pictures they'd like for the article, but I'm happy to take plenty of extras," Nicole said.

Nicole strolled along the shoreline, taking pictures of the marina's storage and maintenance facilities, showroom, restaurant and even pool. As she walked down the long floating docks, she was glad to have Kevin by her side. Although technically anchored, the docks shifted a little with their footsteps and made her feel slightly off balance. Kevin carried her camera bag so she could have a hand free, just in case she needed it to steady herself.

"You're quiet," she said.

"I was afraid you were concentrating. Didn't want to get in your way."

"I can talk and work at the same time. How are things at the fire station?" she asked.

He drew his eyebrows together and hesitated. "Are you sure you want to hear about that?"

It was a fair question. A few months ago, she would never have chatted casually with a firefighter, much less asked him about risking his life that day.

"Was it that bad?" she asked lightly.

"Boring, actually. Slow couple of days, which is, technically, a good thing in my line of work. But it makes for a long day."

"Did you rescue cats or chop holes in roofs?" she asked as she knelt and took an artistic shot of a shiny white boat's bow.

"No cats. A couple of tourists who hadn't been on a bike

in years made the mistake of renting one. Those bike rental places should warn people."

"Uh-oh," Nicole said.

"Turns out you *can* forget how to ride one. Or at least how to use the brakes before you crash into a parked car."

"Are they okay?"

"Mostly. I'd say his collarbone is broken and his wife will never get on a tandem bike with him again."

"I hope that was the worst thing that happened today," Nicole said. She was starting to relax, thinking perhaps that Kevin's job was not always facing infernos and putting his life on the line. Tourists on bikes, an occasional trash can fire—maybe it wasn't as dangerous as she'd imagined.

"After lunch we got a call to the mini golf course. Two brothers tangled on the seventh hole."

"They were fighting?" Nicole asked. *That sounded dangerous.*

"No. They were only six and eight, just little kids. One left-handed boy and one right-handed. Guess their mom didn't think how that would play out when they swung side by side."

Nicole covered her mouth with one hand. "I'm afraid to ask."

Kevin grinned. "One was fine, but the other one got six stitches above his eye. He'll have a scar, but it'll just make him look mysterious. The girls will love it."

"Was that a pretty typical day for you?"

"Sadly, yes. It's a resort town with thousands of people operating on vacation brain. I always hope they bought trip insurance, especially if they have the misfortune of seeing me on vacation."

Nicole laughed. "The poor tourists." She cocked her head and looked at Kevin. "Do you buy trip insurance when you travel?"

He shrugged. "I never go anywhere. I have six years' worth of vacation time saved up."

"And you've been in Cape Pursuit all that time?"

"Believe it or not, I did go to Canada for a training session with our water rescue team last year. I even had to get a passport."

"Why Canada?"

"They have a lot of inland lakes, which are good for training. A group of us went to a special school there." He held her camera bag open while she exchanged lenses. "How about your work in the shop? Going pretty well?"

"I'll put it this way. We saw dozens of tourists at the gallery. They didn't break any bones or need stitches—they just hurt their credit cards. And we didn't mind at all."

"Good business?" Kevin prompted.

"Very good. Jane's becoming a real success."

"You're helping," he said.

Nicole shook her head. She was helping, but it was still Jane's business. When the long, quiet winter season came, would she still be needed? Would she stay in Cape Pursuit? Jane would have a baby by then...

"Jane and I make a good team," Nicole said. "I'm afraid she'd be exhausted by the end of the day without my help."

"She's a hard worker. Running her shop, being in the town government." Kevin's mouth straightened into a serious line. "We admire her a lot, but she should slow down. Take care of herself."

Nicole lowered her camera and scrutinized Kevin's face. Did he know something?

"It's easy to overdo it," Nicole said cautiously. "Especially during the busy season."

He nodded. "Charlie and I were talking about that a few days ago."

"Talking about what?"

Kevin raised an eyebrow and bit his lip. "We were talking about…making time for the right things. Doing the right things."

There was no way she was going to come out and ask him, but Nicole would almost bet her camera lens that Kevin knew about Jane's baby. She was tempted to just go ahead and say it, but she couldn't risk her friend's privacy. Not until Jane was ready. After what had happened with the failed proposal, Jane and Charlie had not spoken. That would have to end, but they both needed time.

"Where do we catch this boat we're going out on?" she asked, changing the subject. "I'd like to get some pictures of Cape Pursuit from the water, maybe the lighthouse if we could take a little extra time—or the mermaid statue. I love that story."

"The tourist story about the pirate and his mermaid girl-friend?" Kevin asked.

"Must be some truth to it," Nicole insisted. "A story like that wouldn't come out of nowhere."

Kevin laughed. "The part about the pirate hiding his stash I believe. I don't know about the rest. I've been hear-ing that story since I was a little kid."

"Have you ever looked for the treasure? I'd think local boys wouldn't be able to resist."

"My cousins went on an expedition once. I missed it be-cause I had a broken arm at the time."

"How did that happen?"

"Haunted house gone bad. The church set up a haunted house in the Catholic school, and some big high school kid jumped out and scared the daylights out of me."

"He broke your arm? How old were you?"

"I was seven. He scared the heck out of me and I fell down the stairs."

Nicole smiled. "Not funny, sorry. I'm trying to picture you being so afraid you'd crash down a staircase."

"My brother made fun of me until Mom told him to stop," Kevin said, grimacing. "And I missed the pirate expedition."

A powerful engine rumbled to life and Kevin pointed to a large boat at the end of the dock. "He's waiting for us."

As Nicole walked down the dock to the beautiful boat framed by the sparkling blue ocean, she reminded herself to be careful and keep her footing. No matter how appealing Kevin was, she was there in Cape Pursuit to build a new life for herself, and now also to help Jane with the new life inside her. Losing her heart to Kevin Ruggles was the wrong thing to do.

HOURS LATER, when Kevin pulled in the driveway at Jane's place, there was already a distinctive blue truck with one orange fender in the driveway.

"Huh," Kevin said. "That's my cousin Tony's truck. What's he doing here?"

"No idea," Nicole said. A sinking feeling glued her to the seat of Kevin's truck. Was Laura okay? Her heart raced, but she tried to use logic. If there was a medical emergency, there would be an ambulance there, not a blue pickup truck. Would Laura…be with a man she'd just met?

No. Not her conservative teacher sister. At least not the Laura Nicole thought she knew. Before their family came crashing down with Adam's death.

Kevin parked and pulled the keys from the ignition.

"Can I come in with you? Just to…make sure things are okay with your sister? I don't want her to think I stole a boat and kidnapped you or anything."

Nicole knew what he was doing. And she didn't mind. Whatever the reason for Tony's visit, having Kevin by her side could only help.

"Sure," she said, forcing a smile. "Maybe your cousin stopped by to check the fire extinguishers at our house."

Before they stepped onto the porch, Tony opened the front door and put a finger over his lips.

"What's going on?" Kevin asked.

"I was waiting for you."

Nicole stepped in front of Kevin. "Is my sister okay?"

Tony glanced over his shoulder and gestured outside. He stepped through the door and closed it almost all the way behind him. The three of them stood on the small front stoop. Late-afternoon sunshine washing over them, but a sense of doom darkened Nicole's heart. It reminded her of the morning a representative from the fire service came to her parents' house to confirm their worst nightmare. It had been almost a year, but the pain was as raw as if it was thirty seconds ago.

"She's asleep," Tony said in a low voice.

None of this made sense.

"She had…car trouble?" Nicole asked, her words slow and uncertain.

Tony shook his head. "Your car is in the parking lot at the bar. I made sure it was locked and I have the keys."

"Thank you," Nicole whispered. Her throat felt like she'd swallowed wool socks. "How did…this happen?"

Tony shrugged. "I was driving by on my way home from work and I saw a woman trying to get into your car but she kept dropping the keys and seemed unsteady." He gave Nicole a lopsided grin. "Your car is familiar to me because of the…uh…door incident. Anyway, I thought the lady was trying to steal the car, but when I looked closer I realized I'd seen her with you and Jane one night."

"She went to the bar after I left this morning? That wasn't what I thought…what she planned…" Nicole stammered. Her sister needed more help than she'd realized.

"The good news is I think she only had three or four drinks. The bad news is your sister can't hold her booze. I don't think she's a very experienced drinker."

"Was she sick?" Nicole asked.

Tony nodded. "She'll be okay, though. Needs sleep and carbohydrates. Lots of water."

"I'm sorry," Nicole said. The wool sock in her throat was now making her eyes sting. "She's going through a tough time right now." A tear escaped and she brushed it away, even though it was useless because she knew both men saw it. "I should have been with her."

"I don't mind," Tony said. "Your sister was a heck of a lot nicer than most drunks when I held her hair back while she puked."

Kevin slid an arm around Nicole's shoulders and gave her a reassuring squeeze. The gesture was friendly, and it was tempting to lean into him, but she had to be strong herself...strong for the one sibling she had left.

"Your car keys are on the kitchen table," Tony added. "I'd suggest Gatorade as soon as she wakes up, if she can keep it down."

Nicole squeezed her eyes shut tight, but she could picture the look Kevin was probably giving his affable cousin right now. A look that said *shut up*.

"I should get going," Tony said.

"What can I do?" Kevin asked. "Anything you need?"

Nicole shook her head, unable to say what was in her heart, even though she thought Kevin would understand.

I've already lost a brother. I can't lose a sister, too. Laura was clearly on a destructive path. If Tony hadn't taken away the car keys...

"Good luck," Tony said, directing his words to Nicole. He turned to his cousin. "Can you move your truck so I can get mine out of the driveway?"

Kevin nodded. "How about I drive you over to the bar and we pick up Nicole's car?"

"You don't have to do that," Nicole said.

"No, that's a good idea," Tony agreed. "You might need

wheels to go to the store. Gatorade and ibuprofen. Toast and crackers. Stuff like that."

Nicole blew out a breath. "Okay." She tiptoed into the house, retrieved the keys, and met Kevin in the driveway.

"Thank you," she said.

"Call me later. Sooner if you need something."

She nodded. Tony had the window down on the passenger side. Nicole leaned in the window and touched his shoulder.

"Thank you for not letting my sister drive like that. She could have killed someone, or herself."

Fresh tears stung Nicole's eyes at the thought.

"Right place at the right time," Tony said.

CHAPTER FIFTEEN

"FOOD TRUCK NIGHT," Jane announced as soon as the last customer cleared the shop at closing time on Saturday.

"I've got cash and a giant appetite," Nicole agreed. She could practically taste the delicious food and feel the salt air. They'd indulged twice already in her stay in Cape Pursuit, and Nicole loved the festive food event by the harbor. "I hope the burger truck is there again."

Jane laughed. "You're right next to the ocean and you're going to skip the seafood trucks?"

"Hey, I'm from the Midwest where burgers are king. We'll go for a walk after we eat so my body has a fighting chance at defeating the cholesterol."

"Walking is a good idea for me, too. Although burgers aren't the reason I've switched to elastic-waist pants and stopped tucking anything in."

Nicole put her arm around her friend's shoulders as they locked the back door and walked to Nicole's red car. "That's exactly what's supposed to happen. You'll be twice as beautiful when you can hardly fit through the door."

"I'm almost five months along," Jane said. "And still only a few people know. Just the people I love and trust. My parents are supportive and excited about being grandparents, despite the circumstances, but you're my lifeline right now."

Nicole got in the driver's seat and waited while Jane

buckled up. "Charlie would be supportive, too. You're far from alone."

"I know. I need to figure out what to do about him."

"Maybe the decision is not as hard as you're making it."

"Huh," Jane said. "Believe me, this is as hard as it gets."

"If you didn't care for him…if it was just a one-night stand…what would you be doing right now about his involvement?"

Jane was silent as they negotiated the crowded streets, and Nicole was afraid she'd pushed too much. It was a hot summer evening with ocean breezes and food trucks waiting. She should let her friend off the hook and just enjoy the evening—should, but she knew Jane needed to talk it through. Several times every day the new life inside Jane had made its presence felt. And Charlie was always right there in the room even though Jane had pushed him away.

"I'd be practical. Draw up an agreement, maybe talk to an attorney about financial and custody arrangements."

"So why aren't you doing those things?"

"Because it's Charlie," Jane said, exasperation in her voice. "He's not a stranger."

Nicole tightened her fingers on the steering wheel. "Do you love him?"

Jane let out a long breath. "You wouldn't ask that question if you didn't already know the answer. But love has to go both ways for it to work."

"Maybe it does go both ways?"

"His proposal didn't come with any words about love. And I'd think that's where those words would come from if they were in his heart."

Nicole's heart ached for Jane as she swung into a spot in the city lot near the park. The lot was almost full, with locals and tourists thronging the sidewalks and lining up at the food trucks.

"Let's eat and figure this out later," Nicole said. She

smiled at her friend. "It's not like you're on a tight time frame or anything."

"Tell that to my stretch pants," Jane said.

"Smell the joy," Nicole said as she stepped out of the car. "I hope the truck that has the little donuts is here. They're the perfect size for dessert. Or maybe ice cream. You should have more calcium in your life."

"I'll eat something healthy, and then maybe I'll have ice cream. And we could go shopping for new clothes tomorrow," Jane suggested.

They walked down the line of trucks offering burritos, stir-fry, steak and cheese, vegan meals, fried everything, and custom sandwiches. Jane waved to locals and said hello to tourists they passed. Nicole recognized quite a few people, and every time she nodded and called someone by name, she felt a little more at home. Back in her hometown, there was a festival once a year that brought in food trucks, too, and she almost never recognized anyone out and about. In Cape Pursuit, it was every weekend for more than half the year.

She should get serious about finding a place of her own. She could ask Charlie if anyone had snapped up that yellow house with the blue shutters. Kevin had touched every inch of it with his painting magic, and when she saw the place she'd felt an instant connection.

As she and Jane finished their first pass of all the trucks, a scouting mission to decide which ones would get their business, they turned around and saw Kevin and Charlie crossing the lawn from the overflow parking area. Both men wore shorts and T-shirts, Charlie's a faded red Virginia Beach souvenir, Kevin's a navy blue fire department one.

"I hope you haven't eaten yet," Charlie said as they met. He stood close to Jane, and Nicole noticed his tense body language. He seemed torn between reaching out and hugging her or running away.

"Not yet," Nicole said. She smiled at Kevin. "We just

did a reconnaissance run. I can give you the full report of trucks if you like."

"I'm having a burger no matter what you say," Kevin said. "But I'd be happy to hear about your mission."

"What would you like, Jane?" Charlie asked.

"I'm not sure."

"I'll have whatever you're having if you'll let me buy," Charlie said. He touched her arm lightly.

Jane didn't brush his hand away. "Are you willing to try the vegan truck?"

"Anything," he said.

"Sorry," Kevin said. "I'm out. Want to get in line at the burger truck with me?" he asked Nicole.

Nicole glanced at Jane, trying to judge whether she would welcome some time alone with Charlie.

"You two go ahead," Jane said, her smile genuine. "I'm going to educate Charlie on the wonders of tofu."

Charlie kept his hand on Jane's arm as they turned and headed for the far end of the line of trucks.

"Is that a good thing?" Kevin asked, nodding after the departing couple.

"I think so. They have a lot to talk about."

"I know," Kevin said. "I wonder if maybe they're both making this harder than it needs to be."

Nicole had wondered the same thing, but she also believed people had to figure things out for themselves. "What would you do if you were in Charlie's situation?" It was obvious Kevin knew about the pregnancy, so Nicole didn't see the harm in asking.

Kevin swallowed and looked at the ground before raising his eyes to hers. "I'd say what was in my heart even if it wasn't what someone wanted to hear. Even if I didn't think I'd be believed."

The temptation to step into his arms was one of the hardest things Nicole had ever fought.

She tried to smile even though her heart was racing. "You must be the bravest man I've ever met."

Kevin took her hand. "No, I'm not. There are things I'm afraid of, just like everyone else."

Crowds of people jostled past them and a stroller clipped Nicole's ankle. Kevin tugged her hand and pulled her next to him. "Let's get our burgers and find an empty table."

As they waited in line, Nicole's bare arm brushed Kevin's. There was so much noise around them, Nicole felt as if they were alone in their conversation.

"How's your sister doing?"

Nicole sighed. "Okay. I've talked to my parents about her...unhappiness. They've encouraged her to see a counselor, and I'm trying to check in with her at least every other day."

"You're a good sister."

"Trying."

"Tell me more about your life back home," Kevin said. "You worked in a furniture factory?"

"Yes," she said, "but don't ask me to build furniture. If I do move into a house in Cape Pursuit, I'm buying everything preassembled and delivered."

"I'd come over and put it together for you," Kevin offered. "Are you thinking about staying here? That yellow one with blue shutters is pretty and cheerful. Like you."

He was going to kill her if he kept up being so nice. *What am I doing?*

"I was just thinking about that house. It has a spare bedroom for my sister in case she wants to visit or even move here."

"Do you think she's considering that?"

"I don't know." Nicole shrugged. "I know she's unhappy where she is, but it would be a major change for her to drop her job and move."

"You did it."

"Yes, but I had a friend and a job waiting here for me."

"She'd have a friend—even better, a sister."

"It would leave our parents all alone," she said quietly. "I'd feel guilty every day about that."

Kevin nodded. He didn't issue the usual platitudes she might have expected from someone else. *You have to live your own life, etc.* Perhaps because he saw people at their worst, he seemed to accept people wherever they were.

"So your furniture job where you didn't make furniture," he said. "I think you have time to tell me about it before we get to the front of the line. If we ever do."

"Hungry?"

"Starving. I missed lunch because we were out on a call, and then it seemed too late to eat. I didn't want to kill my appetite for tonight, but now I'm thinking I made a mistake."

"I'll distract you with tales from the furniture factory in Indianapolis. Fascinating stuff," Nicole said. "I have a business degree with a concentration in human resources, so I worked in the HR department. I helped with hiring, firing, contracts, training, insurance."

"Things that matter to people."

"Yes. I liked it, for the most part. I was also an informal assistant to the president. He had a secretary, but he kept asking me to help him manage events, plan meetings and things like that."

"He liked you."

Nicole grimaced. "Apparently. I was flattered that he thought I was so capable."

"What happened?" Kevin asked.

"I was young and foolish."

"How long ago was this?"

"Last year," she said, a grin replacing the grimace she felt whenever she thought of her former boss, Bryan.

"Did he mistreat you?"

"Not technically. He led me on, but I went willingly. We

had a brief relationship which ended with a mutual under-standing that it wouldn't work."

"But he kept his job and you didn't."

Nicole shrugged. "It was good for me to leave anyway."

They reached the front of the line where they both or-dered the same thing, and then they moved to the side win-dow with their drinks to wait for their food.

"You landed on your feet," Kevin observed.

"With help," Nicole said, laughing. "And I'm not sure living with my college roommate and helping her run an art gallery that she doesn't really need help running is land-ing on my feet."

"But you're enjoying it."

Nicole sipped her wine and nodded. "I'm happier than I've been in quite a while."

Kevin dipped his chin and smiled. The evening light framed his head and shoulders and made him seem even more handsome. "I'm glad."

"Tell me about your fire science degree," Nicole said, struggling to resist his charm.

"Not much to tell yet. I'm starting in the fall. It'll take me almost two years going nights and doing some online, but I'm in no hurry. I love the job I have right now, but I'm looking at the future."

Could he consider giving up firefighting? Was that what the degree was about?

"What will you do with the degree?" Nicole asked.

"Same thing I do now, but I can advance and be an of-ficer, maybe even chief someday. I can also do fire inspec-tions, approve building plans and fire suppression systems, stuff like that."

"Oh," Nicole said. "It sounds like a wise career move."

But still a dangerous job. One more reminder that she should keep things light between them.

Their food order came out the side window and they

picked up their baskets of food. "Let's sit over here," Kevin said. "I think they're still in line down at the vegan truck, and we'll leave it up to them if they want to join us."

Nicole swung her legs over the picnic table bench and Kevin sat across from her. He picked up his burger and stopped, head cocked, apparently listening. A woman was speaking in a hysterical tone bordering on a scream. Nicole couldn't make out what she was saying, but she saw the speaker at a picnic table three rows behind Kevin and pointed.

The crowd noise stilled and everyone seemed to be listening. The high-pitched words *can't breathe* carried on the silence and Kevin was on his feet before Nicole had any idea what was going on. *Does the man live in emergency-readiness mode?*

Kevin already had his legs disentangled from the table. "Come with me, and bring your phone," he said.

Kevin strode toward the distraught woman, and Nicole followed, purse in hand. Kevin muscled past bystanders and leaned in close to a man whose face was blotched with red as he gasped for breath and clutched his throat.

Nicole watched in horror, glad Kevin was there to handle whatever happened. No one else was doing anything.

"Food allergy?" Kevin asked the man.

Despite his struggle for breath, his hands desperately fluttering from his chest to his neck, the man nodded.

"EpiPen?" Kevin asked.

The man shook his head.

"Nicole," Kevin said, turning to her. "Run to my truck." He pointed to the overflow lot. "It's unlocked. Bring the red bag you'll find under the seat. You—" he pointed to someone in the crowd "—call 911 and give them our exact location."

Nicole ran as fast as she could and found Kevin's truck at the end of the first row. She whipped open the door and dug under the seat, thrilled when she found the bag. Slamming the door shut, she raced back to the scene.

Kevin had the man, looking much worse, on the ground. Nicole could hardly breathe from her run to the parking lot, but she couldn't imagine the panic the struggling man must feel. How had Kevin guessed so quickly what the problem was?

Kevin held out his hand when he saw Nicole approach and she gave him the bag. He unzipped it and dug out a yellow box with a syringe inside. Nicole shrank back and watched Kevin open the device and inject the man in the thigh, right through his clothes. She waited, holding her breath. Would it help? Would he keep breathing until the ambulance got there…and then what? And where were Jane and Charlie? Hadn't they noticed the commotion?

Slowly, the man's struggle to breathe diminished. Kevin got behind him on the ground and propped him up, speaking to him in a low, encouraging voice.

The woman who was with him had recovered enough to be helpful and explained it was their first date. She didn't know he had a food allergy and had given him a bite of her lobster roll without telling him what it was. Her tears flowed freely and Nicole's heart went out to her. She put an arm around the woman and sat with her, uncertain what else she could do.

Sirens echoed in the evening air, and Charlie came racing out of nowhere. Kevin gave him the thumbs-up. "Anaphylaxis. Food allergy. I used my EpiPen. Breathing better already."

Charlie squatted down and assessed the patient. "Sorry, I didn't know what was going on until I heard the sirens," he said.

"Where's Jane?" Nicole asked, worried.

"She went to the bathroom and I was supposed to be holding our place in line."

The ambulance pulled up, following bystanders who were waving vigorously to guide it. Kevin and Charlie talked to their colleagues and helped load the patient in the back. Jane came up just as the ambulance doors closed. She grabbed Charlie's arm. "What happened? Is everything all right?"

"Kevin saved the day before I got over here. Allergic reaction to food," Charlie said. "I lost our place in line, though, and I know you're hungry. Want to give it another try?"

Jane glanced at Nicole, and Nicole tried to smile encouragingly. She wanted to give her friend the opportunity for an honest conversation with the father of her baby. Jane and Charlie walked away, his hand on the small of her back.

Charlie stopped before he was out of earshot. "Don't forget to replace your EpiPen, just in case your brother runs into an angry bee."

"I'll do it tomorrow."

"Your brother is allergic to bees?" Nicole asked.

"Deathly. That's why I have my own EpiPen."

Kevin draped an arm around Nicole and they walked back to their picnic table. The crowd had dispersed as soon as the ambulance left, and the festival atmosphere slowly revived.

"I swear I'm going to starve to death before I get to eat tonight," Kevin said, sitting down and picking up his cold burger.

"I don't think I could eat a single thing after what just happened." She felt as if she might vomit. *That poor man's face...he almost died.*

Kevin shrugged, his expression rueful as he held up a soggy french fry. "You get used to it. It ended well."

"How can you do this?" Nicole asked. Her heart was still hammering.

"Do what?"

"Be so calm?"

Kevin focused on her, studying her face. He reached over and grabbed her hand. "I'm sorry," he said. "To me, it's not scary anymore. An emergency, yes, but as long as I can do something about it, it's okay. I forget sometimes what something like that looks like to other people."

"What would have happened if you weren't here?" Nicole asked, her voice sounding small and high-pitched. She tried to calm her breathing.

"I don't know. I hope someone would have called 911 and the squad would have gotten here in time. We do our best to save people, but we don't always get there in time."

Nicole knew he was thinking of the drowning victim he'd tried so hard to save. "I'm going to go wash my hands," Nicole said, emotionally overwhelmed. She headed for the park's restroom building.

Kevin was right behind her. He stopped her before she'd made it ten feet. "Talk to me, Nicole."

She shook her head. Her hands were shaking. She just wanted to go in the restroom and splash cold water on her face. She'd be okay if he'd just let her go.

Kevin took her by both shoulders and looked closely at her. "Breathe in through your nose and out through your mouth. As slow as you can."

She tried following his directions, tried not to think about that man struggling to survive because of something silly like a piece of lobster. Her hands tingled and her legs shook.

"I'm going to count," Kevin said. "Breathe in for four and out for four. Look straight at me. Ready?"

Nicole nodded. She stared straight into Kevin's stormy eyes and did exactly what he said. Her breathing slowed, feeling returned to her hands, and she felt steadier. Maybe it was because Kevin was holding her, his words and eyes encouraging her. Why did she feel so safe with him?

The answer was obvious. He seemed like the kind of man who could handle anything. But what if he got in a situation that he couldn't handle? What if a fire advanced on him and took his life, no matter how healthy and strong he was?

"You look better already," he said. "Anyone would be shook up by that."

She took a deep breath. "I'm okay now. I just needed to clear my head. I'm going to wash my hands and I'll meet you at the table."

He held her shoulders for a moment longer.

"Really," she said. "I'll be right there."

"Maybe I'll wash up, too," he agreed.

Nicole took her time in the small concrete block building. She held a wet paper towel to her cheeks. *I'm in control of my life. I just helped save a man's life. I can make it through the next hour with Kevin and then be strong for Jane no matter what's happening with her and Charlie.*

When she got back to the picnic table, Kevin was already there. He'd shoved away his basket of food and was sitting with his arms crossed on the table.

"Sorry," he mumbled. "This burger and fries don't look good anymore."

Nicole could hardly look at the cold, greasy food. "You're right. We could skip dinner and have ice cream," she suggested. Jane and Charlie had not come back, and if she was going to hang out by the ocean on a beautiful summer night, she might as well make the best of it.

"I like your thinking," Kevin said. He picked up their ruined dinners, dumped them in a nearby trash can, and then held out his hand to her. "We deserve something sweet."

Nicole didn't take his hand, but she linked arms with him and walked closely by his side as they made their way to the ice cream truck down by the water.

CHAPTER SIXTEEN

JANE WAITED IN line next to Charlie, remembering all the other summer nights she'd gone out with friends from the fire and police departments, and other Cape Pursuit business owners. She had a wide circle of people she enjoyed spending time with, had dated a few local men, but her heart had always come back to the most illogical choice. Charlie Zimmerman. The man who stayed in relationships for two weeks at the most and kept his feelings right at the surface level. Not with his colleagues—Jane had no doubt he would lay down his life for the other firefighters at his station.

She glanced up at him as he stood next to her in front of the vegan food truck. He would lay down his life for her and their baby, but she didn't want his life. She wanted his love.

When they reached the order window, Jane ordered tofu stir-fry for both of them, and Charlie pulled out his wallet.

"I'll buy," Jane said. "It's the least I can do for a man who's trying a new kind of food."

He shook his head and withdrew cash from his wallet.

"And I owe you for that bottle of wine you sent to our table at the bar."

He laughed. "Wine you didn't drink, and you know Kevin sent that anyway. He's in love with Nicole."

Jane's eyes widened and Charlie flushed as he accepted change and they moved to the side window to wait for their food to come up.

"I mean, he...uh..." he sputtered.

"I'm not surprised," Jane said lightly. "Nicole is quite lovable."

Charlie laughed. "But is Kevin?"

"I'll let Nicole be the judge of that. They're still getting to know each other, and you've probably heard what happened to her brother when he joined the fire service."

Charlie nodded seriously. "Kevin told me. It's awful." Charlie shoved his hands in his pockets. "I want you to know that I visited my insurance agent and doubled my life insurance. I made you the beneficiary in case...you know."

Jane's mouth fell open but she couldn't think of one thing to say. She felt sick at the thought of ever receiving that life insurance policy.

Charlie wrapped an arm around her and held her close in a quick hug. It was over in a second, but it lasted long enough to remind Jane what she could have. She could have his arms around her. His smile and his strength in her life every day.

"I'll wait here for our order," he said. "I want you to go sit down."

She was torn between needing to sit and sort her thoughts and wishing Charlie would wrap his arms around her again and never let go.

"I'm fine," Jane protested. "They said it would only be five minutes."

"Consider it saving us a table then," Charlie said, his hands on her shoulders.

"We could join Kevin and Nicole." Jane enjoyed the sensation of his fingers rubbing circles on the backs of her shoulders.

Charlie shook his head. "They abandoned their table and headed for the ice cream truck down by the beach."

"How do you know?"

"I can see over the crowd. It's just us for dinner."

Jane nodded and picked up both their drinks. "I'll be over there," she said, tilting her head.

A family of four got up and left as Jane walked toward the tables with a drink in each hand. She sat and propped her feet on the seat of the picnic table, keeping Charlie in her view where he leaned against the side of the food truck, arms crossed. Several groups of young women—tourists—slowed down as they passed him. His height, muscular body and ocean-blue eyes caught their attention, and Jane didn't blame them for looking. But he didn't appear to notice them. Instead, he waved to Jane to let her know he saw where she was sitting.

His handsome face had never been the thing that drew Jane in like the tide. It was something else in him, that spot of vulnerability that had never asked a thing of her. It was his soft core inside his carefree shell that had suckered her in on Valentine's Day when she'd caught an unexpected glimpse of it.

"Sorry you had to wait so long," he said, placing two identical plates on the table. "That medical emergency really delayed our dinner."

"It's your job."

"I didn't do a thing. Kevin had it handled before I got over there."

"I don't mind about dinner, and I'm glad there are guys like you in case I ever need you."

Charlie swung his legs over the seat and leaned forward to speak quietly. "You do need me."

Jane's hands trembled as she pulled her plate closer and unwrapped a plastic fork and knife. They ate in silence for a few minutes.

"This is surprisingly good," Charlie said. "Tastes like chicken."

He polished off his plate quickly, but Jane ate slowly, enjoying the beautiful scene. The ocean took on a deep blue shade that would be stunning in watercolor if she could find a way to capture it.

Everything should be perfect. She'd had more dinners with Charlie and the other firefighters than she could count. Her relationship with him had always been made of something different from her other relationships, an easy friendship that shouldn't be shaken loose by something wonderful growing inside her.

Why was she letting the baby tear them apart? Was she being selfish demanding his love in exchange for a wedding ring?

"Do you know why the entire roster of the Cape Pursuit Fire Department worships you?" Charlie asked after he balled up his napkin and shoved his plate aside.

What kind of a question was that?

Jane laughed. "I'm sure they don't worship me. They treat me like a little sister."

"You're one of the very few people in our lives who asks nothing of us. You show up with coffee when we're out late. You always vote in our favor on the town council when we need new equipment or training. You cooked three tons of spaghetti for us that terrible week last summer when it was one call after another."

"My dad was a fire chief. My mother did the same things. I get it."

"You more than get it. You give us your time, you listen to us and you never ask anything in return."

Jane didn't know what to say. It was a very nice speech. A speech Charlie could use if she was ever awarded the "friend of the fire department" medal by the mayor. But it wasn't what she needed from him. What she *wanted* from him.

"Let me help you. Take care of you," he said. "I can cook spaghetti if you want me to."

Jane laughed. "I'm sure you could do anything."

"Except be your husband."

"Charlie," she said, her voice unsteady. "I didn't say you wouldn't be a good husband."

"You said no when I asked you to marry me."

He picked up her empty plate and his and dumped them into a trash can. When he returned to the table, he sat next to her.

"Do you think because I've dated a lot of other women that I wouldn't be faithful to you? Is that it?"

Jane considered her answer. It was a logical question given Charlie's reputation.

"You were out with another woman on Valentine's Day when I…when we…"

"She didn't mean anything to me."

"I'm sure she would be happy to hear that."

"You were at that party with a date, too."

"Someone I hardly knew," Jane said. "And he left before I could even learn if he was a cat person or a dog person."

"I meant what I told you that night," Charlie said quietly. "When I said I had never let anyone get as close to me as you have. Other women, friends even, come and go. But you, Jane…"

She waited, hardly breathing. Was he finally going to say it? Was this the moment he said he loved her and changed everything? She waited five seconds, ten. How much longer?

"I don't regret what happened that night," he said. "And I meant it when I said I wanted to marry you."

Her shoulders dropped. If he was ever going to say the words she needed to hear, the moment had passed.

"I still want to," he said earnestly.

"Why?"

"For the same reasons I already told you," he said.

Jane closed her eyes and rubbed her temples. Her throat was thick but she didn't want to cry. It was a moment for the truth. "There's only one reason why I would marry you."

"The baby?"

"No."

"What then?" He took both her hands. "We've been friends forever, Jane. You can tell me."

Jane stood and put her hand on Charlie's shoulder. He looked up at her with such open vulnerability on his face she almost surrendered and accepted his offer, even if it didn't come with the one thing that had to be there. He would care for her, support her, do his best to be a good father. Wasn't that more than some women ever got?

It wasn't enough. She had to say the one thing that would split her heart open—for better or for worse.

"I could only marry a man who asked because he loved me."

Without waiting for a response, she turned and started walking toward the beach where she imagined Nicole and Kevin had already finished their dessert. Charlie fell into step beside her. Neither of them said a word as they passed through the crowd. Charlie put a hand on Jane's back as they negotiated a tangle of people near the end of the line of trucks. He was by her side, showing he cared for her… but it wasn't enough.

Jane saw Nicole and Kevin sitting on a bench by the water and almost broke into a run. The silent march with Charlie was pure agony.

"Ready to go home?" Nicole asked when she glanced up and saw Jane. Although Nicole's face was cheerful and re-laxed at first, her expression deepened into concern.

Jane nodded as Kevin stood and offered Nicole his hand to pull her up. She noticed that Kevin and Charlie exchanged a quick look, and she knew she was responsible for the ter-rible awkwardness hanging over them all. She and Charlie were responsible. Did it have to be this way? Did her easy friendships with the firemen have to end?

She waited while Nicole said a quick good-night to

Kevin, but she didn't have the courage to say anything to Charlie before turning and walking toward the parking lot with Nicole at her side.

"You don't have to say anything," Nicole said.

Jane took a deep breath. "It will be a lot more interesting if you tell me about your evening. I swear I see wisps of happiness coming off you."

"It was the ice cream. Nothing has changed between Kevin and me."

"Nothing has changed between Charlie and me either."

He had had his chance to tell her what was in his heart, and the only conclusion she could draw was that it was not love.

CHAPTER SEVENTEEN

As THEY PREPARED to open the art gallery on a cloudy Friday morning, Nicole and Jane spread new pictures and mats on the worktable in the back room.

"Do you think this double mat with the blue inside the white is too...cutesy nautical?" Nicole asked. She held up a photo of the Cape Pursuit lighthouse she'd taken the day she'd gone out on the boat with Kevin.

"It's supposed to be nautical."

"I know, but I don't want to overdo it. I'm having fun matting my pictures, and I'm still surprised every time one of them sells."

Jane laughed. "Your gorgeous pictures sell every day. You should get used to it." She pointed out a sunny corner of the back room. "Do you think I could put a playpen there?"

"It's a great place for one," Nicole said. "And speaking of places, I'm almost ready to commit to my own house, so we can start clearing my stuff out of your guest room. It will make a great nursery."

"I have about four months, and the last thing I want to do is rush you out of my house. I was hoping you'd help with diapers and feeding and figuring out why it's three in the morning and we're all awake and crying."

"I won't go far," Nicole said, laughing. "And you can call me anytime you're pacing the floor or somebody's crying. I'll come over and cry, too. That's how good a friend I am."

Nicole's cell phone rang and she eyed the screen. *Kevin.* She held the phone in her hand, considering whether to answer.

"Telemarketer trying to sell you a vacation time-share?" Jane asked.

"Kevin," Nicole said.

"What are you waiting for?"

Nicole swiped the screen and held the phone to her ear.

"I know I'm asking a lot," Kevin said without even saying hello. He sounded like he was running. Or possibly sobbing.

"What's the matter?" Nicole asked. She'd seen Kevin in tense situations, but the chaos in his voice was new.

"I'm in over my head," he said.

In the background on Kevin's end, Nicole swore she heard the kind of silly songs and noises usually only on—

"Turn those cartoons down," Kevin shouted. He lowered his voice. "Please."

"What's going on at your house?" Nicole asked.

Nicole heard a door shut and Kevin lowered his voice to a near-whisper. "My sister-in-law's father got hit by a car while he was out biking. He's in bad shape, and my brother and his wife left an hour ago to see him. They dropped off their girls on the way."

"I'm so sorry," Nicole said. No wonder he sounded breathless and had to compete with cartoon soundtracks. "Will her father be okay?"

"I don't know. The details are unclear. He lives about two hours away and I'm waiting for Tyler to call when he knows something."

"So you have your nieces for the day?" Nicole asked. She kept her tone therapy-couch neutral.

Jane gave her a questioning look, eyebrows raised.

"I called my parents to see if they could take the girls, but they're out. Dad has a colonoscopy today and Mom's his driver. He won't be in any humor this evening to entertain his granddaughters when all that gas starts working its way out."

Nicole didn't say anything. She didn't even know Kevin's dad, but she was reasonably sure she didn't want to imagine his gastric distress. Or anyone else's.

"Maybe that was too much information," Kevin said. "Sorry."

"Don't be sorry," Nicole said. "Maybe I could help you out when we close the gallery. I could come over and make dinner for you and the girls later. If they're still there."

She heard Kevin breathing on the other end of the line. She waited. Jane continued with the full-face question and Nicole shrugged.

"Here's the thing," Kevin said. "My brother and his wife were taking the kids to Busch Gardens today. They have four nonrefundable tickets good for today only."

Nicole took a breath. "How old are these girls?"

"Three and five."

"And you're planning to take them to a giant amusement park filled with sticky surfaces, junk food and spinny rides."

"Uh-huh," Kevin said. "I have my sister-in-law's minivan, so I don't care if they puke on the way home."

"You're stoic."

"I'm desperate. I need backup. I can't take two little girls in the men's room and I don't know the names of the Sesame Street characters."

"The red one is Elmo and the yellow one is Big Bird."

"Please, Nicole. Come with us. I'm begging you."

The man actually was begging, a note of panic in his voice. Nicole pictured him pacing outside the ladies' restroom and juggling lollipops in lines for rides. Tripping over strollers and tying Hello Kitty shoelaces. Carrying a niece in each arm after they fell asleep on the way to the car. *Adorable.* She sighed.

"Just a minute. I'll check with Jane and see if I can slip away today."

She put her finger over what she thought was the microphone and gave Jane a summary.

"If you want an excuse to avoid amusement park duty," Jane said, "I'm happy to say I can't spare you today. I could make up a good reason."

Nicole considered it. Bail out or buckle up in the minivan. She thought of Kevin trying to apply sunscreen evenly to wiggly girls with ponytails swishing like horse's manes.

"Can you spare me?"

"It's a good opportunity," Jane said. "He'll owe you a year's worth of anything you want."

"Thanks, Jane."

"You may hate me later."

Nicole smiled, shook her head, and uncovered the microphone on her cell phone.

"I heard all that," Kevin said.

"It's not polite to listen to other people's conversations."

She could *feel* Kevin smiling through the phone.

"I'll pick you up at your house in an hour," he said. "I'll be the one wearing ear protection and driving a faded Chrysler Town & Country."

ALTHOUGH SHE WAS dressed as if she were headed for a battle—gray T-shirt, black shorts, sneakers, ball cap and sunglasses—Nicole cheerfully shook hands with Maureen and Paige before buckling up in the front seat of the van. Kevin would be happy to spend time with Nicole under any circumstances, but having her along as backup made him feel as if he might survive the day ahead.

"Thanks for coming," he said. He wanted to ask her about what he'd overheard on the phone. A year's worth of anything she wanted? What did Nicole want?

"I'm excited about it. I love kids and amusement parks, and I've never been to this one."

"You haven't spent the day with these kids either."

Nicole glanced in the back seat. "They don't look dangerous."

"Are you Uncle Kevin's girlfriend?"

At five, Maureen was observant, inquisitive and adorable. He also knew from experience she would report every single thing that happened that day to her mother at bedtime. She'd told her mother every word Kevin said when he took the girls fishing and Paige hooked him in the ear with a wild cast. She had faithfully reported how much pizza and ice cream Kevin let his nieces eat when he took them bowling. And, of course, she enjoyed telling exactly what happened last Christmas when Kevin took the girls to the amusement park for the holiday spectacular. While their parents were shopping and playing Santa, he was running his jingle bells off keeping up with two toddlers. Maureen threw up peppermint ice cream on his shoes and he later found what was left of a candy cane in his coat pocket after he ran it through the washer and dryer.

He got new shoes and a coat at the after-Christmas sales.

Maureen would spin out the whole day as if it were a film reel. He should warn Nicole not to give her the start of a story she could develop into a full-blown tale later. The girl was likely to be a novelist or a politician when she grew up.

"I'm just a friend," Nicole said. Kevin saw her twist in her seat and smile at his nieces.

He backed out of the driveway after looking both ways twice. He usually only had Arnold to watch out for, but today there were two sets of chubby legs swinging from their booster seats behind him.

"If you can figure out how to run the DVD player and put in a movie for the drive, I swear I'll win you the prize of your choice at the game booths."

Nicole tilted her head and studied the drop-down DVD player installed in the van's ceiling. "It's a short drive, isn't it?"

Kevin gripped the steering wheel. "Thirty minutes, give or take." *It could be a long half an hour.* Both girls were already supercharged with energy when his brother dropped them off that morning. They didn't know about their grandfather's terrible accident. Instead, his brother had painted today as a special surprise treat for Uncle Kevin.

Uncle Kevin knew there was a beer offering coming later. At least a twelve-pack of remuneration for a day of heat, crowds and kiddie rides.

"I can do it," Maureen offered. "Mommy lets me run it all the time. I'm her helper."

"Terrific," Nicole said cheerfully. "I'll count on you to help all day."

"Do you have kids?" Maureen asked.

"No," Nicole said. "No kids of my own, but I babysat a lot when I was a teenager. We'll get along just fine as long as your uncle behaves."

"Uncle Kevin in time out, Uncle Kevin in time out," Paige sang.

"I'm on your side," Nicole said in a low voice.

Kevin smiled. He never doubted it.

"Who's carrying the princess bag?" he asked when they'd parked the car and were mobilizing in the parking lot. He held up the mini-backpack with the latest sparkly princess to take the kid movie audiences by storm.

"I'll do it," Nicole said. She took the bag and glanced inside. "Your sister-in-law is well prepared. We have sunscreen, Band-Aids, crackers and hand wipes." She looked up and smiled. "We could survive anything."

"I need sunscreen," Maureen said. "Mom always puts it on us."

"No. Sticky. I hate it," Paige protested.

Nicole knelt. "You can put it on me," she said. "I burn. Bad. I hate having a sunburn."

Paige smiled and let Nicole squeeze kid-friendly sunscreen into her chubby hand.

Kevin sucked in a breath. Watching Nicole with his nieces hit him in the gut with the wish that he had a family like his brother's. Maureen and Paige took after their mother with auburn hair, and he could picture daughters with Nicole. Blondes with green eyes.

"I'll close my eyes while you put some on my face and neck," Nicole said.

God, she was brave.

"Hold still," Paige said. "After I do you, you can do me."

"Mmm-hmm," Nicole said, lips closed against the onslaught of toddler-applied sunscreen.

After they were slathered up—and Nicole had discreetly wiped out her ears with a tissue—they held hands and braved the asphalt heat of the parking lot. Kevin presented their tickets and they clunked through the turnstiles. Only ten feet into the park, a photographer stopped them and instructed them to group up for a family picture.

Kevin looked at Nicole. She shrugged and lined up with the girls, smiling.

"Let's get one of just you and the girls to give their parents later," she suggested.

Kevin mugged with his nieces.

"Now just you two," the teenaged photographer said, indicating Kevin and Nicole.

Kevin wrapped an arm around Nicole and held her close for a picture.

"Girlfriend," Maureen announced to her little sister.

"We always buy the pictures," Kevin confided to Nicole. "We're suckers. I usually get the package where they give you two keychains with a little picture. The kids love it."

Nicole wondered if he planned to purchase the picture of the two of them.

"How many times have you done this?" Nicole asked.

"Solo? Only once before. But I've tagged along at least once a year."

"Are the girls tall enough for the kiddie coaster?"

He nodded. "I think Paige just makes the height requirement this year. It's a hike, though, in the back of the park."

Nicole pointed to her sneakers. "I came prepared. Let's head for the coaster, girls."

"Want me to carry the princess bag?" Kevin offered.

She laughed. Kevin's nieces each grabbed one of his hands and started swinging them, leaving him no way to sling a tiny princess backpack over his shoulders.

Dodged a glittery bullet.

CHAPTER EIGHTEEN

THE MIDDAY HEAT blasted their group, sunshine mixing with rising humidity and no breeze. So far, she'd buckled in for two rides on the kiddie coaster, one trip around a miniature racetrack, and ten minutes in the bounce house. When they finished jumping madly with fifteen other adults and kids, Nicole helped both girls find their sneakers and tie the laces. Despite his excellent physical condition, Kevin was sweating and breathing hard after the bouncy ordeal. That kind of thing wasn't for the weak. Nicole had to give him credit—he'd really made an effort in there, doing flips and chasing both girls until they giggled. She'd taken a more moderate approach. Which was why she retained the ability to kneel and tie pink laces while Kevin clutched his side and stood in the shade.

Nicole's chin-length blond hair was plastered to her neck in a slimy mix of sunscreen and sweat. Mercifully, it was lunchtime and Kevin knew the location of an air-conditioned restaurant. While Nicole claimed a corner booth with the two little girls and breathed in the cool air, Kevin solicited orders, nodding sagely as if he were memorizing them in great detail.

"Booster seat?" Nicole asked Paige, offering her a red plastic seat from the stack by their table.

The child shook her head. "I'm a big girl."

"Okay," Nicole said. It was one less thing she'd have to clean before the girls touched it.

Kevin dashed back over with a stack of napkins so Nicole could wipe off the sticky table. She watched him return to the line at the registers. He was easily the most attractive man in line. She should stop staring.

"Do you think your uncle will get our orders right?" Nicole asked.

Maureen shook her head. "My dad never does, so I don't think Uncle Kevin will."

Nicole smiled and shrugged. "I don't blame him. We're hot and hungry," she said. "And it's not easy being a waiter."

Both girls giggled. Nicole dug the hand wipes out of the backpack and helped them scrub up while they waited for food. The three lines were at least four people deep each, and the teenagers at the registers mechanically pushed buttons as if they were treading water. Nicole wished she had thought to pack lunch. A peanut butter sandwich and a pudding cup would be like a gift from heaven right now.

"I got everyone the same thing," Kevin announced a few minutes later as he placed an overflowing plastic tray on their table. "Hot dogs and fries. There was chaos at the register and it killed my confidence. You can add ketchup and mustard if you want."

"Told you," Maureen whispered to Nicole and they both laughed.

"If you make fun of me," Kevin said, "I'll tickle you on every ride. With your seat belt on, you'll be totally at my mercy."

"I like my lunch," Paige said, nodding agreeably.

"Smart girl."

Nicole watched Kevin steal fries from his nieces and pretend not to notice when they stole some from him. He didn't flinch when food fell out of Paige's mouth as she talked and ate at the same time. He made an emergency napkin run in record time when Maureen tipped over Nicole's drink and the orange soda was headed for their laps.

He would be a wonderful father.

Kevin pulled out his phone and checked his messages.

"Mom," he told Nicole. "Dad's thing went fine and she stopped by my house to let Arnold out."

"Good. Any other interesting news?"

He shook his head and glanced at his nieces who were, of course, listening to every word.

"Still waiting to hear if the...um...Yankees will win the World Series."

"I hope they do," Nicole said.

"Me, too."

When they finished their lunches and left the air-conditioned oasis, the first thing to hit them was heat and humidity even worse than before. And a dark, threatening sky. Nicole dug her smartphone out of the princess backpack and checked her weather app. She held it up for Kevin to see.

"Looks like we'll get wet in about an hour," he said.

Nicole held it closer to his face. "Are you sure you're looking at the radar west of here?"

Maybe he was an optimist or perhaps he had zero experience reading the weather radar. Nicole had grown up with a mom obsessed with the weather. Hanging in the hallway of their ranch home was a three-part weather predictor. Thermometer, barometer, humidity indicator. Her mother could predict bad weather better than the meteorologist on television. And she both feared and reveled in approaching storms.

The flashing red lines on Nicole's phone would have sent her mother straight to the basement with flashlights and a change of underwear for everyone in the family. Growing up in the Midwest, she'd always known there was a tornado kit under the basement stairs. When the tornado sirens sounded their warning in Indianapolis, Nicole, Laura and Adam would hunker down in the basement wearing their bicycle helmets while their mother earnestly listened to the NOAA weather radio. Their father would pace up and down the basement stairs so he could peek out the kitchen windows toward the west.

It was the most excitement they got in Indianapolis. Tornado season. The season of adrenaline.

"I think we're in for it and soon," Nicole whispered, not wanting the girls to overhear and panic.

Kevin looked at the screen and shrugged. "Might miss us. I say we go have fun while we can."

Nicole smiled and followed the group despite the sinking feeling in her stomach. The air had changed. Her mother could probably tell exactly how far the barometer had fallen. But Kevin was a local, and a public safety officer. Maybe he was right.

Thirty minutes later as their group huddled in the entrance to the brick bathroom building and lightning flashed across the sky, Kevin leaned close to Nicole.

"I should have listened to you," he whispered in her ear. "I swear I won't make this mistake again."

Their current rain shelter was about six feet square, with the men's restroom opening on one side and the women's on the other. Her clothes were no longer damp with sweat. They were soaked with rainwater instead. The rain hammered on the steel roof and Nicole shrank against the wall with both girls sandwiched between her and Kevin, the princess backpack digging into her back. Kevin's back was to the open entrance and he was probably getting wetter. Nicole was grateful for the drinking fountain digging into her side. Its tiny exhaust fan on one side blew warm air against her bare thigh.

The wind picked up and leaves scattered across the concrete. Both girls huddled closer and Kevin used his broad shoulders to shelter them all from anything that blew toward them—rain, wind, leaves, wrappers from amusement park food and drinks.

"Next time you'll know," Nicole said, in answer to his admission. "My mother was a closet weather forecaster. I have years of experience with these things."

He grinned. "My mother keeps an umbrella under the seat of her car. That's as close as she ever gets to being prepared for the weather."

"I'm cold," Paige complained.

"Here," Nicole said, shifting the three-year-old closer to the drinking fountain. "I'll share my heater."

Thunder ripped the air and both girls cowered closer to Nicole. Kevin moved in and tightened their circle, his back still to the storm. The public address system hissed on and a voice sounded as if it were giving instructions, but they couldn't hear the words distinctly.

Nicole maneuvered the princess pack around to her front and dug through it for her phone. Just as she feared. Severe thunderstorm warning. Hail. Damaging winds. *As indicated half an hour ago by the flashing red lines… I should have spoken up more.*

She got on social media and searched the hashtag for the amusement park. Yep. Park temporarily shut down, all guests asked to locate to storm shelters.

Lightning blinded them and both girls screamed.

"Hate to say it," Kevin said. "But maybe we should move into the actual bathroom."

"We can't go in the boys' bathroom," Maureen protested. "I'm not going in there."

"We're sticking together," Kevin said.

Maureen glanced up and gave him pouty-kindergartener face. Nicole wondered what Kevin would do. She was on Maureen's side. The men's bathroom was not in her plan.

Kevin sighed and rolled his eyes dramatically. "Everyone in the girls' bathroom," he said.

The four of them moved as a group to Nicole's right and they ducked through the swinging door with a skirted figure on the front. It was much quieter inside, although the rain still danced on the roof.

Okay. I'm hiding out in the bathroom during a thunderstorm with two little kids and a man who rattles my internal weather system. This will definitely be funny later when I tell Jane about it.

"Hey," Kevin said as the four of them leaned, dripping, against the brick wall. "This is much nicer than the boys' bathroom. You girls have it made."

A toilet flushed and an older woman edged out the stall door and glared at Kevin.

He smiled. "Sorry. Any port in a storm."

The woman washed her hands while keeping an eye on Kevin in the mirror. She hustled past them and pulled open the door, then paused and turned a less hostile face to the group.

"I think I'll wait this out," she said.

Kevin smiled again and pulled some paper towels from the holder by the sink.

"Think these will get the girls dry?" he asked.

"I can do better than that," Nicole said. "Would you girls like a spa treatment?"

Maureen and Paige stared at Nicole and Kevin raised both eyebrows. The old lady crossed her arms and leaned against the inside of the door.

"I'll show you," Nicole said. She crouched down, ducked under the hot air hand dryer on the wall, and pushed the button. Her wet hair blew around her face in blond clumps while she worked her fingers through it. She pushed the button again when the timer ran out. Although she felt Kevin watching her every move, she tried to ignore him as she smiled reassuringly at both girls, who watched wide-eyed.

"Much better," she said, straightening up and shaking

out her hair. "I'm dry and warm. If there's a brush in the bag, I could give you a nice blow-dry."

"Me first," Maureen exclaimed. Paige pawed through the front zipper pouch on the backpack and produced a small purple brush. She handed it to Nicole.

The old lady exchanged a smile with Kevin. "Your wife sure knows how to make lemonade."

Nicole noticed that Kevin didn't bother to set the woman straight. Maureen stood under the hand dryer and Nicole brushed her hair. Kevin helped out by pushing the big silver button each time the dryer timed out. Paige took her turn, easily fitting under the wall-mounted dryer, and stood stock-still while Nicole brushed her hair as it dried.

"You are both beautiful," Nicole said. It was true. Their long, smooth hair and pink cheeks glowed, even in the dim fluorescent lights in the bathroom.

The storm still raged outside, but Nicole felt like sunshine inside.

"My turn?" Kevin asked. He stripped off his T-shirt and held it under the dryer. Several teenaged girls raced in and stopped when they saw a shirtless man in the women's bathroom. They stared, obviously impressed.

Nicole stared, too. Kevin's broad shoulders and muscles rippled as he wrung out his shirt and held it under the dryer, elbowing the button to turn it on. He glanced up and grinned.

Maureen and Paige giggled.

"This is a first," he said.

The teenaged girls and even the old lady were riveted by the performance, and Nicole felt warm inside because Kevin was, at least temporarily, hers.

But what would happen when they got home? No matter how foolish it was to hand over her heart to someone with Kevin's career, Nicole was inching closer to letting go of the past with every moment she spent with him.

Despite the storm—and despite the fact they were trapped in a women's bathroom with adorable children while a tornado could be bearing down on them—Nicole felt safe. Because of Kevin and his strength, his need to help people. *Even at the risk of his own life.*

A branch crashed on the steel roof, and Kevin gathered his nieces close to reassure them. He glanced at Nicole and held out an arm for her, too. Nicole slid into his embrace and noticed the interested expression on the faces of their audience.

Any port in a storm. *And this was a very nice harbor.*

THE MINIVAN SMELLED like wet dog, despite their efforts to stay dry throughout the rest of the afternoon. Kevin was impressed with Nicole's resilience once the storm had passed, cheerfully dodging rain, riding kiddie rides, and standing in line for ice cream while he found an umbrella table with the girls. It was not the kind of date he'd have wanted to offer her.

He was glad when evening set in and signaled it was okay to give up and go. Halfway home in the van, his phone rang and he answered it after a quick glance showed him his brother's number on the screen.

"How are the girls?" Tyler asked, skipping a greeting.

"Fine. They smell like sunscreen, rain and hot dogs," Kevin said.

"I don't smell like a hot dog," Maureen protested.

"Wasn't talking about you, nosy," Kevin said, sending a quick grin to his niece who was buckled in behind Nicole.

"How are the Baltimore Orioles doing this season?" he asked his brother. His nieces still didn't know their grandfather had been in an accident and he didn't want to be the one to spill the news.

"Beat up pretty bad, but he'll recover with time," Tyler said.

"Good."

"I'll meet you at your place to pick up the girls and the van. I'm at home right now, but Hillary is staying with her mom at the hospital."

"Be there in fifteen," Kevin said.

"Thanks. One more thing—can you take my shift at the station in the morning? I'm supposed to be on at seven, but I've got kid duty until further notice."

Kevin let the question hang for a heartbeat, but only one. Of course he'd take his brother's shift, though if he could do anything he wanted on his day off, it would involve Nicole. He looked over at her and wondered what her plans were for later. He'd been hoping to find a dozen ways to say thank you for braving the theme park with him. Rain check, maybe.

"Sure," he told his brother. He clicked off and set his phone in the console between the bucket seats.

"Your dad is picking you up at my place," he said. "Any chance you'll keep our secret about me being in the women's bathroom?"

Maureen and Paige giggled and swung their legs. "You took your shirt off in the girls' baffroom," Paige said. "I'm telling Mommy because it was funny."

"It was not funny," he protested. "And it will sound bad if you tell it like that."

Nicole laughed and shot him a look.

"Hey," he said. "I thought you'd be on my side."

"I am," she said. "But I can't think of a way to tell that story without it sounding bad. And funny."

Kevin sighed and switched on the headlights as the sky darkened with the coming sunset. He'd be glad to hand off the minivan, but he'd enjoyed the time with his nieces.

When he pulled in the driveway, Tyler was sitting on his front porch with his dog. Kevin's brother and parents had keys to his place, and Arnold owed his fresh air and bathroom breaks to them pretty often.

"Daddy," Paige said as soon as Kevin parked the van. Nicole hopped out and slid open the side door.

"Leave them buckled up," Tyler said, approaching with Arnold on his heels. "I'll head out and get them out of your hair."

"They were no trouble," Nicole said. "Your daughters are angels."

"Uncle Kevin undressed in the girls' bathroom," Maureen said.

"See?" Nicole said. "Angels."

"It's a long story," Kevin said in answer to his brother's questioning look. "Let's just say you owe me."

Tyler laughed and climbed in the driver's seat. "Thanks a lot, both of you," he said. "I appreciate your help today."

His look suggested he wanted to say more, but the ears in the back seat made him choose his words carefully. Kevin knew his brother would have to tell the girls something to explain where their mom was tonight. *Good luck to him.* Sometimes it was nice only having to answer to an old beagle.

"Any time. But we better not have crap runs at the station tomorrow. I swear, every time I cover for you, I end up pulling a raccoon out of a storm drain or getting called to the same false alarm three times before the day's out," Kevin said.

"I could trade you," Tyler said. "You take the girls for the day and I'll work at the station."

Kevin slid the side door shut and leaned in the passenger-side window. "That's okay. I'll take my chances with the raccoons." He grinned at his nieces and waved goodbye to them.

Kevin watched his brother back out of the driveway, then turned around. Would Nicole stay? She was there right now, the pink rays of the sun washing over her. Arnold leaned heavily against her leg and looked at her with adoring eyes as she scratched his head.

"Today was not what either of us had planned," Kevin said, approaching her and putting his hand on her arm. "Any chance you'll let me make it up to you by taking you to dinner?"

She smiled. "We're too grimy to go out."

"Then we could order food and stay in?" he suggested. "Arnold could use some company, and he adores you."

He wasn't the only one.

"He won't mind if we're smelly?"

"Not even a little."

CHAPTER NINETEEN

JANE OPENED NICOLE'S door and peeked in. "Late night?"

Nicole grinned and tossed aside the covers. "Crazy day at the amusement park."

Jane returned the smile. "Any chance I could get you to throw on some clothes and tell me all about it when we have a slow moment at the gallery today?"

"Might need more than a moment," Nicole said, laughing.

Jane picked up a pillow from a chair and tossed it at her friend. "You can start your story in the car on the way to work. I wouldn't press you on it, but it's Saturday and I've gotten in the habit of depending on you this summer. I think it'll be a busy day."

Nicole pulled open her dresser drawer and picked out a sky blue top and slim black pants. With a pair of sandals, she'd look classy and just artsy enough for the gallery. "Be ready in ten minutes," she said.

"I'll have the coffee ready."

Claudette jumped up on the bathroom counter and shoved things around, flicking her tail while Nicole dashed on some makeup and fluffed her hair. She'd showered off the sunscreen before she went to bed.

"Good enough?" she asked the house cat, who rolled onto her back and knocked Nicole's mascara on the floor. "That's a yes," she said.

On the short drive into town, Nicole told Jane about the

trip to the theme park, the rain, the restroom storm shelter and shirtless Kevin drying off for a crowd. She planned to confide in her friend and tell her how dangerously close she was to falling in love. She hoped they'd find time for conversation despite the busy Saturday ahead. She'd just started to share a few details about her dinner at Kevin's when an ambulance barreled past them, headed in the direction they were going. A fire truck passed them next.

"That's the backup truck," Jane commented. "They don't usually take that one out of the station." Jane accelerated and they passed several blocks in silence. "Flashing lights ahead," Jane said, pointing at the exterior of a tall hotel under construction in downtown Cape Pursuit. A crane sat next to the hotel, but it wasn't moving.

"Lots of lights," Nicole said, trying to ignore the sinking feeling in her stomach.

"It's one street over from the gallery," Jane said. "I think we should park at the shop and we can walk over and see if we can help."

Nicole didn't answer. The reality of Kevin's job sat on her shoulders like a wet blanket. She knew he was on duty today. He could be in that building fighting smoke and fire. Why had she thought she could fall for a firefighter and live with this kind of fear?

"If you want to," Jane added when Nicole said nothing. "If you don't want to, you could stay at the gallery and I'll walk over and check it out. Probably just a smoke alarm. They get called to those all the time, especially in a building under construction."

A false alarm. That's what Kevin had joked about with his brother last night. But they were closer now, and the smoke wafting out from an upper floor told her it was no alarm, no matter how much her friend might try to gloss it over.

The hotel was on fire and Kevin was on duty.

Jane turned right and headed down the street where Sea Jane Paint was. She slowed the car to a crawl, almost exactly in the spot where Nicole had first seen Kevin the day she came to town. Jane suddenly pulled to the right and stopped while another ambulance sped past them. It would have taken off her door if she'd opened it.

Two ambulances. That could only mean one thing. The ambulance turned down the next side street and headed in the direction of the hotel fire. Jane carefully pulled back onto the street and turned to drive around behind her studio.

Nicole felt like throwing up the coffee her friend had thoughtfully handed her when she got in the car.

"It'll be fine," Jane said, getting out of the car. She came around to Nicole's side and opened the door. "You have to get out," she said. She reached in, took Nicole's coffee and gently tugged her from the car.

"Come inside and open the shop. I'll go check out the fire scene and come right back. I promise."

"I can't do this," Nicole said.

"Do what?"

"Let myself care for a firefighter. I should never have let things go this far."

Jane closed the car door and leaned against it. "Everything is probably fine. They send the ambulances out on most fire calls and have them on standby. It's protocol. Okay?"

Nicole followed Jane to the back door of the gallery and waited while she unlocked the door. They turned on lights, booted up the computer and flipped the sign in the front window from Closed to Open. All the things they did on a normal day. But the sirens screaming just a few blocks away told them this was not a normal day.

Jane's cell phone rang loudly and she pulled it out of her purse and looked at the screen. "One of my cop friends," she said. She swiped the screen, said hello to the caller and listened intently, her face paling as she raised her eyes to Nicole's. "We're at the gallery. We'll come over."

She thanked the caller and shoved the phone in her pocket, then pulled Nicole into a hug. "There's a problem at the hotel fire. Construction inside made it unstable."

Jane paused and Nicole steeled herself for the worst. "And?" she asked.

"And there might be two firefighters missing or down inside."

Nicole started shaking and Jane held her tighter. She felt Jane shaking, too. The father of her baby could be in that fire.

An image of Adam smiling as he went off to fight fires hit her. Kevin had flashed her a smile last night as he backed out of her driveway. Adam never came home, a victim of his good intentions and a fire that raged out of control. What if Kevin didn't come home today, or tomorrow or someday?

Being with a man in that line of work was no life for her. She'd been a fool to think so.

"Let's lock up and go over there," Jane said. "Maybe we'll find out things are fine. We'll get some coffee for the guys and come back here to work."

"Okay," Nicole agreed. Going along was better than waiting here. But no matter what they found at the fire scene, things were never going to be fine.

But they weren't alone. As they race-walked the two blocks to the hotel fire, they had to fight their way through a crowd. Bystanders stood on the sidewalk across the street from the fire, watching the man on the aerial ladder hose down the upper floors. Hoses snaked through the front door and firefighters hustled everywhere, some on radios, some running the pumps on the trucks, some hauling hoses. Nicole recognized Tony running the pump on the ladder truck. At least he wasn't among the missing.

"Is Charlie on duty today?" Nicole asked Jane.

"I'm not sure. He texted me yesterday to say he'd been out of town for a day helping his father with something and wanted to make sure I was okay. He's back in town, so he could be here somewhere. It looks like the whole department is here."

Police cars, their blue lights mingling with the red lights on the fire trucks and ambulances, blocked the street.

Jane didn't waste time. She walked through the police barricade, waving at her friends in uniform, and approached the chief. Nicole trailed behind her, dread in every step. They weren't really going to walk up to the fire chief and ask what was going on, were they? Jane touched Chief Ruggles's shoulder and he spun toward her.

"What can I do?" she asked.

He shook his head. "Nothing right now. I've got two missing guys. Man down alarms went off. I sent two more in that inferno after them."

Nicole swallowed, willing herself to stay calm. She didn't say anything as she waited for Jane's next move.

"I can mobilize some food and drinks," Jane said, keeping her voice admirably even. "Looks like you'll be here awhile."

Chief Ruggles didn't acknowledge her; he just kept his gaze pinned on the building.

Jane sent a quick glance at Nicole, a question in her expression. Nicole knew what Jane wanted to ask. She wanted to know the same thing. She *had* to know. She nodded at Jane.

"Who's missing, Chief?" Jane asked.

Until he said the words, Nicole could still hope it wasn't Kevin. Not that she wanted it to be someone else. They all had people who loved them. She took a deep breath.

Did she love him?

"Charlie and Kevin," the chief said. He stalked off, radio held to his ear.

Nicole felt like she'd been punched in the chest. She stared at the burning building, hoping for a glimpse of yellow turnout gear through a window.

Jane pulled her back to the sidewalk and they watched the furious fire scene, arms around each other, holding each other up.

"They train for this," Jane said, her voice shaking now. "Work together all the time. Charlie and Kevin will get each other out." She nodded vigorously. "I know it."

Even in her panic, Nicole still noticed her friend's lip quivering and her eyes shining with tears. Charlie and Kevin…it was almost too much to bear.

She and Jane were in this together. Nicole tried to summon up bravery for her friend's sake if not her own. Despair crushed her heart, and she closed her eyes. She saw her brother, imagined his last moments before the fire raced over him and stole his life.

It can't happen to Kevin, too. Her heart wouldn't survive a second time. She pictured Kevin's strong arms, his quiet bravery. He would get out. He would get his partner out. If anyone could, it was Kevin. This wasn't his first fire.

"They'll make it," she said, almost having to shout over the noise even though she was shoulder to shoulder with Jane. She didn't know which one of them she was trying to reassure.

As they stood tensely, hoping for news, Tyler muscled past them. He wore street clothes and shoved his way directly to the chief. Nicole knew he had the day off because he was taking care of his daughters. Had he left them with his parents? Would Tyler race into the burning building to save his brother—the brother who was working his shift? He had no protective gear, no helmet. He wouldn't be that reckless…would he? He had a wife and two beautiful daughters…

A shout went up as a two-man crew came through the

front door hauling another firefighter with them. They carried him a safe distance from the building and laid him down on the ground only feet from Nicole and Jane. The crowd moved back, silenced by the scene. Nicole held her breath as the two rescuers pulled off the man's face mask and helmet.

Next to her, Jane gasped and put her hands over her mouth, tears spilling down her cheeks.

It was Charlie. He sat up and rubbed his face with both hands. He looked around desperately.

Nicole guessed what he was looking for. She had the same question squeezing the air from her lungs. The firefighters with Charlie shook their heads and Charlie jumped to his feet, lost his balance and sat down hard. The chief strode over and squatted next to him, talking with him. Nicole watched as they gestured broadly, their movements exaggerated by the heavy yellow coats. What was Charlie saying? Where was Kevin?

Tyler Ruggles listened for a moment and then headed for the building.

Nicole and Jane watched as the chief raced after him and grabbed Tyler by the back of his shirt, holding him in an iron grip while he spoke into the radio in his other hand. Tyler was a big man, but his uncle was taller and broader. Tyler struggled and Nicole wondered how far he'd go. Would he punch his own uncle to get free and go in the building?

Was it already too late for Kevin?

Jane hurried over and knelt next to Charlie, talking to him while the ambulance crew rolled a gurney over. Charlie waved them away, but they didn't budge. Finally, Nicole watched Charlie walk to the waiting ambulance and concede to sitting inside with the back doors open. He never took his eyes off the building, waiting, she knew, for his partner to come out alive.

WHERE THE HELL was Charlie? Kevin groped his way through smoke and darkness in the interior stairwell of the hotel. His partner had been right in front of him a second ago and now he was gone. The whole building was an unpredictable mess. An old fifteen-story hotel, it had practically been gutted on the inside as construction crews modernized everything. He'd heard about the plans. Whole suites were being added. There were several restaurants planned. A pool on the roof. It was a major job and still had a long way to go before it was finished.

But something had gone wrong. The early-morning call with smoke already pouring from upper windows suggested the fire had a head start. Maybe a piece of construction equipment had been left on overnight, or sparks had smoldered inside a wall until something encouraged them into a full-blown flame. The chief wouldn't have sent crews into an unoccupied structure, but there'd been a report of two guys on the construction crew who were unaccounted for. Stories conflicted. Had they shown up to work early? Coworkers reported an extra truck out back. It could mean a lot of things. But the fire department couldn't take a chance. If there were victims inside, they had to try to save them.

Knowing two men might be trapped in the burning building, several crews had moved in to attack the fire from the inside. The building was a disorienting maze from the first entrance. Half floors, a missing wall, an elevator door gaping open with no elevator inside. Dangerous as all hell.

He and Charlie had knocked down a fire on a lower story and nearly fallen through a half-finished section of floor. Following a search pattern, they moved as swiftly as they could, looking for the possible missing construction workers.

About five seconds ago, as they were moving carefully

up a stairwell hauling a charged hose with them, Charlie was suddenly gone.

And the next second Kevin knew why.

He was falling, fast and hard. Flailing. The hose gone, his partner gone. He hit something hard, his air pack and helmet rattling, blackness swirling in front of his eyes. How far had he fallen? One story? Two?

The force of his landing knocked the wind out of him and he lay still, stunned but forcing himself to stay calm. Kevin struggled not to breathe rapidly and kill his air tank. He still had air. He still had a chance.

But where was Charlie? Maybe he'd fallen onto a different floor and gotten out. Found the hose. Followed it.

Kevin rolled to his knees. Was anything broken? Did it matter? He only had one choice if he wanted to live, and that was to move. Something was not right with his foot… why did it feel funny? He breathed, ragged pain stabbing him in the ribs. He compartmentalized it, controlled it. He had to find a way out.

Where was Charlie?

On his knees, ignoring the pain and exhaustion, he opened his eyes. Focused. Saw gray concrete floor through his mask. Smoke passed over him like clouds, obscuring his vision and confusing him. He'd trained for this. *Stay low. One hand on the wall. Breathe. You have to find an exit sooner or later.*

He hoped for sooner. How long did he have on his air tank? Five minutes? One minute? He tried to remember how long he and Charlie had been in the building. Had he lost consciousness when he fell?

As if in answer to his question, the low air alarm sounded. He had only two minutes to find a way out.

He crawled to a wall, put his gloved left hand on the surface and started to move along it. Five feet. Ten feet. How much longer? If he passed out or ran out of air, he was done.

He'd die there in the stairwell. He thought of his parents, his brother, his uncle, shaking their heads in grief at the loss. A vision of Nicole flashed through his mind. Even in his confusion, he remembered. The feel of her skin under his fingers. The light in her eyes. *How much she'd already suffered losing her brother.*

He had to get out. Just to see her again. It was worth everything he had.

He lunged forward, moving down the wall faster now. Where was the exit? He knew he was in a stairwell, maybe even at the bottom. How far had he fallen?

Suddenly, the wall was different. Where it met the floor, there was a doorstep. A threshold. Hope surged through him. He moved his hand up, struggling to see and feel. The low air alarm on his tank ticked down, measuring off the seconds. He had no time left.

Kevin shoved on what he hoped was a door. He rolled through it, expecting to fall down another staircase, maybe an external fire escape.

But he was on the ground outside the building. He caught a glimpse of an industrial-sized construction Dumpster. A truck. Heavy equipment.

He had to be at the rear of the building. He'd gone in the front...hadn't he? Wasn't that where the fire was? How did he get here? He couldn't breathe. Knew his tank was empty. But he was disoriented. He tried to think.

Where was Charlie? He had to save his partner.

Kevin tried to drag himself to his feet. He had to find someone, tell them Charlie was still in there. He rolled off his back. Made it to one knee. Tried to push himself to standing. He made it halfway up and his body collapsed. Why did his foot feel so strange and leave him so unbalanced?

He fell on his back, his aluminum air tank striking a piece of steel on the ground and clanking loudly. Kevin tried again, fighting his way to his knees, but a dark wave of nausea and heaviness took him back down.

The last thing he heard was shouting as he felt his face mask being torn away.

CHAPTER TWENTY

TYLER AND CHIEF RUGGLES finally stopped their wrestling match and listened to one of the police officers who had stepped between them. They dashed around the building where the cop pointed, and Jane and Nicole followed them. Although the trucks and firefighters were concentrated out front, something interesting was happening in the rear of the hotel, facing the beach.

Nicole followed them around the corner and saw one of the cops on the ground next to a fallen firefighter. The cop was struggling to remove the helmet and face mask from the man on the ground, who appeared to be trying to get up.

She ran closer, the need to know outweighing everything else. The firefighter rolled away from her, his air pack and bulky coat hiding his identity. It had to be Kevin. He was the only missing man. Tyler and the chief reached the fallen man first and their reaction told her the truth before she got close enough to see for herself.

Kevin. His brother's face was pure relief and joy, as if he'd just dug up gold in his backyard and his favorite team won the World Series. At the same time.

Nicole ran up behind Tyler and saw for herself the man she'd spent the entire previous day with, whom she'd spent the previous thirty minutes terrified for. His face was contorted with pain and he breathed hard and fast, but he was alive.

Kevin saw her and a brief flash of happiness crossed his face. His eyes focused on her for only a second, but Nicole knew the emotion in them. She saw the one thing she feared most. Love. Overpowering love that could only lead to heartbreak.

Kevin held her gaze and Nicole wondered what he saw in her eyes. Her emotions were on the surface, as uncontrollable as the sea. She was glad when Kevin looked away and gripped his brother's shirt front.

"Charlie," he gasped out. "I lost him."

Tyler shook his head. "Charlie's out front getting a massage right now." Tyler swiveled and addressed the small crowd. "Somebody ought to run around and let him know—"

"I'll do it," Jane said. She took off running and Nicole pictured her delivering the news to Charlie that Kevin, too, had made it out of the building. She and Jane had been friends for years, but never had they waited together for two men they cared about to emerge from a smoky building. The look on Jane's face could not be mistaken. Jane loved Charlie desperately, whether she would agree to marry him or not.

Nicole felt shy outside the group of men forming a circle around Kevin. Should she squeeze in there? Jane hadn't hesitated to fuss over Charlie, but that was different. She knew these men. Her father was a fire chief. Jane was comfortable in situations like this.

Nicole was not. And she felt certain she never could be.

Still, she tried to see what was going on. An ambulance crawled around the building and backed as close as the construction equipment would allow. Tyler and another man were unbuckling Kevin's air tank and easing him out of it.

The other firefighters were all business. Was this kind of danger and heart-punishing fear part of their daily lives? How did they stand it?

One man propped open the back doors of the ambulance, like he probably did every day. As soon as he'd determined that Kevin was alive and talking, Chief Ruggles walked off, shouting into his radio and running the fire scene. Tyler knelt, assessing the patient as if he had done it a million times, no matter that it was his only brother.

His only brother. Nicole closed her eyes as an image of her baby brother so painful it almost took her to her knees crowded her vision. Who had been there when they pulled the blankets away and found Adam's crew? Were there shouts of joy when they discovered some of the crew alive? Who had assessed her brother and learned he'd never graduate from college? Did that scene in the wilderness a thousand miles away look like this one?

This is different, she reminded herself. *Kevin is alive.* She should go to Kevin. Kneel next to him and ask if he was all right. Be glad to see his smile. Wipe the dirt from his face, smooth the lines from his forehead. Take his hand.

All those things she wished she could have done for her brother, but fire stole him from her. She couldn't face that again. Ever.

She backed off a few steps. The paramedics and his fellow firefighters would take good care of him. She put more distance between herself and Kevin...until she was far enough away to get back her sense of perspective. The sense that told her getting into a relationship with Kevin had been a dangerous idea from the start.

Maybe she should start listening to that voice in her head, the one that told her to put up her guards or risk crushing her heart.

If she didn't love him, it would be easier to stay.

Tears blurred her vision, but she kept going. Jane met her as she came around the front of the building and gripped her upper arms, stopping her.

"What happened?" Jane asked. "Is Kevin all right?"

Nicole nodded. "I think so. They're taking care of him now."

"Did you talk to him?"

Nicole shook her head. "Not my place. I would be in the way."

Jane cocked her head to one side. "Are you kidding? Come on. We're going back there. Just for a minute. You'll feel better if you talk to him, even one sentence."

Nicole wanted to protest, but Jane had a firm grip on her arm as she pulled her back toward the ambulance. They stood together, watching as Tyler hovered over Kevin. She saw Kevin glance in her direction and wondered if he wanted her by his side.

She wished it was that simple.

Jane smiled reassuringly and put an arm around Nicole, but nothing would make her feel better right now. Jane meant well, but she had misjudged Nicole's reasons for running away. Jane probably thought she was leaving because she was afraid. Because today's near-catastrophe had taken her right back to her brother's death.

Absolutely true. But there was more. She was afraid to look into Kevin's eyes right now because he knew she would see his feelings reflected back. It wouldn't do either of them any good. Because the nearly fatal fire had shown her something clearly today.

She loved Kevin. And that was why she had to leave.

Cape Pursuit had lulled her into thinking she could let go of the anguish in her past. But she'd been drawn right into the lion's mouth—the one thing she couldn't face. And her punishment would be leaving town before her heart broke all the way.

"I DON'T NEED an ambulance," Kevin told his brother. "Just get this coat off me before I roast and see if you can get my boot off. My foot feels weird."

Kevin stayed still, his head pounding, sweat soaking his fire department T-shirt. He still wore his turnout pants with suspenders snaking over both shoulders. The ambulance idled and added diesel exhaust to the other smells of the fire scene. He was used to those smells. And the sounds of trucks, radio traffic, water moving, shouting.

He was not used to being on the ground with a crowd circled around him. Between the group of men, Kevin saw Jane and Nicole. He could find Nicole in a crowd of a million people.

So why did Jane have her by the arm as if she was dragging her back here? Nicole must have fled as soon as she saw he was alive.

His chest tightened even more than it had against the ragged breath and possibly broken ribs. He could guess the reason for Nicole's expression. Her agony was imprinted on her face. He'd made it out alive, but her brother hadn't. All the time they'd spent together…he'd started to think she could let go of her fear and let herself love him despite his profession.

He was kidding himself. Believing what he wanted to. And today's disastrous fire had taken a greater toll than bruising two hundred percent of his body. He had to talk to her. It was now or never, before she ran away again.

He tried to meet her eyes and smile reassuringly, but his brother interrupted him.

"Which boot are you talking about?"

"The right one," Kevin said. He didn't care about the stupid boot. He wanted to go to Nicole. He propped himself up on one elbow and tried to force his body off the ground.

"Stop," Tyler said, putting a hand on his chest and pushing him down. "Did you hit your head when you fell?"

"Heck if I know. Why?"

"Because you aren't wearing a boot on your right foot. Must've lost it in there."

Kevin lay back on the hard concrete and breathed deeply. He closed his eyes. He wanted to talk to Nicole, but he did *not* want her to see him like this. Maybe Jane would realize and pull her away. Get her some coffee and take care of her. He wished he could take care of her.

"You're going to the hospital for a date with a CT scan right now," Tyler said. "I think you might have damaged your tiny little brain."

Kevin heard the gurney from the ambulance rolling up. If someone would just make the world stop spinning...

He put his forearm over his eyes. Was Nicole still watching? He had to show her he was fine.

"I'm okay," he said. "Just help me up and we'll get back to work."

"I don't think so," Tyler said.

"You think I can't get up?"

Tyler laughed. "You're just stupid enough to go back into the fire. But I don't have any turnout gear, so I get the job of hauling you to the hospital."

Tyler stood and reached a hand down to his brother. "But we can do this your way if you want. Easy now."

Kevin took the offered hand and got his knees underneath him. His brother pulled him slowly to his feet and leaned close. "Now smile for the ladies and wait until you get in the back of the squad before you puke or pass out."

Stars orbited in a frenzied pattern in front of Kevin's eyes. He was afraid to look up to see if Nicole and Jane were still watching. He just hoped to get behind the closed doors of the ambulance.

"Better hurry," he told his brother.

HOURS LATER, Tyler drove Kevin home from his emergency room visit. Bruised ribs, a concussion, a puncture wound on his foot that required three stitches and a tetanus shot that hurt like a son of a gun were the extent of the damage.

"You were lucky," Tyler told him.

Kevin hobbled up his front steps, his sore foot slowing him down. "I feel like the luckiest guy alive."

"Take some of the painkillers they gave you. And be glad you *are* alive."

"And Charlie," Kevin said. Being sore and having to lay low for a few days was nothing compared to the way he'd feel if he lost his partner in a fire. Getting separated was bad enough.

Kevin sat on his couch and Arnold laid his head on Kevin's knee, looking up with soulful eyes as if he understood what a miserable day his owner had had. Tyler went in the kitchen and came back with a glass of water and a prescription bottle. He handed them both to Kevin and sat in the armchair across from him. "I had no idea they cut the staircase out of that place and gutted that much inside."

"None of us knew. Chief wouldn't have sent us in."

They were silent a moment while Kevin swallowed two pills.

"They found those missing construction workers," Tyler said.

Kevin's chest felt hollow. Were they dead? Had he and Charlie failed to save them despite nearly dying themselves?

"They were with the construction boss looking at another job before they got started for the day. Met up at the site and took the boss's truck. Drove over to Virginia Beach for a quick look at something."

Kevin nodded, able to breathe again. They weren't dead. They were never in the building. You never knew with reports of people missing in fires. You couldn't take chances.

"The doc said you needed someone to stay with you for the rest of the day because of your concussion."

"I don't need a babysitter," Kevin said. "It was only a mild concussion."

"You didn't even know you were missing a boot," his

brother said. "And you need someone to get you dinner anyway. I'll give you a choice. You can have either Mom or Dad, but one of them has to stay home with my girls because Hillary's not coming back until at least tomorrow. I'd do it, but I'm going in to work my shift since you bailed on me."

"Mom will fuss over me and Dad will eat all the stuff in my cabinets he's not allowed to. He'll go into a diabetic coma and we'll both be out."

"So...how about Nicole?"

Kevin blew out a breath. "I'm not sure."

"What are you talking about? She went with you to the theme park. She was there at the fire scene with her eyes glued on you. I'm sure she's forgiven you for slicing off her car door a few months ago."

"It's complicated. I'm afraid what happened today might scare her away."

Tyler sat back, waiting for an explanation.

"Her younger brother volunteered with the forest fire service last summer out West," Kevin said. "He was only twenty-one. A fire got away from them, and his team got trapped and hunkered down under fire blankets." He shook his head.

"Didn't make it, did he?" Tyler asked, his expression somber.

"No. When she moved here, she was trying to get away from...that."

"Oh," Tyler said. "I see. That's why she held you at arm's length for so long." He got up and crossed his arms. "This is messy, but you don't know what she's thinking until you ask."

Kevin nodded, but the movement hurt his head. He rubbed his eyes. He just wanted to go to sleep, whether someone was there or not.

"What if I call Jane?" Tyler suggested. "She'll either come herself or she'll send Nicole. Either way, you'll know where you stand and either one of them will fuss less than Mom or Dad."

Kevin thought about it. Even if Nicole was scared away by what happened today, even if it opened a raw wound, he knew one thing. She would come over. He closed his eyes and sank into the couch while he listened to his brother talk to someone on the phone. He didn't hear the end of the conversation as he let sleep take a shot at healing his sore body.

CHAPTER TWENTY-ONE

As NICOLE WALKED up the front steps of Kevin's navy blue house, she steeled herself for one of the toughest things she'd ever have to do. Not the toughest. She'd faced the loss of someone she dearly loved a year ago and survived. But she'd had no choice in that.

She had a choice now. She chose to be here, to check on Kevin as his brother had asked her to do.

Emotionally, this was no time to tell him what was in her heart and on her mind. He was already down and probably hurting. She couldn't tell him that whatever was between them was over. Not today anyway.

Tyler had said the front door would be unlocked and his brother was sleeping, so Nicole turned the latch as quietly as she could, hoping not to awaken Kevin. It would be easier if he were asleep—the coward's way out, she knew.

But the choice was taken out of her hands when Arnold's beagle-baying sounded the alarm as soon as the door latch turned. Trying to minimize the damage as much as possible, Nicole stepped quickly into the front living room and showed herself to Arnold, who made a sudden switch from howling to begging for her attention.

Kevin was there on the couch. Soot streaked, wearing his fire department uniform and only one sock. He swiped a hand over his face and sat up, confusion in his eyes.

"You came," he said, in a tone a person might use when they find out Santa truly exists. Happy, but surprised.

Nicole smiled. "Of course. Tyler said you needed someone, and Jane closed the gallery. She's with Charlie."

"She is?"

"Yes."

"I don't need a babysitter, but I'm glad you're here."

Kevin pushed off the couch as if he meant to stand, but Nicole dashed over to him and put a hand on his shoulder. "Don't. You're supposed to be resting."

Kevin closed his hands around her waist and pulled her down next to him on the couch. He put an arm around her. Her plan to keep her distance physically had been completely derailed ten seconds after she'd walked through the door.

"When I was in that building trying to find a way out, I pictured your face. I thought of you." He swallowed hard. Nicole was so close she could almost feel the movement.

She brushed his hair back from his face and wiped a streak of dirt from his forehead. He pulled her into a hug and kissed her cheek as he held her.

This was not going as she planned. She should put her guard up. Make it easier to leave as soon as she figured out where she was going to go.

"Thank you," he said, his lips brushing her neck. "Even though I'm the one in the business of rescuing people, it seems like you're always helping me out. The amusement park yesterday and now coming over here today."

Was it only just yesterday they'd gone to the theme park and everything seemed so perfect?

Nicole struggled to keep her breath even. Her heart raced and she closed her eyes. Despite the smoky smell that clung to Kevin, she still found his scent lingering underneath.

Why had she let herself go this far? It made turning back almost impossible.

Kevin pulled away and dipped his chin, looking her in the eye. "I'm sorry," he said.

Nicole breathed in a lungful of air that bore the smell of fire and smoke.

"You have nothing to be sorry for," she said. "What happened today wasn't your fault." She smiled, trying to lighten the weight hanging between them. "I'm sure you didn't ask to get trapped in a fi—" She stopped, unable to say the word. A guttural sob came out of nowhere and suddenly she was crying. Her eyes welled with tears and distorted her view of Kevin's face. She couldn't stop.

Kevin pulled her close and leaned against the back of the couch. Her cheek was on his chest and her tears soaked his shirt. He said nothing, just held her tight as she sobbed.

She was glad he didn't ask why she was crying. It was for her brother, trapped and killed by a fire. It was for Kevin, trapped but very much alive. It was because of her love for him that she couldn't bear, a love that hurt too much to continue.

Nicole completely gave in to her tears, her sorrow. Kevin's arms felt safe, providing her a haven to let her feelings rush over her without the fear of falling. She wished he could have been there to hold her as she grieved her brother's death a year ago.

She didn't know how long she cried, but when she could finally take a breath, she remembered why she was here. If she ever had to cry over Kevin, lost and dead in a fire, she would never stop crying.

She had to end this.

Arnold laid his head on her knee and whimpered.

Kevin's shirt under her cheek was drenched. He kissed her temple and rubbed her back.

"I'm sorry," he whispered. "I know what today put you through."

Nicole shook her head. "Today had a happy ending," she

said. She met his eyes. "I'm so glad you and Charlie are all right." She put her hand on his chest and pushed herself up.

Kevin winced for only a second, but it was enough.

"Where are you hurt?" she asked.

"Nowhere serious." He brushed a leftover tear from her cheek. "Some bruised ribs, a small hole in my foot. Mild concussion."

"That sounds serious."

"It isn't. I'll be on light duty in a few days." He smiled. "And I'm not supposed to drive or sign any important legal documents for the next day or so."

"How did you get a hole in your foot?" she asked. Talking about practical problems was a welcome distraction from the elephant in the room.

He shrugged. "Lost my boot when I fell a couple of floors. Must have encountered something sharp."

She touched his chest lightly, running her fingers over the ribs she imagined were damaged. "You fell a couple of floors?"

"Charlie and I were on a staircase that dropped off into nowhere. Buildings under construction have all kinds of surprises, but we didn't expect that one. He only fell one story, but I went down a few more. Lucky for me, I ended up on the ground floor, not too far from an exit."

"And your concussion? You were wearing a helmet. I saw it on you when you were first out of the building."

The image of him on the ground struggling with his mask and helmet was something she would not forget.

"That's why it's only a mild one. I think I hit fifteen things on the way down. Knocked the wind out of me." He smiled. "I'm okay, but I just realized how disgusting I smell."

"And your shirt is soaked. Sorry."

"I'm supposed to keep the stitches in my foot dry, but I

can manage a bath if I hang my foot out of the tub. Feel like helping me?" he asked, a hint of a smile curving his lips.

She stood. "I'll fill the tub for you and wait outside the door."

Kevin's grin faded. He opened his mouth as if to speak, but closed it and nodded.

Nicole headed for the bathroom before she lost her nerve. She closed the tub drain, turned on the warm water, and swiped the bar of soap from the shower. Kevin's bathroom was the old-fashioned kind with a separate tub and shower. Nicole put down a bathmat and took a towel from a recessed cabinet. When she turned around, Kevin stood in the doorway.

He pulled his T-shirt over his head and tossed it through his bedroom door on the other side of the hall. Dark bruises colored his back and ribs. Nicole gasped.

"Do I look that bad?" he asked.

She pulled him into the bathroom and put his back to the mirror. "Can you twist your head and see that?"

Kevin grimaced. "It feels just as good as it looks. Must be where I landed on my air pack."

"You're lucky you didn't break something."

Kevin leaned against the bathroom counter and put two fingers under Nicole's chin. "Are you okay?"

"Sure," she said, looking down instead of meeting his beautiful eyes. "I think the water is ready for you."

Nicole looked away while Kevin finished getting undressed and climbed into the bathtub. He left one foot hanging over the rim. Because it was suspended in the air, Nicole could clearly see the bandage covering stitches on the bottom.

"It's no big deal," Kevin said as he noticed her gaze. "The tetanus shot they gave me was worse."

He leaned back and dipped his head under the water, letting it cover his hair and face, then scrubbed himself and rinsed his face off. He started down his chest next. She sat on the closed toilet lid and watched, the rim of the tub concealing his body from her eyes.

"Want me to get your bathrobe?" she asked.

"If you don't mind. It's hanging on the back of my bedroom door. But don't hurry—I'm enjoying this bath."

Nicole exited, and glanced around his bedroom as she retrieved the robe. Neatly made bed, simple but effective blinds, no dust bunnies rolling around on the floor. Arnold lay on a rug at the food of the bed, watching her. She rubbed his ears. "He'll be all right," she said, reassuring the dog with the perpetually sad face. She glanced at the clock on his bedside table. Almost six. She should do something about dinner.

Nicole took the robe into the bathroom and put it next to the tub. "Be right back," she said. "Call if you need me."

She went to the kitchen and rummaged in the cabinets, finding pasta and a jar of sauce. She looked in the freezer. Frozen chicken. Frozen vegetables. She could do this. The man needed to eat and she needed to keep her hands busy so her heart wouldn't break.

A sound in the doorway made her turn. Kevin, wet-haired and wearing the blue robe, leaned on the door frame. "If you're thinking about cooking dinner for me, I won't object. I haven't eaten at all today, except for a few crackers they gave me at the hospital."

"Good, you have to eat," she said, indicating the prescription bottle on the counter with a nod of her head.

"I could have something delivered. If you'll stay and eat with me. Please," he said.

"I'm staying. And I'm happy to cook. It gives me something to do."

"Do you want to talk about this?"

"This?" she asked.

"The reason you're so anxious to be busy."

She faced him and leaned against the counter. What could she say? He was everything she wanted, except for one glaring flaw. And she would never ask him to give up a career he loved. She had no right. Falling in love with him was not what she had in mind when she came to this town. But it was the one thing that meant she couldn't stay.

"When I came to Cape Pursuit, I needed to start over." Her voice shook. She didn't want to have this conversation here and now. It wasn't fair to him. Not today.

"You've been really successful with the gallery and your photography. That's a pretty big start." He smiled. "You even got a new door for your car."

She wanted to laugh, could see that Kevin was trying to make this easier.

"And what do you need now?" he asked. He dipped his chin and looked up at her. She loved it when he did that. It was one of the things she would miss most about him. And his eyes. His strength. His sweetness. Even his dog.

She glanced at Arnold, who had followed her into the kitchen, waiting patiently next to his food bowl. His empty food bowl. Poor old guy.

"I don't know," she said. She walked over and took one of the cans of dog food from a neat stack on the counter. She peeled the lid back and scooped the food into Arnold's bowl. "But maybe I'll figure it out while I'm cooking." She straightened and pointed toward the living room. "Go put your feet up and I'll call you when dinner's ready."

No matter how tired his body was, his brain wouldn't surrender. He heard Nicole working in his kitchen, cooking for him. The act was so intimate, yet so everyday. He was starving, but he'd gladly sacrifice food to talk to Nicole instead and hear what was going on in her head.

He was afraid he already knew. Something about the way she'd said she *didn't* know what she wanted made him pretty darn sure she *did* know but didn't want to tell him. He'd known for months that she never wanted to risk the heartbreak that comes with loving someone who has a dangerous job. She was no coward—that was obvious from the way she came through for other people. But she'd been hurt so badly by the shocking death of her brother, who could blame her for steering clear of someone who could die in a similar way?

Almost *had*. Kevin hadn't allowed a morbid thought to enter his mind about how close he'd come to getting measured for a coffin today. It was a risk he'd always accepted.

But he couldn't ask Nicole to accept it, too. He'd been a fool for thinking of a future with her when she'd told him she wasn't interested from the start. It had certainly started to feel like that was changing lately, but he'd lost more in today's fire than just a boot.

He closed his eyes and inhaled the aroma of chicken. It would be so nice to have dinner with Nicole tonight and tomorrow night and the night after that.

"Wake up."

He heard the soft voice and the touch on his shoulder. When had he fallen asleep?

"Do you want me to keep it warm and you can eat it later when you're not so tired?" Nicole asked.

He opened his eyes and turned his head on the pillow. Nicole knelt next to the couch. Her face was pink from the heat of the stove.

"I love you," he said.

Nicole's eyes flew wide and she sat back on her heels. *Holy moly. Did he really say that out loud?*

A red glow radiated along Nicole's cheeks. Judging from the heat in his own, Kevin knew he was flushed like a traffic light.

Nicole stood. "You've been taking medication on an

empty stomach." She took his hand and pulled him off the couch. "You better eat now."

Kevin followed her to the kitchen, misery dogging him with every step. Had he just made a bad day worse? If he wanted to blurt out something like that, there had to be a dozen better places and times.

The table was set for two with plates full of delicious-smelling food. Kevin waited for her to sit before taking his chair.

"This is wonderful," he said. "Thank you."

"You haven't tried it yet," she said.

"I know a good thing when I see it."

Nicole didn't answer, but he saw a hint of her smile.

They ate silently, with an occasional groan from Arnold who laid his head on Kevin's good foot.

"Sorry there's no dessert," Nicole said.

"We could go out for ice cream. But you'd have to drive."

She shook her head. "I think I should leave you alone to get some rest."

It didn't sound good. The way she said *I should leave you alone.*

Kevin picked up both empty plates and hobbled over to the sink. He rinsed them and left them for later. Nicole had already washed the pots and pans she'd used. The whole kitchen was spotless.

"There are leftovers in containers in your fridge. For to-morrow," she said.

"I was hoping you'd come back tomorrow."

"Kevin, I..."

He leaned on the sink and opened his arms, hoping she'd step into them. But she didn't.

"I have to go," she said.

"No, you don't. Nicole, I understand. Today freaked you out. But things could be so great between us. I don't want to give up on that. On us."

Her eyes shone with tears, and when she looked down, one streaked over her cheek. He couldn't stand it. He closed the distance between them and hugged her tight.

"Promise me you'll think about it," he said. "And I promise you I won't let you go without a fight."

CHAPTER TWENTY-TWO

JANE CLOSED THE GALLERY, fatigue in her every movement. The hotel fire had riveted all the tourists until the drama simmered down, and then they had turned to shopping full force. She was appreciative for every piece of artwork that sold. Each sale was a step toward her financial independence, and that of her child. She had already worked with Nicole to design a budget based on average summer and winter sales that would accommodate an extra health insurance policy, child care and the necessary days off that came with a baby.

She could do this. But she wasn't going to do it alone—not when there was no reason except her own stubbornness. She'd wondered all afternoon how things were going with Nicole and Kevin, but she hadn't heard from her friend. That was either the best or worst sign, and she suspected the worst. Nicole's tender heart when it came to loving and losing a firefighter had been so sorely tried, Jane doubted Nicole could withstand the storm of emotions. Jane would be there to help Nicole pick up the pieces. Later.

There was something she had to do first.

She parked in front of Charlie's house, rang his doorbell and waited. He didn't answer right away, but his car was in the driveway, and she wasn't leaving until she'd said what she had to say. After the second ring, Charlie opened the door. His hair was wet, and he was wearing a dress shirt and pants. Handsome as ever, he appeared unscathed by his harrowing escape. She wanted to reach out and hold him tight.

"I'm sorry," Jane said. "Are you going out?" She pointed to his button-down shirt and the necktie wrapped loosely around one hand. *He went home from a terrifying fire scene, showered, and had plans to go somewhere?* Maybe she was making a mistake.

"I was," he said, his tone serious. His eyes lingered on her face as if he wanted to memorize her.

"Oh," Jane said. "I could…come back another time."

"Come in," Charlie said. "Please."

"I only stopped by to tell you something."

"You don't need an excuse. You've been here dozens of times, and I was happy to see you every single time." He put an arm around her shoulders and drew her inside. "Sit," he said, pulling her next to him on his couch and keeping her hand in his.

"Today was horrible," she said, her voice shaking. "I was terrified just watching and waiting outside that building, and I can't imagine how you must have felt being trapped in there."

Charlie dropped his tie, wrapped both his hands around hers and rubbed them gently. "I'm sure it was worse for you. I wasn't trapped, just disoriented. I kept my mind on two things so I wouldn't panic."

"Two things?"

"Well, actually three. I was desperate to find my partner. Losing your partner is one of the worst things that can happen in the fire service. And I thought about you. I pictured your face and wondered what our son or daughter would look like. Just thinking about it kept me calm—and hopeful."

"The fire was awful."

"It was, but it could have been so much worse. Kevin's a little injured, but he's okay. And I'm here with you." He put a cautious hand on her belly, where a gentle swell protruded. He spread his fingers and held them still. He waited, silent and smiling.

But hadn't he planned to go somewhere?

"I'm used to the feeling of being lost," he said. "You know as well as anyone that I've often taken the long way and sometimes the wrong way. But today was different. I knew I had someone to come home to."

Jane sniffed and her throat was thick. "While we were waiting outside, a million things went through my head," Jane said. "You've been part of my life for so long, and I should admit to you that I've been half in love with you for years." Her words spilled as quickly as her tears. "And now you're the father of my baby—"

"Jane," Charlie interrupted. He raised her hand to his lips and kissed it.

"I have to say what I came over here to say," Jane continued. "I thought I would pass out from fear this afternoon. I couldn't imagine what I would do without you."

He touched her cheek. "I'm sorry."

"I regretted that I'd said no to your proposal. I had thought it wasn't enough that you cared for me and would provide for me and the baby. I thought that my love for you wasn't enough unless I was sure it was equally matched. But I was wrong."

"Wrong about what?" he whispered.

"I love you enough to make it work. For you, for me, for our son or daughter."

"What are you saying?"

"I'm saying yes, if you still want to be my husband."

Charlie stood up and paced to the window. He kept his back to Jane and scrubbed his fingers through his hair. She couldn't retract what she'd said. She didn't want to. She'd said what was in her heart, and if it wasn't the right thing, there was nothing she could do about it.

"Do you remember that I told you I had to go out of town to help my dad with something?"

"Yes," Jane whispered. He still hadn't turned around. Had he changed his mind about marrying her?

"I was seeing my father, the man I thought was a rock. I thought he had his act together more than any human I've ever known."

"Did something happen to him?" In all the emotion of the day, Jane had forgotten Charlie's sudden trip.

Charlie turned around and the expression on his face shocked her. She'd expected anguish, despair, worry. Instead, there was wide-eyed joy on Charlie's face. His expression danced with happiness.

"Something happened." He laughed. "Boy, did it happen. My dad and I had an honest conversation for the first time in over a decade." Charlie sat down again next to Jane, put one arm around her shoulders again and put his hand on her thigh. His smile faded. "When my mother died of cancer, I was twelve and on the verge of falling apart every single day," he said slowly, enunciating every word. "Seventh grade must be the worst time in any human's life, and it was especially bad for me."

"I'm so sorry," Jane said. She had known he'd lost his mother as a child and grew up with a bachelor father, but he'd always talked about his dad as if he were a hero. What had happened?

"My father was perfect. He played his role as single dad as if he'd trained for it. The man could cook mac and cheese and help me with my homework at the same time. He even took down all the curtains twice a year and washed them, made a collage of pictures to display at my high school graduation party and helped me write the essay I needed to get a scholarship for the fire academy."

"He sounds like an amazing man," Jane said. She hoped that if she needed to be a single parent, she would be able to pull it off. Where was Charlie going with this story? Would he accept her answer, or was it too late?

"My father was strong, supportive, stoic. I held on to him as if he were a life ring and I was drowning."

"It had to be hard for him," Jane commented. She leaned into Charlie as he held her. He smelled of soap and shaving cream.

"Because I was a self-absorbed seventh grader, I didn't think much about what he was going through. I just thought that was how men behaved. They took care of people they loved, offered support, asked for nothing in return."

A feeling of hope began spreading warmth throughout Jane as she listened. She'd talked to Charlie so many times over the years, but she'd never seen him like this. Raw honesty and emotion, but not sorrow. Whatever had happened to his father wasn't a tragedy…it was a revelation.

"So when I got a phone call from my dad that he needed my help, it… I don't know how to explain it. It made me think."

"What did he need?"

Charlie laughed. "You're not going to believe it. My perfect dad, Mr. Do the Right Thing, had gotten himself into a scrape. He went to Atlantic City on a gambling trip with some of his friends. I think they must have had more fun than they'd planned because they all blew through their cash. They could have made it home on credit cards, but my dad somehow lost his car keys."

Jane smiled. "I'm guessing he was the driver?"

"He was," Charlie said, nodding. "So I had to go to his house about an hour north of here, get his extra set of keys, drive all the way to Atlantic City and help get him and his friends home. I even had to spring for breakfast at the waffle house. Those guys ate as if they'd been up all night. Probably were."

"Were you angry with your dad?"

"At first," he acknowledged. "Not because he called and asked for a favor. I'd do anything for him. I just couldn't believe he could be so irresponsible. This is the man who always had dinner on the table, made sure my school clothes fit, made the house payment on time and taught me how to do everything from changing light bulbs to changing tires. How could he screw up so bad?"

"Everyone screws up."

"Yes, they do. Even people you think are perfect. His friends drove my dad's car, and he and I took my car. We talked about a lot of things on the way home from Atlantic City, but he opened up about his fear and loneliness being a single dad. He told me he only had one regret as a father, and that was that he never told me growing up how much he loved me. He said he'd tried to say the words, but he was afraid he would break down if he let too much emotion get in the way."

Charlie grabbed a tissue from the table next to the couch and handed it to Jane. Instead of drying her own tears, she dabbed at the one that had slid down his cheek as he talked about his father's love.

He swallowed. "I got home really late last night, and I almost came knocking on your door to tell you that I'd finally figured something out," he said.

"Will you tell me now?"

"See these clothes? I was on my way to your house just now to repeat my marriage proposal, but this time I was planning to do it right. I wanted to lead with what was in my heart."

Jane put her arms around Charlie and drew close to him. "What were you going to say?"

"I love you," he whispered, his lips brushing her neck. "Will you marry me if I promise to change diapers, light bulbs and tires but still remember to tell you and the baby every day how much I love you?"

"Yes," she said, pulling back so she could see his face. "I can't wait to marry you."

He spread his fingers over her belly again. "Can we do it soon?" he asked. "I'd like to practice being your husband for a few months before the rest of the family arrives."

"Very soon," she agreed, and then she kissed him and held him tight.

CHAPTER TWENTY-THREE

"ARE YOU READY for tough love or is it too soon for that?" Jane asked.

Nicole arranged some newly framed prints in a display by the front window. The August sun was bright, and many tourists were already on the streets.

"Too soon," she said.

"That's too bad." Jane sipped her tea. "Because I was all ready to let you have it. I was going to say things like you can't run scared all your life. You can't let your past steal your future. Loving someone means taking a risk. You can choose a nice, safe insurance salesman to love but there's always a chance he'll get bit by a poisonous spider and die of an ugly, festering wound. Stuff like that."

Nicole thinned her lips into a line and glared at her friend. "That's mean."

"I said I was *going* to say those things. If you weren't so delicate."

"Thanks."

"I also considered adding a few barbs about how indecent it is to leave a guy when he's down. Especially a guy as delicious as Kevin who's worshipped you since you came to town four months ago."

Nicole sat cross-legged on the carpet by the large, sunny window. "The bad thing about having such a good friend is that you know where all my buttons are. But you're not supposed to push them."

"Does Kevin know where they are?"

Nicole glanced at one of her photographs on an easel. It was a picture of the sunset, taken from the boat when she was photographing the marina. Had she been living in total denial? Going out with Kevin on that boat. Going along with his adorable nieces to the theme park. Eating ice cream by the ocean. Having her heart nearly wrenched from her body when she thought he died in that burning building...

"I can't do this," she said. "I told Kevin I needed space when I left him a few nights ago."

"And?"

"Aside from five voicemails and those flowers—" she gestured to a vase full of yellow sunflowers on the gallery counter "—he's given me a ton of personal space."

Jane laughed. "He told you he wouldn't let you go without a fight."

"I don't feel like fighting."

"So surrender."

Nicole sighed. "I can't. You have no idea what it felt like thinking someone I'd just realized I loved was dying in that fire."

Jane raised her eyebrows. "You don't think so?"

"Sorry. Of course you do." Nicole squeezed Jane's shoulder when her friend knelt down beside her. "It was like losing Adam all over again," Nicole said softly.

"But you didn't lose Kevin."

Nicole didn't answer. She concentrated on the pattern of the sun on the blue carpet.

"So what are you planning to do?" Jane asked. "You're going to have to see Kevin at my wedding in a few weeks, and probably even talk to him." Jane paused and grinned. "There could be dancing. I think you should be prepared."

"I'm not making any decisions right now. I'm helping

you with Homecoming and the rest of tourist season since you're going to be very busy with your baby and your handsome new husband."

"And then?"

Nicole shrugged. "Maybe I'll go home. Laura could use a friend right now. I'm worried about her. And maybe I could hit the bars with her and start looking for a nice insurance salesman who is impervious to spider bites."

"You could stay here," Jane suggested. "You'd be the best aunt ever."

Just as she said it, a fire truck roared by, lights flashing and sirens rattling the front windows.

Nicole raised her eyebrows and looked at her friend.

"There's a fire department in every town. You can't run from this forever."

"But there's not a Kevin in every town. I can't stay here and wonder if he'll be around every corner I turn."

Jane sat next to her on the floor by the window. Both of them petite, they fit between the easels.

"I'll miss you, Nikki. How will I run this gallery without you?"

Nicole smiled. "How did you run it the two years before you took me in? I know you didn't really need my help."

"Yes, I did," Jane protested. "You've been a lifesaver, and I love having you around."

"I don't know about staying, going, anything…"

Nicole watched an ambulance fly past, following the fire truck. An image of Kevin injured or dead rushed through her mind and she felt cold all over. *I couldn't live with this fear every day.* She had no choice but to make a permanent break and leave town.

Jane watched the ambulance until it disappeared in traffic down the street. She rubbed Nicole's shoulder. "Love sucks," she said.

Nicole's cell phone chirped and she glanced at the text. It was from Kevin.

Want to have dinner? Comes with dessert.

Jane read over her shoulder. "He's adorable. I wonder what's for dessert."

"I'm not planning to find out."

"Can I point out that Kevin was not in that fire truck, and that the ambulance had nothing to do with him since he's texting you right now?" Jane said. "While I'm at it, I'll also say he's been a firefighter for six years and he's still walking around."

Nicole huffed out a sigh.

"Just saying," Jane said.

THE ONLY THING keeping Kevin sane as he endured daily silence from Nicole was the fact that he was outrageously busy. Charlie had a priority painting job he wanted done so he could make a quick turnaround on a house before his upcoming wedding. Chief wanted the station spiffed up for the fire department's centennial party coinciding with the Cape Pursuit Homecoming Festival. And, now that his ribs and foot were back in firefighting shape, he was working his full-time job again.

He still found time to think of Nicole. Constantly. He thought about her as he and his colleagues muddled through the one hundredth birthday party planning. He thought of how much she might like the house he was currently painting and wondered if she planned to stay in Cape Pursuit. He'd asked Charlie if he'd managed to sell a house to Nicole, but Charlie said she'd put him on hold for now.

She'd put Kevin on hold, too. *When she said she needed space, how long did she mean?*

Kevin thought of her as he prepped the fire station for

the party and wondered if she'd say yes if he asked her to be his date. He thought of her every time he left the station in the fire truck, realizing for the first time that his life was not entirely his own. Someone else—aside from his family—cared that he came home alive.

Or did she? She hadn't returned his calls in a week. She had mailed him a thank-you note for the flowers. *Mailed.*

Maybe he shouldn't have told her he loved her, but it was the truth. And he had to believe she felt the same way or she wouldn't be shoving him away with both hands.

He thought of her every time he drove past the gallery, saw a little red car, noticed someone with a camera.

He had high hopes for the Homecoming Festival. There would be street vendors selling food and merchandise. Games. A parade. All the things that made living in a small town fun. He'd seen Jane's name on the list of vendors on the fire inspector's desk. All temporary vendor tents had to be approved and equipped with a clearly marked exit and a fire extinguisher.

Perhaps he should sign up to inspect the tents. Every day. Especially the one selling paintings and photographs of local landmarks.

"Looking for volunteers," the chief announced, his voice echoing in the station. Kevin was on a ladder cleaning overhead ductwork as part of the preparation for the party.

"For what?"

"Homecoming parade. Need a driver and a candy thrower for each of the trucks. Also need someone to walk alongside and hand out smoke detectors to people on the parade route."

Kevin glanced down at his uncle. "We've never done that before, have we?"

"Nope. But it's our way of celebrating a hundred years of serving the community. And we're getting a head start on fire safety week."

"I see."

"Also need guys who don't have families—or dates—to volunteer to be on duty the night of the party."

Kevin continued knocking dust off the top of the ductwork, letting some sift down on the chief who stood directly below.

"So?" the older man prompted.

"I might have a date," Kevin said.

His uncle snorted. "You can't bring Arnold."

"I can do better than Arnold."

"That's not what I hear."

Kevin knocked down a big chunk of built-up dust and cobwebs, but the chief dodged it and it hit the floor.

"How about the parade?" his uncle asked.

"I've driven a truck in that parade for the last six years. I'll walk alongside and hand out smoke detectors this year. Maybe I'll meet someone and ask her to the party."

"Good luck."

Kevin wondered how much Tyler and Tony had told the chief about his stalled romance with Nicole. He still had a few days. Maybe he could figure out a way to win her over before it was too late. What would it take...and how far was he willing to go?

CHAPTER TWENTY-FOUR

NICOLE AND JANE stood outside the gallery watching the parade. Cape Pursuit had struck gold with the weather for the Homecoming festivities. August heat, sunshine and blue skies were forecasted for the entire weekend. The parade at eleven o'clock on Saturday morning was the official kick-off, and droves of people filled the sidewalks. White tents and food trucks filled the downtown park, waiting for the crowds who would make their way down there after the parade. Nicole would take up her place in their art tent after the parade.

A yearly tradition, the Cape Pursuit Homecoming weekend induced graduates from the local high school and former residents to come back to town. They'd hit the bars, have high school reunion dances, enjoy the parade and bring their families home to the place where they grew up. When Nicole had taken a walk along the beach the night before, she saw a group of people about her age mugging for a photo in front of the mermaid statue. She'd taken their camera and snapped the shot so everyone could be in the picture. And then fifteen cell phones stacked up for her to take a picture with each one when the group appeared to realize she was a reliable photographer. She'd gladly done it, happy to be part of the fun. High school classmates, she guessed.

Growing up in urban Indianapolis, Nicole hadn't experienced any small-town traditions. Cape Pursuit had started to feel like home to her, but she was still convinced she had to leave.

Didn't she?

She focused on the parade. Instead of blocking off the busy road that ran right along the ocean, the parade route snaked along the street of businesses where Jane's gallery resided. The sidewalks were wider here, the shops and restaurants inviting.

A high school band trooped by with baton twirlers flashing their skills. One wildly thrown baton might have taken out a glass storefront, but it bounced off a streetlight instead. The crowd shrank back for a second, cautioned by the shiny missile. A few politicians were working the crowd and handing out campaign buttons and flyers in preparation for the fall election. The local equestrian club went by on horseback. A glittery float was home to the Cape Pursuit Queen and her court.

Police cars. Antique cars. Muscle cars. A classic parade. The largest fire truck in the fleet—a ladder truck—opened the parade, but other vehicles from the Cape Pursuit Fire Department were interspersed throughout the mile-long route. It was probably wiser to spread them out in case of emergency. Or maybe it was a way to keep the excitement alive with the flashing lights, wailing sirens and pulse-rattling air horns.

Jane waved at every single emergency vehicle and called the occupants by name. Nicole glanced uneasily at each cab as it approached, waiting for a sign of the man she most wanted to see but had avoided for a week. Where was Kevin?

The big red ambulance that had taken off her car door months ago crept slowly toward them. The driver wasn't Kevin.

A tall firefighter was walking alongside the ambulance wearing full turnout gear. It had to be eighty degrees. He carried a big box, and he was handing out small white boxes to people in lawn chairs or standing on the side of the street.

As he got closer, she knew for certain now that it was Kevin.

"Look who's coming," Jane whispered. "If you try to run inside, you'll find out the hard way I locked the door behind us."

"Not funny. And I'm not going to run."

"Have you returned a single one of his phone calls or messages?" Jane asked.

Guilt and a stab of pain washed over Nicole. Because Kevin had stopped calling. There had been only silence for the past two days.

What was he handing out, and why was he walking along in such heavy gear? He'd have a heatstroke in the August sunshine.

"Maybe I should go inside and get him a cold drink," she suggested to Jane.

"Now you care about his well-being?"

"I always cared," Nicole muttered. "That's the problem."

He was almost to their spot in the shade of the gallery awning. Nicole held her breath. Ignoring him in theory was much easier than ignoring him in person.

And he was right there. Tall and handsome, he had the attention of every woman along the parade route. He stopped walking and let the ambulance creep ahead of him. He dug in the big square pocket of his turnout pants and stepped onto the sidewalk in front of the gallery.

Removed his helmet.

Dropped to one knee.

And handed Nicole a smoke detector in a white box.

"There's a note inside," he said.

The crowd applauded at the display and Nicole thought for a moment she had just been proposed to. *Oh. My. God. Was that what this was?*

Kevin didn't stick around. He stood, put on his helmet and jogged off to catch up with the ambulance.

"I wouldn't mind knowing what that note says," an old lady in a lawn chair told her. "If you're interested in making my day."

"I was kidding about the door being locked," Jane said. "You better go inside and cool off. Read your note."

Nicole thought she would combust if she didn't get away from the crowd and into the air-conditioned gallery. The foghorn door alarm nearly gave her a heart attack in her emotionally fragile state. She retreated into the back room and pried open the cardboard box. Had Kevin prepared this one before the parade and stuffed it in his pocket, hoping to find her along the way?

The note was folded inside the box. She opened it with shaking fingers.

Nicole,
Nothing in the world is more important to me than fighting fires and saving lives. Except you. I would risk everything to do my job. Except risk losing you.
Kevin

What did it mean? Was he saying he would quit his job for her? Ridiculous. The man lived and breathed firefighting. It was his family tradition, and he poured his heart into it. She was reading something into the note that wasn't there. She was sure of it.

Kevin had told her himself that day at the beach he would never give up firefighting. *And she would never ask him to.*

The foghorn signaled someone's entrance and rattled Nicole's train of thought.

"It's just me," Jane called.

"Back here."

Jane swept the curtain aside. "Well? Is it a marriage proposal?"

Nicole laughed. "I've only known Kevin four months. And we haven't even talked in over a week."

"So?"

Nicole handed her friend the note. "What do you think this means?"

Jane looked at the note for a long time, then returned her attention to Nicole.

"Do you love Kevin?"

Nicole sat at Jane's desk and put her head in her hands. "I thought I did. But then I thought I couldn't. And then I thought I could forget him if I just didn't see him or talk to him."

"And how did that work out?"

"Honestly, not very well. And then when I saw him today, I wanted to snatch him up and keep him all to myself."

"Every woman on the parade route was thinking that."

"But they can't have him," Nicole said. "He's mine."

Jane laughed. "Really? When did that happen?" She flipped the note over and looked at the back. "Nope. Nothing here."

"You know what I mean."

Jane shook her head. "I'm not sure I do. Are you saying you're willing to fall in love with a firefighter after all?"

"I have no choice," Nicole said. "I already have."

"Ah, geez. This is lousy timing. I got suckered into going to that stupid fire department party tonight with Charlie. And now I have to keep my mouth shut all night about you and Kevin being in love."

"Sorry. Maybe it won't come up."

"You should come along, too," Jane said.

"I wasn't invited," Nicole said.

"Kevin never asked?"

"He didn't ask."

"I just assumed you turned him down. Maybe he's not going," Jane suggested.

"Are you kidding? He probably sleeps in fireman pajamas. Of course he's going."

"Not necessarily. Some of the guys are on duty tonight, which means they may technically be at the station for part of the party, but they're more likely to be on squad calls. Have you seen all the extra people in town looking for trouble tonight? If Kevin's on call, he'll be running his adorable ass off."

"That's probably it. Right? You don't think he asked someone else as his date?" Nicole asked.

Jane held up the note. "No man writes a woman a note like this when he's got a date with someone else."

"So what should I do now?"

"Follow today's game plan and head to our tent in the park while I man the gallery. I have no doubt you'll have more fun there than I will here."

Nicole and Jane loaded Nicole's car with the paintings and framed photographs they planned to sell at the festival in the park. They had set up the tent and table in advance but left the merchandise in the gallery for safekeeping. With the artwork and the business supplies stowed in her car, Nicole got in the driver's seat and headed for the park.

There wasn't a single parking space anywhere near Nicole and Jane's spot. The back seat and trunk of her little red car were filled with heavy framed prints and paintings, and it was Nicole's job to lug them all across the grass to the row of white tents flapping cheerfully in the ocean breeze.

It was not a happy thought. She cruised past the parallel parking spots twice, hoping someone else was just unloading merchandise and would pull away.

No luck.

It was almost noon, the official opening time for the booths and food vendors. Crowds of people were already walking around. Kids played on the swings and monkey bars, while adults took pictures and chatted in small groups.

She had to get the car unloaded and the tent open for business. They could be missing out on sales right now with the crowds of nostalgic locals and tourists. There was only one choice. Nicole activated her four-way flashers and double-parked in the street as close to the back of her tent as she could. Feeling guilty, she stole a glance both ways and hopped out of the car.

She'd hurry. No one would mind. It was a carnival atmosphere anyway, right? She could run back and forth across the grass and carry all the pictures, stow them in the back of the tent and then move her car. It was the only way, and it would only be a few minutes.

Nicole put two framed paintings under each arm and lumbered across the lawn as fast as she could. Why had she chosen this linen dress today? The sky blue color was perfect, but she would be a wrinkled mess by the time she opened the tent flaps. And her delicate sandals with narrow heels and slender ankle straps were no match for the grassy park grounds.

She ran back to her car, got four more framed pictures, and hauled them across the lawn to the back of the tent. Her trunk empty now, she opened the car's back door and leaned in. A car whizzed past her, ruffling her skirt. She was flirting with danger and a parking ticket.

She had two paintings under one arm and was reaching into the back seat when an air horn right behind her startled her and she jumped, hitting her head on the ceiling of the car. She dropped two paintings onto the floor of her car and straightened up, rubbing her head.

A giant red ambulance blocked the street entirely as it idled next to her, lights flashing. Kevin got out of the passenger door and towered over her. He grabbed her hand

and held it while he examined the place on her head she'd been rubbing.

"Are you okay? I told Tony not to blow the horn and scare you."

She glanced up at the cab of the truck. Tony leaned across the seat and grinned. "Double-parking sons of guns," he said.

Nicole smiled. "Hello, Tony. I'm glad you were driving this time." She poked Kevin in the chest. "This guy might have taken my car door off."

"I thought you might have learned your lesson last time," Tony called.

Nicole shook her head. "I'm a glutton for punishment."

Kevin still held her hand. He kissed it, never taking his eyes off hers. Nicole felt all the nerves in her body sigh at the same time. Kevin wore his uniform, the fire department symbol emblazoned over the left side of his chest.

And it didn't bother her. Finally. She reached up with her free hand and traced the Maltese cross with one finger. It had taken months, but that symbol now meant something other than her brother's death. It meant something new, thanks to Kevin. Rescue. Safety. Giving someone a second chance.

"I got your note," she said, her face tipped up to his. She didn't care that there were hundreds of people around. All she cared about was another chance with Kevin.

"I meant every word," he said.

He stepped closer and slid an arm around her waist. Traffic began to back up in both directions because the street was completely blocked. Someone honked a car horn. Repeatedly.

"What exactly did you mean?" Nicole asked.

"I meant I would give up anything but you."

She shook her head. "You can't."

"Sure I can. Why not?"

"Because," she said. She moved closer to him and put her head on his chest, reveling in the way it felt to be held by him with the sunshine on her back. "Because I love you. And I want you to be happy."

His arms tightened and she heard his heart thudding.

"You love me," he whispered.

"You had to know that."

"I hoped."

More car horns honked and Tony leaned across the seat again. "Think you can speed this up, partner?"

"No," Kevin said.

"I'll drive around the block and come back," Tony said. "You've got a radio."

The ambulance pulled away, leaving diesel fumes in its wake. A car flew past them, nearly taking off Nicole's door. Kevin shut it and pulled Nicole onto the sidewalk.

He held her at arm's length, assessing her. She was glad she was wearing that impractical dress and dainty shoes now. He ran a hand through her chin-length blond hair. "I can't get you out of my mind," he said.

"I have the same problem."

"We could help each other with that problem," Kevin said. "I have a solution."

Nicole's heart filled with liquid heat that radiated all the way to her fingers. "What is it?"

"I visited the travel agency downtown yesterday."

"Really? I thought you said you never went anywhere on vacation. That everything you wanted was right here."

"Right. I haven't taken a vacation in six years."

Her curiosity was killing her.

"Turns out if you cash in six years' worth of vacation time, you have enough money for a trip for two to Italy."

Tingling started at the top of her head and raised goose bumps along her neck. Her eyes suddenly stung.

"Do you know anyone who'd like to go on a ten-day trip to Italy with me?" Kevin asked.

Nicole flung herself into his arms and held on tight. Could this really be happening?

"But wait," she said, her words muffled against his shirt. "If you cashed in all your vacation time for the money, how can you go on a ten-day vacation?"

She pulled back so she could see his face.

His eyebrows drew together and his smile flattened into a serious expression. "I put my resignation on my uncle's desk right before the parade."

All the breath rushed from Nicole's lungs. "No," she said.

Kevin nodded. "I did. I told you I'd give up anything except you. And if my career choice was keeping us apart, I have other options. I happen to be quite a decent house painter."

Nicole shook her head.

"Really," Kevin said. "I'm always turning down painting jobs because I don't have the time. And Arnold will be so happy when he hears the good news." Kevin smiled, the lines in his forehead disappearing. "He likes riding along on painting jobs."

"You can't quit," she said.

"I did."

"You have to take your resignation back," she said.

"Think about what you're saying, Nicole." He ran a finger down her face. "I don't want you to live in misery, always wondering if I'm going to come home from work. You deserve better than that."

She grabbed his hand and turned it over, touching the calluses, running her finger over a small scar on his palm. She took a deep breath and looked up. "I used to think I couldn't live with the fear of losing you, but I know now loving you is worth it. Even if that means I'll worry like crazy about you."

Kevin bit his lip. "You mean you'd be willing to take me as I am, dangerous job and all?"

"I'd be lucky to have you as you are."

Kevin kissed her as they stood on the sidewalk. Nicole closed her eyes and gave in to her love for Kevin. The sounds and smells of the festival were all around them. Music. Laughter. Sweet aromas from the food trucks. Cars cruising down the street.

A loud diesel engine idling close by.

"Hey, Ruggles," Tony shouted. "Want me to take another lap around the park?"

Kevin broke the kiss and nodded at Tony.

"And you might want this," Tony said. He shoved an envelope out the window. "Dad asked me to clean off his desk this morning, and I thought this might be trash. You decide."

Kevin took the envelope and stared at it as his partner drove away.

"Is that what I think it is?" Nicole asked.

"My resignation," he said.

"Give me that."

Nicole took the envelope and tore it in half. "I hope you saved enough vacation time for a ten-day trip to Italy," she said. "But then it's back to work. Cape Pursuit needs guys like you."

"I still had a couple of weeks left over," he admitted. "And I can't think of a better way to spend them."

She kissed him and laughed. "Wait until you see the pictures I take on our trip. I may have to open my own gallery."

"How about we start by opening your tent and getting your car off the street?" Kevin suggested. "It's a safety hazard sitting there."

"I'm living dangerously these days," Nicole said.

"Then it's a good thing you have me to keep you safe. Always."

Tony came back by with the ambulance and idled next to them.

"One more lap," Kevin told his partner.

Tony laughed, shook his head, and drove off as Kevin and Nicole kissed in the ocean breeze of Cape Pursuit.

* * * * *

COMING SOON!

We really hope you enjoyed reading this book. If you're looking for more romance, be sure to head to the shops when new books are available on

Thursday
26th July

To see which titles are coming soon, please visit
millsandboon.co.uk

MILLS & BOON

Coming next month

CARRYING THE BILLIONAIRE'S BABY
Susan Meier

'Go ahead. Just lay your hands on either side.'

He gingerly laid one hand on her T-shirt-covered baby bump.

She reached down and took his other hand and brought it to her stomach too. 'We may have to wait a few seconds...oops. No. There he is.' She laughed. 'Or she.'

Jake laughed nervously. 'Oh, my goodness.'

'Feeling that makes it real, doesn't it?'

'Yes.'

His voice was hoarse, so soft that she barely heard him. They had a mere three weeks of dating, but she knew that tone. His voice had gotten that way only one other time—the first time he'd seen her naked.

Something inside her cracked just a little bit. Her pride. He might be a stuffy aristocrat, but there was a part of him that was a normal man. And she had to play fair.

The baby kicked again, and she stayed right where she was. 'Ask me anything. I can see you're dying to know.'

He smoothed his hands along her T-shirt as if memorising the shape of her belly. 'I'm not even sure what to ask.'

'There's not a lot to tell. You already know I had

morning sickness. At the end of a long day, I'm usually exhausted. But as far as the baby is concerned, this—' she motioned to her tummy '—feeling him move—is as good as it gets.'

'I care about all of it, you know.'

'All of what?'

'Not just the baby. You. I know you want to stay sharp in your profession, so you don't want to quit your job, but...really... Avery. If you'd let me, you'd never have to work another day in your life.'

She studied him. This time the offer of money wasn't condescending or out of place. It was his reaction to touching his child, albeit through her skin.

Continue reading
CARRYING THE BILLIONAIRE'S BABY
Susan Meier

Available next month
www.millsandboon.co.uk

LET'S TALK
Romance

For exclusive extracts, competitions
and special offers, find us online:

📘 facebook.com/millsandboon

📷 @millsandboonuk

🐦 @millsandboon

Or get in touch on 0844 844 1351*

For all the latest titles coming soon, visit
millsandboon.co.uk/nextmonth